THE SUN

STEVIE COLE

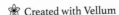 Created with Vellum

To my momma and daddy, I hope you would be proud of the life I've written. . .

Three things cannot be long hidden: the sun, the moon, and the truth.

— BUDDHA

PLAYLIST

The Sun is set in the 90s. So if you guys would like a little nostalgia, just check out the playlist on Spotify to relive your own glory days for a second.

xx- Stevie

Music Playlist

1

SUNNY

The day Elias Black came to my house was the first day it hadn't rained in over a month. Sometimes I thought that must have been an omen.

The springs in the old Victorian couch groaned when I hopped onto my knees to lean over its curved back. The window fogged from my breath as I pressed my face and palms to the glass when Daddy's white pickup pulled into the drive.

Momma's high heels tap, tap, tapped through the kitchen and then the dining room, finally coming to a halt behind me.

I waited for her to fuss at me for getting smudges all over her clean windows, but she didn't scold me that day. I guessed her nerves had gotten the better of her.

Momma said she wanted a house full of kids, but there was only me. After six years of trying to give me a little brother or sister, Daddy and she finally agreed they would serve those less fortunate by fostering children in need, and that was why Elias Black sat in the passenger seat of Daddy's truck. He was a child in need.

"He's here, Sunny." Momma sounded hopeful and a little scared.

My heart pounded when Daddy rounded his car and opened the passenger door. The night before I'd been so excited, I'd barely slept. The anticipation had mounted. My imagination ran wild with all the things Elias and I would do: build pillow forts and tell each other ghost stories, even though they'd scare me half to death.

I'd even conceded to let his GI Joe marry my Prom Queen Barbie. Since my friend Daisy Fulmer's brother Bobby always wanted her Barbie to marry his GI Joe, it stood to reason Elias would want one of the ones Momma stocked in his room to marry mine.

Ever since I found out Elias was coming to live with us, I'd imagined a boy hopping out of Daddy's truck, smiling and running straight to the front door. So it all seemed rather anticlimactic when a frowning, gangly little boy climbed out.

His dirty jeans were too short for his long legs. The He-man shirt he wore must have been a size too small, and his tangled, brown hair looked like rats had nested in it. He adjusted a tattered, red backpack on his shoulder, then walked alongside my father, his gaze straying to me in the window.

Taking a breath, I smiled and waved. My heart crumpled right along with all my hopes and dreams of having someone to play with when Elias rolled his eyes. Then I sank onto the couch with a sigh.

Momma ruffled my hair. "What's wrong, honey?"

"He looks mean."

"Oh..." she knelt beside the couch, her pretty, blue dress pooling around her knees. Tilting her head to the side, she draped my braid over my shoulder. "Honey, he's been through a lot, and he's coming to a strange house with people he's never met. I'm sure he's just scared."

"He looks like he smells."

Her eyes set on mine with a sympathetic plea. "You shouldn't judge a book by its cover."

At the tender age of seven, I already found that life lesson hard to adhere to.

That was her favorite saying. One I'd heard at least a thousand times in my short life. With a sigh, she pushed to her feet, then smoothed her hands over the skirt of her dress.

"I don't want to play with him," I lied.

Living in a rural, beach town in Alabama without another kid for two miles made me desperate for a playmate, but still, it was easier to pretend I didn't need him to like me. Even as children, I believed humans were programmed to save themselves from embarrassment and feelings of inadequacy, and it was obvious to me that Elias would not want to play with me.

"Enough!" Momma headed toward the door. "Be sweet to that poor boy, Sunny Ray."

I scowled. I hated when she used both my names.

One, it sounded dumb. Two, it told me she meant *or else*.

Crossing my arms with a determined huff, I decided, at that moment, when I grew up, I would change my name.

The unoiled hinges to the wooden front door creaked, and I peeked around the living room doorway.

Even though Momma made a fuss over Elias when Daddy nudged him over the threshold, he wouldn't look up.

I was just about to walk away when she grabbed me by the elbow and yanked me into the entranceway. "Elias," she said. "This is our daughter, Sunny."

He didn't lift his head, but he peered up just enough that

I could see his eyes. They were speckled with green and brown and blue, like when God made him he wasn't exactly sure what color eyes a boy named Elias Black should have, so he dipped his paintbrush in a few colors and swirled them all together.

Had God asked me, I would have told him to make that boy's eyes black like his name to match the storm cloud that seemed to live on his face.

THAT EVENING, dinner was uncomfortable, to say the least.

Elias picked at his food, mostly shoving his peas around on the plate. Had I done that, I would have gotten in trouble. Playing with one's food was not proper, Southern etiquette, but Momma didn't breathe a word to Elias.

I glared at him, guessing from his looks and the way he had both elbows on the table that he'd never taken a manners class in his life.

When Momma asked if he'd prefer something else, my mouth dropped open. "I don't want to eat peas!" I whined, beginning to shove the little green orbs around on my plate.

"Sunny!" Momma shook her head and gave me her *don't-start* glare as she pushed back her chair. That menacing expression was followed by, "Eat your dinner."

She leaned over Elias' shoulder. "Would you like me to fix you a sandwich?" Her tone was sugary-sweet, and it made me dislike him, even though Pastor Fulmer said we should like everyone.

Elias shrugged one shoulder.

Momma crossed the kitchen with a smile, humming while she made Elias a peanut butter and jelly sandwich.

I banged my elbows onto the table, then rested my chin in my hands while staring at the boy who refused to make eye contact with anyone. He wasn't even *trying* to do anything, but he sure was getting on my nerves.

When a plate was placed in front of him—a sandwich with the crust cut off like *I* ate them—he subtly glanced at me and smirked.

That's when I knew, Elias Black was the kind of boy that would get sent to the principal's office, the type that would pull girls' pigtails and stick toads in their lunchboxes.

It was then that I decided, sometimes it was best to judge a book by its cover, no matter what my momma said.

AFTER DINNER, Daddy showed Elias to the spare room now serving as his, which left me in the kitchen to help Momma clean up. I finished sweeping and dumped the crumbs into the trashcan. When I spun around, Momma studied me with her hands dug into her hips.

"What's the matter?" Concern marred her soft eyes.

A twinge of guilt tugged at my heart. "I don't like him." I knew better than to say mean things. I just couldn't stop myself. "How long is he going to be here?"

Momma's eyes narrowed. "That's not like my sweet girl. Come here." She held out her arms, and I sulked toward her, dragging the broom alongside me. The comforting, warm scent of fabric softener surrounded me when I rested my forehead against her shoulder. "What's really the matter with you?" she asked. "Huh?"

"Is he staying forever?"

"No, baby. Not forever."

I chewed at my lip, then huffed before going limp in her arms. "He doesn't like me."

"Sure, he does."

I shook my head, hiding my face deeper in her blouse when I thought of the nasty way he had rolled his eyes.

"You've gotta give him some time. Be your sweet self, and he'll like you just fine. As different as this is for you, it's much more so for him. Remember the golden rule: Do unto others..." She kissed my cheek, and I stepped back to place the broom in the closet, then I headed toward the foyer.

I stopped at the bottom of the stairs, listening to the shower running in the guest bathroom—now his bathroom, complete with a GI Joe shower curtain. While I glared at the closed door on the second floor, an unsettled feeling washed over me.

There was something invasive about having a stranger in our house, using our soap and washcloths. And to make matters worse, this stranger was here for an undetermined amount of time.

ELIAS HAD BEEN with us for two weeks before he ever spoke to me, and to be honest, that first time wasn't anything monumental.

He bumped into me in the hallway at school and mumbled, "Sorry."

As much as I hated to admit it, there was still a tiny piece of me that wished he liked me.

The weeks droned on, yet I knew nothing more about Elias Black than what I'd learned through my mother and father's discussions in their room—things I wasn't meant to hear.

Earlier that year, I had discovered that if I pressed my ear to the wall that separated the two bedrooms, I could eavesdrop. And oh, the miraculous things I learned: things about their church group and Grandma Alveenie's health...

And that Elias had twin brothers—"God only knew where they were," Momma said.

His dad was in prison, and his mother had disappeared.

It was two months before anyone called CPS, and at the time of Elias' arrival in our home, his mother had yet to be located. Daddy suggested she may be dead. Mother "wouldn't hear of it." Whatever that meant.

That night though, as I held my ear to the cool wall, what I overheard sent a shudder of fear through my veins.

"I found out what his father's in prison for," Daddy said, his voice so low and hushed I thought maybe, just maybe, they'd caught on to my eavesdropping.

"David. I thought they kept that sealed."

"They do…"

"Drugs? Stealing?" Mother asked.

"Murder."

"What?" Momma's voice shook. "David! He killed someone?"

Then silence.

The kind of silence that made me lean against the wall harder, cupping my hand around my ear. My stupid heart banged around in my chest so loudly that it clanged in my ears, which didn't help my spy work, at all.

The uneasy quiet dragged on for what seemed like thirty hours. Finally, I heard Momma sigh. "Why wouldn't the social worker have told us that?"

"Would it have mattered, Clara?"

"I don't know." Then the door to their bathroom creaked, and all I could hear were the sounds of muffled voices.

Murder.

I moved away from the wall, rolling that word over in my head.

Elias' dad killed someone.

A sudden, artic chill wrapped around me, and I sank underneath my pink, fairy covers, staring through the dark at my closed bedroom door. Fathers were supposed to coach t-ball and soccer, take their little boys fishing. Not kill people.

I wondered if Elias knew, and if he did, I contemplated whether that made him a bad person, too. I was curious about a lot of things regarding Elias Black, and my mind traveled down the rabbit hole of my imagination, wondering where he had lived before he came here. Possibly a place similar to an RL Stine book. Dark and dreary, covered in dust and spiders. The house would be small and cramped and located in the middle of an overgrown field with coyotes prowling the grounds.

I thought about Elias and his messy hair and his lost brothers until the unsettled feeling overtook me and I found myself with my covers over my face, whispering the Lord's Prayer before I finally, somehow, drifted into an uneasy sleep.

My dreams that night were plagued by coyotes and villains, and I awoke with a racing heart and sweaty palms.

I sat straight up in bed, then froze. Someone was hunched over in front of my closet door.

My nightlight glowed just enough to make out Elias' messy, brown hair and Transformer pajamas, which was the only reason I swallowed the scream that sat in the back of my throat.

His head lay crooked over his shoulder, his wiry body bent over his knees.

Gnawing at my lip, I swung my legs over the edge of my bed, wanting nothing more than to wake Elias and ask him what he was doing. But the longer I stared at him, the more I thought about the terrible things I'd heard through my wall earlier tonight—dreams of wild animals and mean men— and I was too afraid to wake the boy who wouldn't talk to me.

I grabbed my pink stuff animal, Rattle Bear, the beads inside her belly shaking as I tiptoed into the hallway and then to my parent's door. I intended to climb into their bed and snuggle safely between them, but just as I reached for their knob, something in my room creaked.

I waited. Curiosity tugged and tugged at me until I found myself scooting along the wall. I crept toward my room. When I peeked through the cracked door, Elias was frantically throwing the covers off my bed.

"Sunny?" he whispered, followed by, "Shit. Sunny?"

I'd never heard a little boy cuss before, and for some reason, it excited me.

Using one finger, I pushed open the door. The light from the hallways spilled across my floor and caught Elias' attention.

When his dark eyes landed on me, his shoulders sagged with a hard breath. He sank straight to the floor, cradling his knees to his chest.

I hesitated, scared. Intrigued. Then I took a few steps into my room. "What were you doing?" I asked.

"Looking for you."

"Oh."

"I thought you were gone."

I liked his voice. It was soft and soothing, like water lapping at the side of a boat.

It made me feel. . .something deep inside. Safe or happy maybe.

Whatever it was, I just wanted him to keep talking.

"Do you like your room?" I asked when I sat Indian-style in front of him.

He picked at a loose thread on his pajama bottoms and shrugged. "I don't like the dark."

"Me either." I pointed at my fairy nightlight. "Daddy put a boy one in your room."

"Still dark. I've never slept by myself before 'cause I don't like it. It's not safe."

"It is safe."

"Nuh-uh." He adamantly shook his head. "That's why I watch you. So you'll be safe."

"That's why you were in here?" My silly heart skipped and jumped. I felt like a princess from one of the fairy tales Momma read at bedtime. Maybe Elias was a secret prince sent from a faraway land to rescue me from a danger I was not yet aware of. "To keep me safe?" I said, pointing to the spot where he'd been sleeping, and he nodded.

"From what?" I asked.

"Bad things," he whispered, his voice so low that he must have been worried someone would hear.

That cold feeling seeped through my body again, and I pulled my arms around my waist to ward off the unease. Instead, I focused on the newly discovered fact that Elias Black evidently didn't hate me. We may build pillow forts after all...

"Bad things don't happen here," I said.

His face lifted. "Is that why you sleep so good? Every night, you sleep and sleep."

"I guess. It's what you're supposed to do at night though."

Elias finally jerked the loose string free from his pajama bottoms, balled it up, and threw it. "Wish I could sleep like that."

I glanced over my shoulder at the doorway, knowing what I was about to say was a sin that would make Jesus frown. Momma always talked about boys and girls on TV sleeping in the same bed and how it was shameful, but I felt bad for Elias, not to mention, now I was a little scared myself. If it made us both feel better, surely God wouldn't send me to hell for sleeping with a boy one time.

I hopped up and straight onto my mattress then patted the empty side. "You can sleep up here," I offered. "Then we won't be alone."

Chewing at his lip, his gaze drifted from me to my bed like he wasn't exactly sure if he liked that idea or not. "You don't kick, do you?"

"I don't think so."

He gave one curt nod, then he got to his feet and crawled across the end of my bed. He flopped back on the pillow and yanked the covers over us both as he inhaled a deep breath. "Why do girls smell like candy?"

"I don't know. Candy smells good, though."

I laid stiff and still, afraid to let my body brush against his, frightened he was like a stray cat that I'd scare away. He kept fidgeting under the covers; then, after a few minutes, he exhaled as though he'd been thinking hard about whatever was about to come out of his mouth. "I heard you tell your maw I don't like you. I do like you. I just don't *like* to like people."

I smiled because I was special. "Momma says you're 'sposed to like everyone."

"People hurt you when you like 'em. And they leave."

I rolled onto my side, staring straight into his water-colored-by-God eyes. "I won't leave you, Elias Black. And I won't hurt you. Ever." I held out my pinky finger, and he glanced at it, brow furrowed.

"You want me to pull your finger or 'sumpin?"

I giggled. "No, silly goose. I wanna pinky promise. I won't leave you. You don't leave me. Never."

"Never?"

"Never. Ever." I made my eyes wide. *This* was serious business.

His little finger curled around mine, and we shook on it. "Then I'll let myself like you, Sunny Ray," he agreed.

When Elias used both my names it made me feel all tingly inside.

"I know why you're Maw named you that. 'Cause you're like a warm ray of sunshine."

I stared at my ceiling, thinking about what he meant. The sun was just a giant ball of fire, but it was pretty important, so I took it as a good thing. "Elias..." I whispered, but his breathing was hard and heavy, his eyes closed tight. I waited a few more minutes, then I leaned over and sniffed him, curious what boys smelled like.

And he smelled like soap. That was it. Just Dial Mountain Fresh soap.

THE NEXT MORNING when I woke, the spot beside me was empty. The sheets were crumpled and cool where Elias had been.

The aroma of bacon grease crept up from downstairs and underneath my closed door, causing my stomach to grumble. I rubbed at my eyes before stumbling out of bed.

When I went into the kitchen, the skillet sizzled, and Elias set the table while Daddy read the Sports section of the *Robertsdale Times*. Elias glanced up at me when he placed the last fork next to my plate. I smiled, but the storm cloud was back, heavy and angry on his face.

"Do you want to play after breakfast?" I asked.

"No."

"Sunny, would you"—bacon grease popped. Momma swore under her breath. "Can you grab the milk from the fridge and pour Elias and you a glass?"

"Yes, ma'am." I frowned at Elias on my way across the room.

I thought about our pinky promise when I snatched the plastic Dairy Fresh container from the shelf and closed the door to the fridge a little too hard. After I filled our cups, I took a seat, set the milk on the table, and then glared at him throughout breakfast.

As soon as the table was cleared, I went to my room and changed into play clothes, then lugged my Barbie case down the stairs and out into the backyard. I didn't need some dumb boy to play Barbies with anyway. He'd just mess it all up like Daisy's brother did, trying to boss the Barbies around and look up their skirts...

Two minutes after I dumped the dolls onto the grass, I huffed. Elias wasn't sleeping in my room again. It didn't matter if I pinky promised or not.

A light breeze rustled the leaves of the oak overhead. The sun glinted through the yellow-red and brown-orange leaves, and panic settled in my chest. The sunlight reminded me of heaven, which reminded me of Jesus. Jesus must be sad that I liked sleeping next to Elias and his soap smell. People aren't supposed to like sin—Pastor Fulmer taught us that in church. I didn't want to go to hell, but I didn't know if I was sorry enough to be forgiven, either.

My stomach knotted and kinked as I wondered what eternity with the devil would be like. Demons screaming and screeching, clawing at my skin. Molten fire and all the bad people that died before me. Momma and Daddy would be so disappointed when they got to heaven and looked down into that pit of fire and saw me burning right next to Lucifer.

My eyes watered at the thought, and I closed them to beg for forgiveness, even though I wasn't sorry.

Halfway through my frantic prayer, the kitchen door banged shut.

I opened my eyes to Elias stomping across the yard with his hands shoved deep in his pockets. He stopped in front of me and kicked at a rock. "You gonna take your promise back since I made you mad?"

"You made me sad. Not mad." I lied. I was a little of both.

He released the kind of sigh that made his shoulders rise tall and fall hard. "Shit."

I fought the smile tugging the corners of my mouth. "If Daddy hears you say that, he'll wash your mouth clean out with soap."

"Why?"

"He said those words make your mouth dirty. I guess the soap helps get them out." I grabbed one of my dolls and combed through her hair. "Bobby Fulmer got his mouth washed out, and he said it tasted like fairy poop."

Elias snarled his lip. "How does he know what fairy poop tastes like?"

"I guess it tastes kinda like poop but cleaner?"

He plopped down in the grass beside me, staring at the pile of dolls before he snatched up Ken. He held the Barbie in front of him like it was a snake that might strike. "I said I didn't want to play because I don't know how. Not 'cause I don't like you. I meant it last night." He threw down Ken but didn't make eye contact. "I like you, and I don't want you to take your promise back."

"You can't take a promise back." I shook my head.

"Sure, you can."

"Pretty sure it's a sin if you do."

"Shit." He drew the vowel out, and a slick grin shaped his lips. He wasn't afraid of getting his mouth washed out, and I had a feeling he probably wasn't afraid of the devil.

"My paw said there ain't no such thing as sin." Elias was so different than me. He was what a lot of people in Fort Morgan, Alabama, would call a problem child. Raised by heathens, bred in sin—at least that's what I overheard my best friend, Miss Fulmer say to my momma once. But I thought I liked Elias just fine, heathen sin and all.

"Well, I don't take back promises," I said. "And what do you mean you don't know how to play?"

"We never had toys. Paw would break them anytime the church dropped some off. Sometimes he'd set 'em on fire. He said pretending made you stupid."

Scowling, I combed through Barbie's hair faster. "That's not nice."

Elias snatched one of the dolls with brown hair, flipped her over, and pulled her skirt up before shaking his head and dropping her next to Ken. "Don't seem like much fun," he said.

I exhaled, trying to think of things I'd seen boys play at school.

"You know about Robin Hood?" I asked.

"Sure do." He sat up straight wearing a proud smile. "Read all about him and his merry men and that Friar Tuck. Stole from the rich and gave to the poor. I like him."

"Wanna play Robin Hood?" Before he had a chance to answer, I took him by the hand, then led him to my tree-house in the dogwood at the back of the yard.

I climbed the ladder, and he followed me. We just stood on the platform, staring at one another. I kept looking at his patchwork eyes, at how they changed depending on the way the sun hit them. And he stared at me. Hard.

"You be Robin Hood, and I'll be Maid Marion. Just—" I held out my arm, clutching an imaginary bow, while I pulled an invisible arrow from the bag slung over my shoulder. Elias's eyes tracked my every movement, and his brow wrinkled. "Pretend you got a bow and arrow, and you're shooting the bad guys."

"Like King John?"

"Yep." I stuck my tongue through my lips and closed one eye while I aimed. Then I released the arrow into the air, pretending to watch it arc before it hit my target square in the chest. "I got him!" I bounced on the balls of my feet and clapped.

"You gotta make sure he's really dead." Elias hopped out of the treehouse, scurrying across the yard to where I imagined King John lay.

We ran about the yard for hours, slaying the enemy and giving their riches to the peasants of the land—which ended up being my Barbies and Ken—and then Elias led me to the treehouse again, out of breath and all smiles.

"All right," he said. "I'm gonna pretend to leave, and you gotta call for me. Say Robin."

He started down the ladder. Just before his foot touched the ground, I called him.

With a smile, he clambered right back up to the top. "So you do love me then?"

I froze. My heart pounded in my chest.

"It's from the book," he whispered, like we were actors and he didn't want the audience to be broken from the play's spell. "You're supposed to say, 'yes, Robin, I do.'"

"Yes, Robin, I do."

And with that, he pressed his mouth against mine. My

lips tingled, and my heart played hopscotch in my chest. Elias jumped off the decking and took off across the yard in a flash to fight more bad guys.

I'd sinned twice in one day. And I wasn't sorry for it at all.

2

SUNNY

NOVEMBER 1989

Robertsdale Elementary was a one-level building surrounded by a patch of mostly dead grass and a palm tree by the entrance.

The playground had a single swing set with three swings, a slide, and monkey bars. To be honest, it was depressing. I was certain prisons had more to offer inmates than our school offered children in the way of activities.

Elias was in Miss Thompson's class which was on the other end of the hallway. And while our school was small, I only saw Elias at recess. It quickly became the most anticipated part of my day.

Me, Jenny, and Daisy sat at the edge of the playground, picking clovers and dandelions while the rhythmic creak of the swing set played behind us. Jenny linked a chain of clovers together to make a crown for Daisy. "My brother says he's weird," Daisy murmured. If anyone was strange, it was her brother Bobby.

"My daddy said he's from trash." Jenny held up her flower crown, admiring it. "Said he saw Mrs. Black at the battered women's shelter all the time. He said Mr. Black was an angry drunk, too." Jenny smiled when she glanced at me, and I felt my insides get warm with anger. "Is it true, Sunny Ray? Is he trashy?"

"No. He's nice."

"He told Ben Jones he kissed you." Her smile went crooked like she had one up on me. Then my jaw tightened, and my stomached turned. "Trashy boys kiss trashy girls."

"Jenny," Daisy chastized. "Stop. You're being mean."

Jenny shrugged before setting the ring of flowers on top of Daisy's wavy, brown hair. "He's either trashy or a liar." Her dark eyes cut back to me. "Is he a liar, Sunny Ray?"

I didn't like Jenny Smith. Momma said her mother was a gossiping hen, and I was pretty sure that attribute had passed down to Jenny.

"Stop it, Jenny!" Daisy grabbed the crown and threw it to the ground.

Jenny glared at me, and for some reason, I *wanted* to tell her he had kissed me. Part of me thought it would make her jealous. Part of me wanted her to hate me for it. Evidently, the innate desire to make another girl envious wasn't lost on us, even as children.

"He's not a liar," I said, snatching a yellow dandelion and plucking the petals from it.

Jenny gasped. When I looked up at Daisy, her eyes were all wide.

"Ew!" Jenny curled her lip. "Why would you kiss *him*? Mama said he's poor. His own parents didn't even want him."

"Jenny!" Daisy shoved to her feet. "You shouldn't say things like that."

Just then, the back door to the gym flung open, banging against the aluminum siding and catching our attention.

All at once, a group of kids tried to shove through the

small opening. They wiggled and shouted, then exploded out of the doorway scattering in all directions like a ruptured artery. Elias stepped through the exit, alone, hands shoved in his jean pockets and eyes aimed at the ground.

He looked similar to every other eight-year-old boy that skipped and jumped around him, except unlike the others, he had that cloud of despair that loomed over him. That heavy weight that surrounded him made him seem like a grown-up with all the burdens of the adult world on his shoulders. And it didn't seem fair.

"Well, Daisy," Jenny huffed, then pointed at Elias who took his time to cross the field. "Look at him. My mama told me to stay away from him. You know Pastor Fulmer says that thing about lying with dogs and catching their fleas. I'm not catching his fleas, Sunny Ray. If you aren't careful, you'll catch 'em."

It was like a load of bricks had slammed down right over my chest, and my fingers tingled the way it does when my hand had fallen asleep. Elias drew closer, and Jenny kept talking about how awful his family was and how terrible I was for liking him. Daisy was near tears begging her to stop. And all I wanted was to make sure that Elias didn't hear the ugly things Jenny said. Before I realized what I'd done, my hand balled into a fist and launched itself right at Jenny's nose.

A thin trail of blood trickled over her lip, and her eyes welled with tears. She ran off, screaming for Mrs. Beasley while Daisy lingered beside me, her hand clasped over her mouth.

"Sunny," Daisy whispered, but I wasn't paying attention to her.

Elias now stood in front of me, holding my bloodied hand and inspecting it.

"You okay?" he asked, a worried frown marking his face.

I nodded in a bit of a daze. I couldn't believe I had just punched Jenny Smith. I was going to be in so much trouble.

"What'd she do?" he asked.

I shrugged. I wouldn't dare tell him. Then Daisy opened her big, fat mouth, "Jenny was saying bad things about you, and Sunny punched her."

A crooked smile shaped Elias' lips. "I've never seen a girl punch someone before."

"I never wanted to punch anybody before."

"Did you like it?" he asked.

"No."

The grin on Elias' face was the biggest I'd ever seen. "Well, I liked it. Almost as much as I like you."

ELIAS

OCTOBER 1991

At that point, it had been over two years since Miss Watson—the social work that carted me from foster home to foster home—brought me to the state department to meet Mr. Lower.

Before she opened the door to the building, she bent over, her round glasses nearly slipping off her nose, and she told me that someone in my family would eventually come for me. She grinned when she made that statement and then patted the top of my head as though that thought should make me feel good or something. I guess some kids wanted a family member to take them, but I only had my Aunt Billie. Paw always said she was a lot-lizard. I didn't know what that was, but even at age nine, it didn't sound good.

Twenty-four months and there had been no sign of the lot-lizard. That should have made me happy, I guess, seeing as how I really liked living in the Lower's nice house. It had two stories with one of those wrap around porches and a swing just like I'd see on television shows. Mrs. Lower baked cookies constantly, and always smiled sweetly, except for the time I got sent to the principal's office for yanking Jenny's hair. I tried to tell Mrs. Lower Jenny had it coming, but she wouldn't listen. I bet if she'd let me explain that freckled-face Jenny Smith whispered to Daisy Fulmer that Sunny's dress was ugly, she would have given me a cookie.

But even with the nice house and all the smiles and cookies—even with Sunny Ray as my forever best friend, I couldn't be too happy. Every day when I thought about what happened before Mrs. Watson showed up to take my brothers and me away, my stomach twisted like a wad of snakes around a struggling rat. Sunny wouldn't want nothing to do with me if she knew my paw was bad. That was for sure. So I didn't let myself get too happy or too settled. I felt awful that I'd lied to Sunny, telling her I'd never leave her. I knew one day I would—I'd have to, because she'd want me to. But boy, I hoped that didn't come for a long time.

That's why I tried not to think about that night my paw shot those two men and shoved them in our trunk, and most of the time, I didn't. I was too busy thinking about Sunny and her pretty smile that made me all warm inside. Something about her heated me from the center like I'd just eaten a bowl of soup. But at night, when Mr. and Mrs. Lower were in their room, watching TV, and I was alone in my bed with that dumb He-Man nightlight glowing in the corner, I couldn't help but think about it.

I'd close my eyes, and there it was. A black stain behind my eyelids. By the time the low hum from the Lower's television cut off, my heart usually pounded in my chest like an Indian war drum.

That night, the TV didn't cut off, and I was lost in the memory of how the smell of cigarettes and bourbon made my pulse race and the back of my neck sweat. I needed the scent of candy to help me feel safe.

When the clock on my nightstand blinked over to eleven thirty, I crawled out of bed and tiptoed to my door. The blue flicker of light from the Lower's TV danced on their bedroom wall. From my doorway, I could see Mr. Lower on his back, one arm dangling off the mattress. Even though I figured he was asleep, I counted to one-hundred before I snuck down the hall and slipped into Sunny's room.

The second the floorboards creaked under my foot, she sat up. "What took you so long?" she whispered.

"Your dad fell asleep with the TV on." I hopped onto the bed next to Sunny, bouncing her a few times. It sent her into a giggling fit. Her laughs made me happy.

When I finally settled underneath her sheets, I inhaled that smell of candy that was all Sunny deep into my lungs until she felt like a part of me. I wanted Sunny Ray to always be a part of me because no one else ever had.

She snuggled right into her fluffy pillow, her blond hair spilling over onto my arm. And then we started our nightly game of Have You Ever. We'd ask each other questions until one of us fell asleep.

"Have you ever been to Disney World?" she started.

"No."

"Me neither." She sighed. "Maybe when we grow up we can go."

"Yeah. Maybe." I shifted, fighting with the sheets tangled around my feet. "Have you ever eaten an ant?"

"Eww. No. Have you?"

"Nah. I don't like the thought of their six little legs in my mouth." I wiggled my fingers in front of her face. Pretending they were the prickly legs of an insect and she laughed.

We kept going until Sunny's voice drifted, and I knew

she was nearly asleep. I rolled over, placing my face in her hair. That night, for the first time, when I closed my eyes next to Sunny, that black stain on my soul lingered on my lids, and I smelled the cigarettes creeping around me. My eyes popped open, and I gripped the sheets, staring at the doorway.

My pulse clanged in my ears, and my skin itched with that tingly heat that made me want to jump up and run right out of the house.

"Sunny?" I just wanted to hear her voice. I needed to be reminded that I was here and not back in the house on Rural Route 21.

"Huh?" Her voice was lazy, half-asleep.

"You ever been to the beach at night?"

"No." She yawned. "Have you?"

"Yeah. I used to sneak out when my Paw was drunk and mad and shouting. I'd run right on down to the highway and across the hot pavement until I felt the sand under my feet."

She turned toward me. Thanks to the soft glow of the nightlight, I could make out her blue eyes all wide in wonder. Paw always spoke about feeling like a man, and right then, I thought I knew what he'd been talking about. The way Sunny looked at me in that moment made me feel how I thought men felt. My chest puffed out, and my lips curled into a grin.

"You went by yourself?" she breathed.

I nodded. "Swam out in the water sometimes, too." I thought about lying and telling her I swam with a shark, but used my better judgment and decided against it. After all, Sunny and her family didn't care much for sin, and I'd heard lying was just that. I didn't want to sin against Sunny. Not ever.

I rolled onto my side, placing my nose inches from hers. "Wanna go?"

She stared at me for a long minute before exhaling. "We'll get in trouble."

"Only if they catch us."

Excitement darted through me like a hot liquid until I found myself jumping out of her bed and grabbing her hand to pull her to her feet. She didn't argue with me, just followed me right to her window, stifling giggle after giggle.

I threw back the frilly curtains and pushed the latch on the windowsill until it clicked, the seal popping when I finally shoved up the wooden frame.

I'd already swung both legs over and was sitting on the ledge just about to jump when Sunny placed her hand on my shoulder. "But the dark's not safe," she whispered.

"It is when I've got my sun with me." I kissed her cheek fast, then hopped down, landing on the soft grass with a thud.

Sunny's hair tumbled over her shoulder when she leaned over the ledge. For a moment, I didn't think she'd come, and something in my chest went all tight, but then she threw her legs over and joined me, landing with an oomph at my side.

I took her hand in mine, and we started across the yard, the crickets silencing as we waded through the damp yard.

The sky was clear, lit up by a moon so full it looked like a marble I could catch in my fist like a firefly. By the time we reached the gravel road, Sunny stopped, pulling on my arm. "I'm scared."

"So am I." I grinned. "That's what makes it fun."

Her teeth went to work on her lip again.

"You can go back if you wanna," I said, noticing how sweaty her palm had grown.

"I wanna be with you." She squeezed my hand, and my heart did a weird flip-flop thing that sent heat buzzing over my body.

"I won't let nothing get you. Promise."

"Never?"

"Never. Ever." That had been our promise to each other since the first night I slept in her bed, since the first time in my life I'd known what it was to feel safe. Two words that meant everything to the both of us.

Sunny gave me a quick nod, and we started down the road beside the house. It wasn't but a few blocks to the highway that ran parallel to the ocean, and I was pretty sure I knew the way, but in the country darkness, it was hard to tell one turn from the next.

We passed Rural Route 21, right past the white mailbox with a dent from Paw's baseball bat, and I never breathed a word. I was too scared Sunny would ask questions if I told her that was where I once lived. Afraid that the terrible, bad thing I had done would somehow come to life and chase us both down the dirt road before it swallowed me up, leaving Sunny all alone in the dark.

"You okay?" Sunny asked, out of breath. I realized I walked so fast that her short little legs struggled to keep up.

"Yeah."

"You're squeezing my hand real tight," she whispered. "Like you saw something."

"Nah."

Just then, the rumble of an old engine came from the distance. A car turned onto the road, only one headlight illuminating the thick marsh to the side of the highway.

Nudging Sunny with my shoulder, I guided her into the tall pokeweeds where we hid until the beat-up sedan sputtered past and the red glow of the taillights disappeared. I took a breath. "Let's run. Okay?"

And off we went, sprinting through the grass and narrow pines, across the highway until the sand squeaked under our bare feet.

Ahead of us, I could barely make out the dashes of whitecaps on the ink-black ocean. There was no separation from the sea and sky except for the stars that resembled broken bits of glass strewn about space and the low-hanging, lonely moon.

The waves whooshed as they tumbled onto the shore.

The wind, sticky with mist, slicked my skin.

The second the warm, Gulf water rushed over my toes, weight lifted off my shoulders. This place had been my refuge for as long as I could remember. Beaches stretched on forever, dark dunes provided places I could hide, and there was just enough light from the moon and the stars to assure me I was safe.

Sunny's shoulder brushed mine. The smell of candy caught in the wind, mixing with the saltwater and sand. We stood there in silence, the waves foaming around our feet as we stared out into the endless darkness.

I'd stood here a hundred times before, out of breath. Sometimes angry. Sometimes scared that I'd go home and Maw would be gone. But I had always been alone.

It was much better with Sunny than it was by myself, and I thought life would be better with her. Always.

I reached for her hand and held it because that's what people do before they kiss, and I wanted to kiss her. In my mind, I believed if I kissed her like they did in the movies, all hard and strong and long, she'd love me. Maw always said that love had powers beyond measure, and that's why, even though my paw was horrible, she wouldn't leave him. She loved him.

I needed Sunny to love me so that if she ever did find out about that dark stain on my soul, she wouldn't run away.

"Why do you say I'm like sunshine?" Sunny asked.

"Because you brighten everything up." I hesitated. "Even me."

"Even your storm clouds?"

"Yep."

She sighed, resting her head against my shoulder. "Well, I think you're like the moon."

The water sucked back into the ocean, and another large wave crashed onto the shore, the tide coming up to our knees. "You think I'm dark and gloomy?"

"No. Because I feel bad for the moon, just like I sometimes feel bad for you. It makes the dark less scary, but no one seems to pay attention to it. Except me."

I chewed at my lip, my heart pounding.

"And the sun and the moon belong together," she added.

I smiled even though it seemed like the sun and the moon spent eternity chasing each other, one always rose while the other sank on the other side of the world.

We stood there, knee deep in the dark ocean, side by side, and the world felt right. For the first time in my short existence, it felt right.

Some people grow up with parents who love them and make them feel like nothing in the world matters as much as they do. I didn't have that. Sunny was the only person who made me feel like I was that important, and I was fine with that. Even at the age of nine, she was my world.

"Sunny, when we get older, I'm gonna marry you."

"Okay." And with that, she ran back toward the shoreline, shouting for me to catch her.

I thought I'd chase that girl to the end of the world just like the moon chased the sun if she wanted me to.

I really thought that.

WE SNUCK BACK in her window just as the sky turned a bright pink that Saturday morning.

Her parents never had a clue, and after breakfast, I crammed all the money I'd saved from not buying milk at lunch—which totaled fifteen dollars—in my back pocket, took my bike, and rode down to the beachfront.

Right across from the public beach was a little shop my maw used to take us when she'd come across some money. They had rock candy and soda and hippie jewelry that Magpie Brown used to make. At least that's what Maw said.

The little bell above the door jingled when I stepped inside. A thin wisp of smoke swirled through the air, tickling my nose with the strong scent of incense. The shop was full of clutter, surfboards, and tie-dyed t-shirts, shelves of candy and wax skull candles.

From the front of the shop I could just make out Magpie's salt and pepper hair piled high on her head, stray pieces jutting out everywhere that reminded me of Medusa.

The wooden floorboards creaked when I made my way to the jewelry counter.

"Elias Black," she said, her voice raspy from cigarette smoke. "I haven't seen you in a while." She pushed up from her stool and shuffled toward the counter, her beaded necklaces clattering together. "Did you come in for some rock candy?" She didn't wait on my response. Just reached for the glass jar and had the lid nearly unscrewed before I cleared my throat.

"No, ma'am. I came in for something special."

"Special?" One of her bushy eyebrows shot up. "What kinda special?"

I shrugged a shoulder, then stepped closer to the jewelry counter. "Something for a girl."

"Ah..." she chuckled, which sent her into a coughing fit.

Silver rings filled the display case, some made from spoon handles, some bent in wavy patterns. Then I spotted one with two silver bands and a tiny crescent moon that seem to lock into a sun. I jabbed my finger over the glass. "How much is that one?"

Magpie took the glasses hanging around her neck and placed them on the bridge of her snout-like nose while she peered into the case. "The sun and the moon?"

"Yes, ma'am."

"Oh, she must be very special." The door to the case squealed when she pushed it open to reach inside and grab the jewelry. "Because these are very special rings. Friendship rings." She flipped the little white tag over and frowned, which sent my heart into a spiraling fit of thumps and jumps. "I made these rings under the solar eclipse, and that's what this is." She held them out to me and tapped her long, red nail over the sun and moon. "It's the solar eclipse. The only time the sun and moon ever meet. Tragic if you think about it."

It was then I caught sight of the price scrawled on the tag. Fifty dollars. My stomach sank. It would take me another six months of no milk to save for that. "It's pretty," I said, defeated. "But I can't pay that. Thanks, Magpie."

With a sigh, she leaned her elbows over the glass, still holding out the ring. "How special is she, Elias."

"Special enough that I can't ever lose her."

"And why this ring?"

"Well. . ." I drug the toe of my sneaker over the old floor, then blurted out: "Her name's Sunny, and she's like my sun because she's always smiling and making me happy just by being around. And she says I'm like the moon because I bring light into all the dark places."

A soft smile set on her weathered face, and she pushed away from the counter. "Then I'd say these rings were made for the two of you, Sunny and Elias." She tore the tag off and went to the cash register. "How much did you bring?"

"Fifteen dollars."

She nodded. "Then fifteen dollars it is."

I paid for the ring, thanking old Magpie at least twenty times before I ran out of the store and hopped back on my bike. By the time I reached the Lower's, my back was sticky with sweat, and there was a stitch shooting through my side, but I didn't care. I pedaled past Mr. Lower's Chevy and some beat up Toyota truck parked in the drive, not thinking twice as I rode around to the backyard.

As soon as I rounded the fence, I could see Sunny sitting in her treehouse, facing the corner. I dropped my bike to the ground, the wheels still spinning as I ran through the gate and straight to the dogwood with the rings clutched in my palm.

Halfway up the ladder, I called her name, but she didn't say anything. The second I climbed onto the platform, she glanced over her shoulder. Her eyes were bloodshot and her cheeks stained with tears. She only looked at me for a second before she turned away.

A dizzy heat washed over me, my skin breaking out in a cold sweat.

Swallowing, I sat beside her and scooted closer until my hip touched hers, and she immediately dropped her head to my shoulder.

"What's wrong?" I asked, shifting on the hard decking so

I could wipe her tears. All she did was shake her head. "Please tell me, Sunny."

She inhaled then exhaled, gripping my shirt in her hands. "You're Aunt Billie's here."

And my entire world stopped. For a moment, it did.

My pulse sounded like a train barreling down the tracks in my ears, my throat tightened, and just as soon as the fear of losing her set in, the hinges to the Lower's backdoor creaked.

"Hey, kid!" I could tell from Aunt Billie's voice that she had a cigarette gripped between her lips.

I sat still, praying that if I didn't move, she wouldn't see me.

Sunny dropped her chin to her chest, and a soft sob broke free from her throat. That was like King John had shot a poisoned arrow right through my heart. Then I did the only thing I could think to do, pretended none of this was happening.

"Hey," I said, opening my palm and holding out my hand where she could see. "I got you something." She didn't budge, so I leaned down so low that my head was nearly on the floor of the treehouse. It was the only way I could see her face hidden under all that hair. "I got you something special, Sunny." Her eyes moved to my face, then my hand. "One for me," I said. "One for you. The sun and the moon."

She sniffled, then wiped her face dry. "They're pretty."

"It's a promise. Never. Ever. Okay? I'll never ever leave you."

Tears welled in her eyes again. "But you are leaving. . ." Another arrow in through my chest.

"I'll still see you."

"What if she won't let you?" she whispered.

"Elias. Yoo-hoo?" Aunt Billy had tottered halfway across

the yard in her high heels. Mr. and Mrs. Lower followed closely behind her with deep-set frowns on their faces.

"No matter what, I can't leave you forever," I said. "The sun and the moon, remember? They belong together." I grabbed her hand and slipped the ring with the moon on her finger. It was too big, and when she held up her hand, it slid down over her knuckle. I placed the sun ring in her palm. "Now put mine on my finger."

Sucking back tears, she pushed the ring on my finger. Mine fit a little better, but not much, so I made a fist to make sure I didn't lose it. "This way I always have you with me," I said. "And you always have me."

Sunny's lip quivered, and she threw her arms around my neck, squeezing so tightly that I couldn't breathe. But I didn't care. Had she been able to keep squeezing me until I died, I would have let her. Clinging to Sunny as hard as I could, I stared down at Aunt Billy and her bouffant, bleached hair and electric blue eyeshadow. Then I glanced at Mr. and Mrs. Lower. "Please let me stay with you." My throat tightened and burned. "Please."

Mrs. Lower's gaze dropped to the ground, and she covered her mouth while shaking her head. Mr. Lower placed his arm around her shoulders while shooting a half-smile in my direction. I'd seen that not-a-possibility-smile one too many times in my life. There was no arguing.

"Sunny," Mr. Lower said, and she hugged me even harder. "Elias has to go. But we'll keep in touch with them."

"That's right," Aunt Billie said, taking the cigarette from her lips before flicking the gray ash onto the Lower's nice lawn. "We'll be sure to keep in touch and all that jazz. Now, we gots to go get your brothers." A silver lining at least, I'd be with my Judah and Atlas again. But as much as I loved them, they weren't Sunny.

"Please don't go," Sunny whispered.

"I don't think I have a choice." And with that I untangled myself from her hold, fighting back the urge to cry as I climbed down the ladder.

Sunny's face crumpled from the inside out as she crawled to the edge of the treehouse. I was sure from the way my chest stung, I was going to die.

"I mean it," I whispered where no one could hear us. "I'm gonna marry you when we get grown up."

"Okay."

I clenched my jaw when I turned away from the dogwood, not wanting to cry. I didn't want to hurt Sunny any more than I already had.

Aunt Billie knelt and wrapped her bone-thin arms around me. She smelled like air freshener and smoke which caused my stomach to turn. "It's gonna be all right, kid. It's all gonna be all right."

Mr. and Mrs. Lower hugged me. I turned my emotions off when I thanked them for having me stay with them, then I went to gather my things while Sunny stayed in the treehouse.

I wanted to run back out to the backyard, climb up that ladder, and hug her one more time, but Aunt Billy was at the front door when I came down the stairs with my backpack.

We loaded my stuff into the back of the truck, and Aunt Billy waved at the Lowers when she turned the ignition. The engine choked, then sputtered to life, the entire vehicle rumbling.

I watched that two-story house with the wrap around porch grow smaller and smaller as we backed down the drive, and just before the truck turned around, Sunny stepped onto the front steps, staring down at her hand. I couldn't breathe; I figured it meant I loved her. Maw always said love left you breathless, and abandoning Sunny took every ounce of air from my lungs, leaving them burning and aching.

"Well, kid. I been fighting the courts long enough to get custody of you little terds." The gear shift ground and the truck lurched when Billie put the car into first. Steering with her knee, she reached for the pack of smokes on the dash. "Gonna go fetch your brothers then we're on to Mississippi."

"Mississippi?" My mouth dropped.

"Yep." She grabbed the car lighter, holding the red-orange butt to the end of her cigarette. Her cheeks sunk in when she took the first pull, and a stream of smoke sifted through the cracked window. "You got an Uncle Tommy Jo now. Real nice fella I met at the Jet Pep right across the state line. So yous and your brothers gonna live with us until we find your momma. Which ain't likely."

Crossing my arms over my chest with a huff, I sank down in the seat, while some guy on the radio sang about more than words and his heart being torn in two.

4

SUNNY

AUGUST 1996

Drew, the ninth foster child to come through our house, had colic. Bad colic. The kind where all he did was scream until he was beet red and Momma had to blow in his face to make him suck in a breath.

Daddy was busy taking care of my brother, Simon, who at the age of three had just had open heart surgery, so I tried swinging Drew on the porch while Momma took a shower, but that didn't help; he only yelled louder. From my parents' frazzled state, I felt he may be the last infant to grace the Lower household.

Momma came out on the porch in her tattered robe and a towel on her head. After Drew had been passed to her, I asked if I could go to Daisy's house. Placing him on her shoulder, Momma looked off the porch toward the field. It was already dusk, and while she usually wouldn't let me out after seven, that night she did. She nodded while bouncing the hollering bundle in her arms, kissed me on the cheek, and told me she loved me.

I almost felt guilty when I grabbed my bike from the

garage and swung my leg over it. I wasn't going to Daisy's. I was going to my haven. The place I went when I needed to think when I wanted to remember what it was like to be close to someone the way I was Elias.

Of course, I had my friends, and at fifteen, maybe I should have developed that unmatched bond with someone else, but I hadn't. Not even with Daisy. So every once in a while—when I really wanted to contemplate losing a foster kid to their real family or boys or why people like Jenny Smith hated my guts—I went to the secluded part of the beach Elias had taken me all those years ago.

I was out of breath by the time my tires hit the sand and the pedals locked up. After I hopped off and hid my bike behind a clump of sea oats, I slipped out of my shoes and then took off toward the shoreline, the sand squelching underneath my bare feet. I didn't stop until warm water rushed around my ankles.

Dropping my head back, I inhaled the briny scent of damp sand and the warm, rising tide. All I could see was the blank canvas of night scattered with glittering stars that danced around the nearly full moon, its silvery-white reflection catching on the waves as they tumbled in.

Over the years, I'd memorized each crater, every shadow in that giant orb, how it waxed and waned throughout the months. I had realized that even though it shared the sky with the sun in the early morning, the two celestial bodies were never close.

They simply chased one another infinitely.

The moon and the sun. The first star-crossed lovers doomed to an eternity of almost.

My gaze dropped to the ring on my hand, and an eerie blue gleam to the water caught my attention. The upsurge sparkled as though a million tiny fairies had been trapped inside. I was so captivated, enchanted by each swell that glimmered, that I hadn't notice anyone approach.

"Are you kidding me?" A guy laughed behind me, and I jumped. "Poseidon's Wheel?" He was in the water now. And we were alone on a very dark, very deserted beach.

Screaming, I quickly trudged through the knee-deep surf toward shore.

"Hey," he said. "Calm down. I'm not gonna hurt you."

My pulse raced. Adrenaline scorched through my body. His voice was deep, but not exactly that of a grown man's. Something about it caused a familiar tug on my heart. Which was the only reason I stopped to watch him wade deeper into the water.

"Man, it's been a long time since I've been here," he mumbled.

My breath caught for a split-second because the boy walking toward me had a face like a storm cloud. The glowing waves rumbled behind him, and we narrowed our gazes at the same time, then he froze. "No way...Sunny?"

"Eli—Elias?"

We both struggled to run against the current, tripping and stumbling before we reached one another. It was like one of those moments in a movie where the music reached a climactic crescendo. I didn't think; I just reacted. Before I knew it, my chest was against his, our arms wrapped tightly around each other—just like the last time I saw him in my treehouse, only he didn't smell like Dial Mountain Fresh soap anymore. He smelled like leather and spice with a touch of the ocean in his messy, brown hair.

"What are you doing here?" I asked, my chin over his shoulder while I tried to suck his scent deep down.

I prayed he was going to tell me he had moved back. No

matter how much it may hurt to know he had been here without me knowing, I didn't care. I just wanted him to stay.

"Driving through to Birmingham to see my paw," he said, sweeping my hair from my face. "He's up for parole or some shit. Aunt Billie wanted to visit a trucker she used to fool around with, so we're over at the Motel 8. Just for tonight though."

My hopes crashed and burned. He slowly dragged his knuckles over my cheek, and I bit down on the inside of my lip. That touch felt like everything right and a little wrong, something I wanted to cling to.

"I've been sick trying to figure out a way to see you," he said. "I mean, being right here and not seeing you." He closed his eyes and shook his head. When he reopened them, he said, "Torture, Sunny. Torture."

"Is that why you came to the beach?"

"It is. I guess the universe wanted us to see each other, huh?"

"I guess." I stared into his eyes, black under the moonlight, as I grappled with what to say. I couldn't form words to express every thought I'd had of him every day since he'd left. Sometimes there are no words, only touches, so I hugged him again, resting my head on his shoulder while the warm water heaved and pulled around our feet. "I missed you," I whispered.

"I missed us." He combed his hand through my hair, and for a moment, I let his words suffocate me until it became hard to breathe.

Five years when you are a child is an eternity. Voices change. Faces age. But feelings, so it seemed, did neither. That pull deep in the middle of my chest that tethered me to him was still right there, firmly intact.

When we finally let go of one another, he took my hand

and threaded his fingers through mine with a practiced ease, like he'd done it a thousand times. That was the first time since boys were *boys* that I had held hands with one. I liked the way his hand felt rough against mine and slightly bigger. How safe it was.

We walked to the shore and sat shoulder to shoulder on the sand, close enough that sometimes, when the waves crashed, the glowing water brushed our toes.

Elias pointed to the sea. "You ever seen it glow like that?"

"No. Have you?"

"Once. When I was about six, right before. . ." His brows lowered, and he drew in a hard breath. "Not too long before I went to my first foster home. Anyway, it's called Poseidon's Wheel."

"Like the Greek God of the ocean?" I asked.

He nodded. "Yeah, sailors back in the day didn't get the whole microscopic-plankton-that-glow in the water thing, you know? So they thought it was Poseidon causing the water to light up." Laughing, he nudged me with his shoulder. "It's pretty cool, though, to think that something like that was proof of God to people. Even if it was a god with a trident and a fishtail."

I stared at him, taking in the straight line of his nose, his jaw.

"I think about you every day," he said, turning to face me. Before I could tell him that I thought of him, too, he exhaled. "What time do you have to go home?"

I shrugged a shoulder. "Soon."

Elias' chin dipped to his chest, and he dragged his fingertip through the wet sand. A necklace swung loose from his collar when he leaned forward to make another design. The ring hanging from it caught under the moonlight. Without thought, I reached over and gripped it between my fingers. Stunned, I realized it was the sun to my moon. "You still have it?"

"Of course," he said. "You still got yours?"

I held up my hand and wiggled my fingers.

Elias raked his teeth over his bottom lip, almost concealing a smirk. "Fits now, huh?"

"Yeah. Guess yours doesn't?"

"Not exactly."

I rested my head on his shoulder and watched the white caps. I wanted every millisecond I could get from him. "Where are you living these days?"

He let out a short laugh that wasn't really a laugh. "With whoever Billie's sleeping with."

"Oh."

"Found out my mom died." The waves crashed, filling the silence. "That's why she never came back for us."

"I'm sorry." It felt cheap to say, but saying nothing seemed too callous. I wanted all the details of the years I'd missed, even if I didn't know how to go about getting them.

Elias draped his arm around my shoulder and pulled me tight against him. "It's all right. Life, you know?"

We sat in the dark, listening to the soothing pulse of the ocean and the muted laughter from people far down the beach. I should get home before Momma called Daisy's house, but I didn't want to leave him. After all, the chances I would ever see him again were slim.

His hand absentmindedly swept up and down my arm.

Being beside him like that, it felt like a missing fragment of my soul had finally been snapped back into place. That was the moment I learned what being whole meant. The very second I realized how impulsive love is. "Come home with me?" I whispered, and my heart stalled.

Elias kept his gaze aimed at the sea like I hadn't just

asked him to do something neither one of us had any business considering. "Okay." Standing, he brushed sand from the back of his legs and then offered me his hand to help me to my feet. And we walked back through the dunes, arm in arm like we hadn't spent the last seven years apart.

MY INSIDES TWISTED and knotted when I walked through the front door into the quiet, dark house while Elias waited out back below my window. Momma stood at the sink, washing bottles with Drew asleep in the swing beside the counter. Daddy was on night shift, which meant he wouldn't be home until eight the next morning.

The picture of Jesus that hung on our foyer wall seemed to judge me when I walked past that night. Had I been seven, that painting may have been enough to make me march upstairs and never open my window, but I had found the older I grew, the more able I was to justify my sins when I want them vindicated.

I told myself that it was all right to sneak Elias into my room. If God had not moved him so far away, if my parents hadn't hidden the fact that his Aunt Billie was coming to get him and given me time to say a proper goodbye, I wouldn't have to try and soak up one lone night with him. By the time I'd reached the dining room doorway, I had convinced myself that I'd eventually feel true guilt over it and be able to ask forgiveness. After all, Pastor Fulmer said death row inmates were forgiven of murder all the time—if they truly were sorry. Sleeping next to a boy was nowhere near murder.

"Sunny? That you?" Momma called.

"Yes, ma'am."

"I was thinking maybe tomorrow we could go down to

Betty's and get our nails done. Let Daddy keep Simon and Drew for the afternoon."

"Uh. Yeah." I swallowed, and my heart hammered like a judge's gavel. I walked through the dining room and into the kitchen, stopping beside the sink to kiss Momma on the cheek. "Goodnight."

She shut off the water and placed the last bottle on the drying rack before she turned toward me. Her soft smile faded a touch, and somehow, I thought she knew. "Your cheeks sure are red," she said, placing the back of her hand to my forehead. "You aren't coming down with a summer cold, are you?"

"No." I took a step back. "I just rode my bike really fast to get home on time. It's hot." My gaze strayed to the window. I worried how long Elias would be out there waiting.

"I think I'll sleep on the couch. Drew seems to do better in his swing."

"Okay." I started toward the steps.

"Just come get me if you need me," she said on her way into the living room.

I waited at the foot of the stairs until the lull of the television cut on before I went up.

When I brushed my teeth, my hands shook.

A lump formed in my throat when I pushed my bedroom door open.

My chest heated when I slipped into an old band shirt and sleep shorts. And when I stepped to the window to lift it, I thought for a second that I might pass out. I was going to hell and all for a few extra hours with a boy I never stood a chance with simply because he was too far away.

No sooner had I raised the sash than Elias' fingers curled around the wooden frame. I grabbed his wrists and helped pull him up, thankful for the thick area rug that muted his subsequent tumble onto the floor.

While I could make out his face on the beach, his features had been shrouded in darkness. But here, in my room, I could see each tiny detail: the way his jawline had grown more defined, the subtle chestnut undertones in his hair, and his eyes that had a color not yet named.

Without a word, he clamored to his feet and took the few steps needed to close the space between us, then cupped my cheeks in both his hands. An unyielding heat seared through me as he inched his face closer and closer. It terrified me and thrilled me at the same time.

"I've been saving this," he whispered, then pressed his mouth against mine in a feather-light touch, as though it were meant to be a question. Then his lips parted, and he kissed me harder.

My stomach flitted—butterflies—and my hands were clumsy, reaching for his neck, his hair.

I tried to mimic what I had watched in movies, but after a few seconds, I no longer cared how perfect it looked because the way his soft lips moved against mine was seamless. My pulse clanged in my ears, and parts of my body felt different, tingly like they'd just woken from a deep sleep.

When Elias finally pulled away, I was left against the wall with my eyes closed and my lungs desperate for air. That first kiss left me breathless, and I was pretty sure that I no longer owned my heart.

"And that's proof," Elias said.

"Of what?"

"That it'll always be you and no one else." He swept his fingers through my hair then crossed the room, kicking off his shoes before sitting on the edge of my bed.

"Always me what?" I asked.

"I've gone on dates with girls," he started, and my heart clenched. "But I was never able to kiss 'em because when I close my eyes, the only thing I see is you, Sunny Ray." He touched the middle of his chest. "The heart is only meant to love one person."

Shakespeare had forever lost meaning to me because those words Elias had just uttered were mine. Only ours.

I crawled across the bed on my knees until I was right in front of him, my pulse skipping and jumping and my mouth unable to form words.

He stared at me, and I stared at him, each of us taking shallow breath after shallow breath.

"I think I love you," I whispered.

"I love you, and I'm certain of that, because you always know when you find what you've been looking for."

We kissed for what seemed like hours until my lips ached and my eyes were heavy with sleep. I laid beside him, sweeping my fingers up and down his arm, wishing he could somehow stay. "What do we do?" I asked.

"Wait for each other."

I swallowed.

"Three more years, we'll be out of high school. I'll move back here for you."

"You promise?"

"I saved my first kiss for you, Sunny Ray. I'll save you my first of everything." He pulled me onto his chest.

That was a strangely satisfying feeling—lying on him like that and listening to his heart beat. And then, just like that, I was asleep.

"What in the hell?"

I sat straight up in bed when my door slammed against

the wall—straight up to my daddy looming in the doorway, teeth clenched, cheeks hellfire and brimstone red.

Elias shot up, dragged his hands down his face with a groan, and mumbled "shit" beneath his breath.

"Sunny Ray Lower—" Daddy took one ominous step into my bedroom that I swear shook the floor—"what in God's name is a *boy* doing in your bed?"

By this time, Momma had run to the doorway with Drew cradled in her arms, a bottle clutched in his tiny hands. When her gaze landed on Elias underneath my sheets, her face went stark white. Her mouth opened and then closed before she looked at the floor.

"Get." Daddy took another step, and I felt Elias tense beside me. "Out."

Elias held up his hands like he expected to block a blow. "It's, uh." He swallowed hard. "It's not what it looks like, Mr. Lower. It was just that I. We. . . shit."

The vein in Daddy's temple bulged, throbbing with each thump of his heart. I had only seen that happen once, when Henry Watson, the town drunk, called Momma a bitch.

"Did you hear what I said, son? Get the hell outta here."

My entire body shook, and my vision blurred. I had let my parents down, and no amount of words or sincere apologies would ever convince them Elias in my bed was much more innocent than it appeared.

"Daddy," I whispered. "It's not what it looks like. It's—"

"You're fifteen, Sunny. Fifteen!"

By now Momma sobbed in the hallway, and Simon had tottered out of his room, crying.

Daddy's gaze cut to Elias. "And you, I'll be speaking with your parents."

"I don't have any parents, sir."

"Daddy, it's Elias!" I shouted, and my voice trembled as I

fought the urge to cry. "He just came in for one night, and I didn't want to leave him, so I asked him to come stay. I know it was wrong, but I just wanted to see him, and I'm"—I choked on a sob. "I'm sorry."

Momma called on Jesus before pacing the hall. Everything washed from Daddy's face, and for a split moment, I thought he would forgive us both. I thought maybe he understood. But then, a new wave of anger tore across his face. "Get out of my house, son." He pointed at the hall, his finger shaking. "Now!"

Elias tossed the covers off and climbed out of bed. His eyes remained trained on me while he shoved his feet into his shoes, not bothering to lace them. He stalled for a moment, gnawing at his lip.

"Son?"

His brows pinched together, and he nodded once before he turned his back to me. Something in my soul crumpled like a shoreline wasting away under the rising tide.

"Daddy?" I pleaded. My throat burned so badly that I either had to let the tears out or scream.

Elias stopped at the end of my bed. "I meant what I said, Sunny. I love you." He went to move past Daddy. "And I'm sorry, Mr. Lower. I didn't mean any disrespect."

Daddy's nostrils flared when Elias brushed past him and into the hallway, and I fell forward into a heap on my bed, balling the sheets in my hand and crying. Every breath I sucked in smelled like leather and spice, and all that did was twist the proverbial dagger deeper into my chest.

"We need to talk when I calm down," Daddy said.

I continued to weep as his footfalls traveled the length of the hallway followed by the bang of his bedroom door. I was ashamed and upset, but mostly, I was afraid I would never see Elias again.

But I couldn't expect them to understand that. They were so far removed from fifteen years of age, tainted by life and bills and unfulfilled dreams. I expected the way I felt for Elias to seem silly and ridiculous. After all, I hadn't even spoken to him in five years, and suddenly, there he was, snuggled down in their only daughter's bed.

The floorboards creaked. Momma's hand gently touched my back. "Sunny?" She used the voice she reserved for when I was sick—or when Elias didn't want to eat his peas. "Honey?"

"Go away." As soon as the words left my mouth, another pound of guilt weighed down on my shoulders.

"Listen." She paused, and Drew cooed. "I'm not mad at you. We're human, and you're at the age where your hormones can take over and cause you to make rash decisions. I just. . . I just don't want one mistake to ruin your life, and—"

"I didn't sleep with him, Mother. He didn't even touch me!"

There was a long beat of silence only broken by the intermittent gasps I took between tears. "Okay." She inhaled. "If you say you didn't, then I believe you. But love—honey, love is something that you can't possibly understand at such a tender age."

My jaw tensed. Too young to understand love? Then why was there an aching feeling in my chest when I watched Elias leave? If that wasn't love, what was it? "You don't understand," I said.

"Yes, I do. I've been your age before."

"But you're not me!"

Her hand left my back. "You're right. I'm not."

I glanced through the curtain of hair covering my face. Momma appeared defeated, confused, worried, as if the sleepless nights with Drew and Simon hadn't been hard enough on her, there I was adding to it.

"I'm sorry."

She nodded, cradling Drew before she walked through the door, slowly closing it behind her.

I STAYED in my room that entire day, afraid to come out and face my father. Little girls never want to let their daddies down. No matter how old a girl got, I didn't think that changed, and I had let him down a hundred times over that day.

I finally went downstairs for dinner, keeping my eyes on the floor when I pulled out the dining room chair. The legs scratched the hardwood floor when I scooted up. I stared at my plate but could still see Daddy's elbows on the surface, his hands clasped. I wondered if he was praying.

"I've been thinking all day about how to handle this, Sunny." His words hung heavy in the air like a thick, black cloud of smoke attempting to choke me out.

Momma took a seat with a glass of wine. That was the first time I'd seen her drink since Grandma Alveenie had died six years before.

I twirled the spaghetti around my fork anticipating the worst: grounded until I graduated. Community service down at the police department for the unforeseeable future. Daddy took a sip of water. "You're grounded for the rest of summer. And you're never to speak to that boy again."

Pound. Pound. Pound. My heart threatened to crack my ribs as I stared at the noodles wound around my silverware.

"Did you hear me, Sunny? Not a phone call. Not a letter. Nothing."

What I wanted to do was scream, push my chair back

and let it topple to the floor with a loud clatter before I pounded my fist on the table and told him no. But I didn't. I just stared at my spaghetti, fighting the flood of tears.

"Sunny?"

"Honey, your father's talking to you." Momma's voice was hushed.

"Why?"

Daddy exhaled through his nose. "Boys like him—"

"You don't know him!" My cheeks burned.

"And neither do you."

"I do know him, Daddy. I know that he—"

"I've kept up with him, and I hate to say it; he's nothing but trouble. Not to mention that no decent boy is gonna sneak in your room and sleep in your bed!" His jaw ticced. "There's only one reason a boy would do that, and the thought of what he had on his mind makes me sick."

"Daddy, it's not like that," I whispered. "You don't understand."

He shook his head. "I understand better than you do, and I raised you better than this, Sunny Ray."

"Whatever," I mumbled and dropped my fork.

"Excuse me, young lady?"

I glanced up at him, my nostrils flaring as I fought the urge to cry. "I said. Whatever!" And then I shoved away from the table, stormed out of the kitchen, and up the stairs. My father called for me while my mother told him to let me be. I went to my room, slammed the door, and I sulked. At fifteen, my parents owned my life, and a boy I could never see again owned my heart.

5

SUNNY

The chain to the porch swing groaned when I pushed back as far as it would go. I picked up my feet, and the humid air blew over my face, catching my hair.

It had been nearly three weeks since Elias was caught in my room. Twenty-one days since my father had banished me from having any contact with him, and with each day that passed, the seed of anger in my chest sprouted and grew.

My parents opened up their home to those "less fortunate." They had, at one time, opened up their home to Elias, and yet, I wasn't allowed to see him because suddenly he wasn't good enough. The entire ordeal took a toll on my parents as well, though. Having your pride and joy slumming it with a guy from "the wrong side of the tracks" was enough to make any parent question where they went wrong—at least that was the conversation I overhead a few nights before when I pressed my ear to my bedroom wall. And the fact that Momma mentioned the incident to Daisy's mom, well, that meant she was really troubled with it. She was never the type to air out dirty laundry, especially not to the preacher's wife. I guess she must have asked her to say a special prayer for my soul. Which would explain why Daisy sat on the porch step staring at me. "Mother told me what happened."

"What?" I played dumb.

Tilting her head, she raised both brows. "Elias Black."

I shrugged, and she rolled her eyes with a huff.

"In your bed, Sunny! You had a boy in your bed, and you didn't tell me?"

I shrugged again, then we sat in silence for a minute.

"So, what was it like?" She chewed at her lip, anticipating, afraid.

"What was *what* like?"

"Sleeping with him."

Sighing, I hopped off the porch swing and took a seat on the step beside her. "I didn't have sex with him, Daisy."

She deadpanned me. "I'm your best friend, Sunny. Come on."

"Come on, nothing. He slept in his shorts and T-shirt. All we did was kiss."

"Okay well, what was that like?" She grinned.

"Like. . ." I took a breath and closed my eyes, recalling the way his lips felt, the way my heart beat like it wanted to break out of my chest. "How you feel when you see a shooting star. In awe and breathless."

She didn't make a peep, and when I opened my eyes, there was a small crease in her forehead, her brows scrunched inward. "That sounds deep. I'm not going to lie. I'm disappointed that you didn't lock your door. That was a bad, bad mistake."

"I did lock it. The stupid lock didn't catch." The house had settled, causing a few of the doors to no longer line up the way they should. I found that out *after* I'd been caught."

"That sucks."

"Yep."

"So you can't see him?" she asked. "That's what I heard your mom tell mine."

"Can't talk to him. Write him. Nothing."

Daisy inhaled, a nostalgic smile shaping her lips as she leaned over her knees. "It's tragically romantic."

"It's tragically stupid."

We sat, watching the mail truck sputter up to the mailbox at the end of the drive. After he shoved a handful of letters in, he waved as he drove off. I pushed up from the step and headed down the long drive. Daisy followed me. "So you think you love him?" she asked.

"I know I love him," I said.

"How?"

"Because," I remembered what Elias had told me, my chest going all tight. "You know when you've found what you've been looking for."

Daisy's face crumpled. "You should be a poet, Sunny. Gosh. Shooting stars and looking for love."

The hinges to the mailbox creaked when I opened it to grab the envelopes. Daisy started jabbering about Billy Weathers—this private school kid in her youth group at church. She knew she was in love with him because he looked like the blond hunk from "Saved by the Bell." I had seen Billy, and he looked nothing like Zac Morris.

I was about to roll my eyes when I glanced down at the letter on the top of the stack, addressed to me without a return address. Adrenaline snapped through me like a live wire, and I couldn't have hidden the grin had someone threatened me with death.

"What?" Daisy asked, peeking over my shoulder. "Oh. My. God. Is that him?"

"I don't know."

"Open it!" She grabbed my shoulders and shook me. "Open it. Now!"

I flipped it over and jammed my finger underneath the sealed flap, tearing it open with one swipe. Just before I pulled out the letter, I eyed Daisy. "I swear to all that is holy, Daisy Fulmer, if you breathe a word of this to your momma or your daddy or your dumb schnauzer Pepper, I'll never talk to you again."

She made an *X* over her heart. "I would never."

One last, stern look, and then I tugged the letter out, quickly unfolding it.

Sunny Ray,

Sorry I haven't written or called before now, and sorry that this will probably be all you hear from me for a while. I just wanted you to know that I think about you every day. You mean everything to me. There may be hundreds of thousands of galaxies in the universe, but I'm pretty sure there's only one sun for each. You're my sun. And we only belong to each other. I love you.

I'll write you back with an address as soon as I can.

Elias

"What's it say?" Daisy waved her hands around in a panic. "I can't take the anticipation."

I read the letter to her, gushing and swooning while she clutched her chest. "I swear, love letters are a lost art," she said. "At least that's what my Aunt Gertrude says." She looked from the letter to me. "What are you going to do when he sends you another one?"

And that swell of happiness shrank like a deflated balloon. I didn't have an answer to her question. I had always been the good girl who did exactly as my parents said—aside from sneaking Elias into my room—but at some point, I had to make my own decisions. At some point, I had to do what I felt was best instead of what they thought was best. That was just part of growing up.

"I don't know. If Daddy ever caught a letter from him, I'd be grounded until I was thirty-five."

Daisy's eyes lost focus, and she chewed at her lip while slowly shaking her head. "There has to be a way. You love him, so there has to be a way." I stared at the note, at his perfect handwriting, at the words I love you until Daisy snapped her fingers. "Oh my God. Too easy. Write him back, and tell him to send the letters to me."

"What?" I frowned.

"Tell him to mail me the letters. Put—put the name Betty Smith on the return address, that's a girl I used to go to summer camp with. I'll tell my mom I ran into her at the Piggly Wiggly or something."

"And your mom's gonna believe you've slipped back into the archaic ways of pen paling?"

"I'm not allowed to have AOL or the internet because it's the eye of the devil or some crap, Sunny. They force me to live an archaic life. She'll believe it."

Swallowing, I nodded. The fire of rebellion lit in my soul. I respected my parents. I did, but I loved Elias, and I couldn't stand the thought of losing that.

THAT NIGHT I laid in my bed unable to think, worried about

when he would send the next letter. Worried that I might get caught but fully convinced it would be worth the repercussions.

I wanted to speak to him, write him, but I didn't even know where he was.

I imagined Juliet must have felt the same way when she received letters from exiled Romeo—in awe and heartbroken and helpless—hopelessly in love with a boy she couldn't touch or see except within daydreams.

Elias Black was my very own, tragic love story, and what teenage girl wouldn't drown in the epic depression of such a thing?

And drown I did—until I got caught.

6

ELIAS

DECEMBER 1996

Aunt Billie lay sprawled out, snoring on the sofa with a lit cigarette in her hand, the ash half-an-inch long. I placed my football helmet on the TV tray that served as a makeshift table and took the smoke, then stubbed it out in the ashtray.

My twin brothers Judah and Atlas came stampeding up the front steps of the single-wide trailer, causing the entire thing to rock. When the flimsy door banged closed behind them, Billie snorted and rolled onto her side.

"She's drunk," Judah said.

"No shit. She's always drunk." I ruffled his brown hair when I stepped around him, and he jabbed me with his elbow. They were fourteen, hormones raging, testosterone trying to flare up like a rooster's wattle, but they were still a foot shorter than me. I couldn't help myself.

I almost had made it to the hallway before I noticed they were still in street clothes. "Why aren't you wearing your practice jerseys?"

Judah shrugged. "JV didn't have practice."

I glanced at Atlas, and he stared at the floor. He was the one who had a bit of a soul, and he wore mistakes on his face, so I knew that excuse was bullshit. "Look," I said. "You're both up shit creek because either you didn't have practice and you went screwing around instead of coming home, or you got in trouble and coach sent you home— which actually, then you're up shit creek without a paddle."

Atlas punched Judah's arm. "I told you he'd know."

"What'd you do, shitheads?"

"Ah," Judah sighed. "I got Mary Peters to show us her titties, and Coach Brenner caught us."

The big brother in me wanted to laugh, high-five them, but they were already delinquents, and the sad thing was, I was the only somewhat responsible person in that trailer.

"You suspended?"

"Just from the team," Atlas said. "Not from school."

"Yeah, a load of bull." Judah sank onto the old recliner in the corner of the room. "I barely saw her nipple."

"Her boobs were small anyway, Judah." Atlas groaned. "If you were gonna try to see a girl's tits you should've asked Wendy Michaels."

"No," I said, grabbing the pile of mail on the table and sorting through it until I came to a letter from Sunny. "You shouldn't be asking any girl to show you her titties. Jesus, what's wrong with you?"

"I get boners in class, Elias. That's what's wrong with me." Judah snorted before snatching up a *Playboy* that Billie's latest love interest had left over. "Guess I'll stick to Miss November."

Shaking my head, I dropped the rest of the mail back to the table.

"Elias doesn't have to try to see titties 'cause I bet his girlfriend sends him Polaroids of her hooters." Atlas laughed before ripping the dirty magazine from Judah's hands.

I turned around, squaring my shoulders and glaring at both of my idiotic brothers. "Don't say shit like that about her, or I'll put ghost pepper juice on your toilet paper."

Judah held up his hands. "Sorry, butt munch."

"That's the lamest name. Don't go around calling people at school a butt much or you'll end up shoved in a locker, dipshit."

I went to my room, shut the door, and fell back on the only thing in that trailer that was clean—my bed.

The smile I had on my face faded when I tore open the envelope and noticed Sunny's letter only consisted of two lines.

ELIAS,

I want to break up. There's no changing my mind, so please don't write me. I'm sorry.

Sunny

SITTING on the edge of the bed, I clenched my jaw while staring at the paper. Her dad must have found out. That would be the only reason Sunny would do that.

The last letter she had sent contained a small, two-year calendar she'd printed off with little notes on each day, counting down until I'd be eighteen and could move back to Fort Morgan. After that, the days counted down to her eighteenth birthday when her parents could no longer tell her what to do.

My brothers and I were supposed to go back to Birmingham in two weeks to see my paw, and I'd talked Billie into stopping in Fort Morgan to space out the ten-hour drive. Sunny and I had planned to meet at the beach. Leaning over my knees, I wadded up the note and tossed it at the wall.

Something in the living room shattered. I shot up from the bed and through the doorway with my fist clenched at my side. Billie stood in the middle of the crappy living area, her hair going every which way like she had stuck her finger in an outlet and gotten zapped. The window behind the TV was broken, and Atlas and Judah both had sick smirks on their faces.

"What the hell happened?" I asked, glaring at my brothers.

"Those little shits," Billie said, then went into a coughing fit that doubled her over. "Drank the rest of my vodka."

"Like you need it you ole' drunk," Judah grumbled, and Billie flipped him the bird while whispering she wished she could kill him.

"Who broke the window?" I asked.

"She did," Atlas said, pointing at Billie. "Threw the vodka bottle clean through it."

I glanced at Billie, disgusted that these were the cards I had been dealt in life. A mother addicted to love and meth, a convicted murderer for a father, and then passed on to an alcoholic prostitute for truckers of an aunt—turned out that was what "lot-lizard" meant.

No wonder Mr. Lower nearly had a coronary when he found me in Sunny's bed. Looking around this filthy trailer, at the hell I had come from, I couldn't say I blamed him for not wanting his daughter tainted. This was not a life most people escaped.

Dejected, I reached for the door.

"Where the hell you going, kid? I need more vodka."

"That's your problem." And I slammed the door behind me.

I wound my way through the trailers that littered London Village Mobile Home Park until I came to the old brown one right by the entrance.

I plodded up the cinder block steps and knocked on the door which sent Benny's dogs barking. He cracked the door and peeked out before opening it wider and shoving his three wiener dogs back to let me inside.

"You need to use my intraweb doohickey to do another report?" The dogs followed him as he shuffled to the side of the room to move papers from his desk.

"No, sir. Can I... Can I use your phone?"

"Course you can." He grinned a toothless smile, the wrinkles around his eyes creasing so much his eyeballs looked like nothing more than slits. "Callin' your girlfriend again?"

Billie didn't make enough money to pay for a phone much less the internet. I relied on Benny when I couldn't get to the library and needed to type a paper or do some research. I brought him his groceries once a week, so I guessed it was a fair exchange.

About a month ago, Sunny and I had worked out a day and time for me to call her at Daisy's house. Benny pulled his hearing aids out to give me privacy, but ever since that night, he's always asked about Sunny with a grin.

"Well, something like that," I said. "I guess."

His eyes went wide as he reached for his phone and untangled the cord. "Uh-oh. Trouble in paradise?"

I ran my hand over the back of my neck and gave him a shrug.

"Women can get to be real hassles," he said.

"More like fathers." I took the phone and punched in Daisy's number.

"Oh." He pulled a cigar from his pocket and lit it while the phone rang in my ear. "Let me guess. Not good enough?"

"Nope."

"Rich girl?"

The phone rang for the third time. "Not exactly, but sure as shit not poor. Sheriff's daughter."

Benny cocked one of his crazy, white brows. "Damn, boy. You lookin' to get yerself killed, ain't ya?"

The line clicked and, thankfully, Daisy picked up.

"Sunny there?"

"Oh boy," she sighed. "No."

"Her dad made her break up with me, didn't he?"

"Look, this isn't any of my business."

"Oh," I laughed. "You made it your business, letting me send letters to your address. Sunny told me you were invested in this like some soap opera bull crap," I said, and Benny chuckled.

"Yeah, well." There was a pause where I thought she may be about to tell me. "I'm bowing out."

"Damn it! Just tell me if he made her do it, Daisy."

Daisy's mother called for her in the background. "I've gotta go," she said. "But really, Elias, how did you think it was ever gonna work out? I'm sorry." Then the line went dead.

Benny shuffled into his kitchen, and I hung up the phone and then dragged my palm over my face.

"Ain't nothing else to do when your heart done got broked than drink." Benny shoved a Miller High Life against my chest, and I fell back on his sofa with no intention to drink it.

My life was officially shit.

TWO WEEKS LATER, I pulled Billie's 1974 Toyota into the Motel 8 in Fort Morgan.

Groaning, Billie climbed out and strutted to the office in her ridiculous heels, leaving us to wait.

An old Camaro with T-tops and louvers on the back windshield pulled in right beside us. A group of girls in skimpy skirts climbed out, one with a cigarette pinched between her candy-red lips. Judah banged on the back window from the bed of the truck. I turned in the seat just as he plastered his face to the glass and nodded in the direction of the girls, and I waved him off.

He and Atlas hopped down anyway.

It may have been Christmas, but it was still humid as hell and warm when I opened the door and stepped out. My brothers were already right in the middle of the girls, every single one of them smiling and twirling hair around their fingers. Those girls were probably a year older than me, but none of the Black boys ever looked like *boys* once puberty hit. We were all tall, broad-shouldered with muscles we didn't really have to work for—compliments of my old man. So Judah and Atlas could easily get away with being eighteen if they wanted.

I snagged a pack of smokes from the dash before closing the door. "You dipshits stay outta trouble, would you?" I started toward the highway.

"Where are you going?" one of the girls asked in that annoying sing-song voice teenage chicks think is cute. It wasn't.

"To think."

Heels clicked over the pavement. "Oh, come on. Hang

out with us. We're going to get some beer and go to the beach."

"Come on, Elias. She's hot," Judah shouted. The girl giggled. I didn't even turn to look at her. I couldn't have cared less what she looked like. All I could think about was how close I was to Sunny and couldn't see her.

"Yeah, *Elias.*" She grabbed my arm, and I snatched it away.

"It's all right. My brothers'll keep you company." I hopped over one of the faded yellow parking blocks.

She mumbled, "Whatever," beneath her breath.

I couldn't stand girls like that—normal girls who were all giggly and fake and desperate for attention.

I walked a mile down Beach Front Road with no particular place to go, and somehow, I ended up standing in front of First Baptist of Fort Morgan's sign, staring at the metal letters with that week's message: *Be devoted to one another in love. Honor one another above yourselves. Romans 12:10.*

I was halfway through the parking lot when the door to the chapel opened, and a tall, slender man stepped out, followed by a rail-thin guy that looked to be about my age. Adults don't age the way kids do, they just end up looking like an older, more tired version of themselves which is why I knew the man who had just walked out the door was Pastor Fulmer, and I was able to figure out that the kid was Daisy's brother Bobby.

The pastor glanced in my direction and smiled. "Hi there."

"Hey."

He slowed his pace as he approached the lone Buick in the parking lot. I noticed the way his gaze swept over me, assessing what kind of person I was.

Jeans. Band T-shirt. My first tattoo of a tribal sun—in

honor of Sunny— on my forearm, the ink only a month old. I bet he was banking on me being a possible vandal.

"Can I help you?" he asked, stopping halfway between the church and his car.

"Nah, just cutting through." I headed across the lawn and overhead him ask Bobby if he wanted a ride down to the waterfront carnival to meet Daisy.

Maybe, I thought, just maybe that's where Sunny was.

It took me half an hour to walk to that damn carnival, creatively named, Carnival Beach. There were only about ten rides—the Tilt-A-Whirl, the swings, The Scrambler, and some kiddie crap—but it had been there for as long as I could remember. By the time I had slipped through the gate, my shirt stuck to my sweaty back, and the sky had gone from a bright orange to a purplish-blue as the last remnants of the sunset dipped below the horizon.

Britney Spears "Oops, I Did It Again" blared from The Scrambler, the screams of the thrill-seekers fading in and out as the ride spun in a wide circle; and Kids with cotton candy-covered mouths ran wild around the merry-go-round.

I shouldered my way through the crowd, inhaling the fried, sugary smell of funnel cakes as I walked toward the picnic tables. Bobby sat on one of the wooden benches with his arm around a redhead wearing a midriff that would have given Pastor Fulmer a coronary. When Bobby leaned down to wrap his arms around her waist, I caught sight of Sunny sitting alone on a bench. She stared down at her lap, looking just as sad as I felt.

A girl with brown hair pulled into a ponytail came bouncing over to her who I assumed was Daisy, and I started toward them, my pulse going haywire. If Sunny's dad was hell-bent on keeping us apart, that was fine, but I was going to kiss her lips and tell her I loved her in person one more time before I let her go. Part of me believed that was all it would take to convince her we were worth waiting on, and that in a few years' time, it would be worth having pissed off her dad.

After all, love was the noblest of causes.

A group of touchy-feely couples walked in front of me, blocking my view and stopping me dead in my tracks. When they finally moved out of my way, a blond guy had sat next to Sunny on the bench, his arm draped around her shoulders, and he snuggled way too close. My heart faltered. I gritted my teeth. And then the asshole leaned over and pressed his mouth to the lips of the girl who owned my heart. More people shuffled in front of me, obstructing my view. They laughed, completely unaware of the arrow that had just been shot through my chest.

Thump. Thump. Thump.

That's all I heard, my vision pulsing right along with my heart. I wanted to walk right over to Sunny, let her know she hadn't gotten one over on me, but then. . . I didn't see the point. Take the higher road, I thought and turned around, my chest aching while I told myself I should have known better, that I wasn't good enough.

The colorful carnival lights strung overhead blurred together, and each stride I took grew more determined, harder, angrier until I elbowed my way through the fairgrounds, not caring when I nearly knocked some guy to the ground.

Sunny broke up with me because she wanted to. Because she had found someone else. And while I should have expected that—because that's what people do, let you down and leave you—I never expected it from her.

Just like that, I gave up.

On her.

On me.

On ever being someone that would matter to anyone, and I made a promise to myself. From then on, it was, to hell with everyone else.

7

SUNNY

AUGUST 1999

Aloud crack of thunder rattled the single-pane window to the classroom. Dark storm clouds churned the sky. Gloomy and foreboding, much like I assumed my senior year would prove to be. I halfway smiled at the irony while twisting the silver moon ring on my finger. Sometimes I wondered why I still wore it. Maybe I had kept it because even though I hated that I lost him, I loved the memory of him.

Students filed in, groaning and moaning about the summer's end. The jocks strutted through the door, wearing football jerseys. Two emo kids slunk in, dressed in long-sleeved black T-shirts and jeans despite it being hotter than the devil's butt crack outside. And the populars—Jenny and Valeria and Kristen—all sauntered in with their sundresses and wedges, nails freshly painted.

Flicking her hair over her shoulder, Jenny took the desk diagonal from mine and in front of Daisy. Then she gave me a glance that was just quick enough for me to catch an eye roll. Jenny had hated me with a passion ever since I punched her in second grade.

"Oh, I like that shirt," Daisy said, snagging the sleeve of my new Nirvana tee and tugging. She gave me a once over. "You know, you look kinda like a rock star and a pageant queen had a baby."

"Um." I wrinkled my brow. "Thanks?"

Daisy was—unique. She desperately wanted to be part of the populars, for reasons unbeknownst to me, yet she dressed. . . well, there were no words for how Daisy dressed, although Momma said she looked a little on the slutty side. Especially to be a preacher's daughter.

That day Daisy had opted for a red-lace fly away over a leopard-print leotard and black jeans. It was actually cute and stylish until the Airwalks on her feet came into view.

Rain pelted against the roof. Lightning bounced off the walls, and I threw my head back, fighting the urge I had to close my eyes. Boredom and the lull of the storm would easily put me to sleep.

I had halfway dozed off when one of the guys in class whistled, and Daisy leaned over the aisle, swatting my shoulder. "Oh my God." Her eyes motioned toward the new teacher at the front of the class. The first thing I noticed as the teacher leaned over to put her purse away was the insane amount of cleavage her low-cut dress revealed.

"Daddy said she's new in town," Daisy whispered. "Fresh outta college. He said she was gonna tempt the boys into sin." She smiled as though the idea of those boys sinning sent a tingle of excitement darting through her.

It turned out, my first day of the twelfth grade was Miss Weaver's first day of teaching. Ever. Which meant she was at best twenty-three, so not much older than us. All the guys in class stared at her with drool dangling from their chins. Thomas Radcliff, Robertsdale High's classic troublemaker, whom all the girls swooned after, nudged quarterback Ben

Jones with his elbow, then pretended to grope a pair of boobs.

The guys all snickered while Jenny sunk down in her seat, mumbling the word slut.

The bell rang, and Miss Weaver stood, smoothing her hands down her inappropriately tight dress. All I could think was that the length of that skirt and the height of those heels had to be against dress code, but I had to give it to her; the woman had curves.

Just as she cleared her throat, the door banged against the wall, catching everyone's attention.

"Day-um," Jenny whispered, straightening in her chair and primping her hair.

The guy in the doorway stared down at the slip of paper in hand while rain puddled around his combat boots. From where I sat, and thanks to the damp, ebony hair matted to his cheek, I couldn't make out his face. But everything else I could see was enough to keep my gaze locked on him. His soaked shirt clung to muscles teenage boys shouldn't possess—much like the sleeve of tattoos covering his arm and the stubble on his jaw. Until that day, Thomas Radcliff had been all I'd known of a bad boy, and while I saw the certain allure in Thomas' rough-around-the-edges looks, the guy in the doorway made Thomas look as innocent as a choir boy. And Thomas must have known, because he slouched in his seat, grumbling, "Who's the dipshit?"

Ben and the football players at the front of the class chuckled. Miss Weaver shot them a disapproving glare. "May I help you?" she asked, taking a slow step away from her desk.

"I think I'm in this class." His voice was deep, ominous, almost identical to the thunder rumbling outside.

Miss Weaver leaned over the desk to check the roster,

putting her cleavage on full display. Of course, the guys all grinned. "Oh? What's your name?"

"Elias Black. Ma'am."

My heart stopped for two full seconds. Daisy spun around in her chair, her eyes wide, mouth agape. "That can't be? Is it?"

I shrugged even though I knew it was him.

"Yes. You're in the right place," Miss Weaver said, her voice entirely too peppy. "Just take a seat at one of the empty desks."

Elias adjusted his backpack on his shoulder and then ran his hand over his hair, the movement creating a fine mist of rainwater.

Mine and every other girl's eyes—including Miss Weaver's — were glued to him as he moved through the class and took a seat by the window. Elias slouched in his chair as he opened his notebook, not even bothering to glance around the room.

Daisy still stared when Miss Weaver went to the whiteboard. "Sunny, did he look that hot the last time you saw him?"

"Kinda." But definitely not that grown.

"Holy crap." She faced the front for a few seconds before she spun back around. "You think he's been in prison? I mean, look at the tats," she whispered.

"He's not old enough to have been in prison."

"Right. Juvie."

Rolling my eyes, I placed my elbow on the desk and rested my head in my hand, making a conscious effort not to look at him.

That entire period, my heart remained in a panicked flutter, an inconsistent rhythm that swung between slow, hard thumps and erratic palpitations, and the few notes I had jotted in my notebook by the time the bell rang were incomplete.

People around me grabbed their books. Desks scraped against the floor as kids bolted toward the door, pushing and shoving one another. By the time I collected my belongings and stood, Daisy leaned in the doorway, tapping her foot over the tile floor.

"What are you doing?"

Stalling. "Nothing," I said with a shrug.

When I glanced back at Elias' empty desk, my cheeks stung and my shoulders dropped. I couldn't blame him for ignoring me, but part of me hoped he just hadn't recognized me.

THE CAFETERIA BUZZED with conversation and the clatter of trays hitting tables. The medley of fried food and mop water had a magical way of stealing most of my appetite.

In high school, lunch was nothing short of political. Akin to the United States during the Civil War, there were just some lines you did not cross. Non-populars didn't sit with the popular crowd. Nerds didn't sit with slackers. And no one sat with the loners. To the far side of the room, there was the catch-all table where everyone not assigned to a group sat. That was my table and much to Daisy's dismay, it was hers also.

I started toward it, but Daisy nudged me, nearly knocking her milk off her tray. "Where are you going?"

"To sit down."

"Not over there. Over here." She nodded toward the populars' table, and I exhaled. Daisy's goal in life was to sit at that table, to rub elbows with Kristen Dowdy and Valeria

Bedrouex—no matter how popular Jenny was, Daisy still hated her.

"I'm not going to sit over there. And if you roll your eyes any harder, you're going to be looking at your brain, Daisy."

"I swear. Sunny, you are the only person that *could be* in the popular crowd that doesn't want to be in the popular crowd." Daisy lived in this fantasy world where she believed that just because people didn't hate me that I could be part of the "in" crowd. What she didn't realize was that people were civil on the pure principle that my dad was the Sheriff, and that those popular kids were just as miserable as the rest of us

"You do realize popularity is a load of bullshit?" I asked.

She gasped.

"Seriously, Daisy? Look at them?" I started toward the catch-all table.

"Yeah, they look amazing."

"Really?"

"Straight outta *Clueless*."

"The fact that movie is your Bible or whatever is almost enough to make me disown you."

She flipped her hair over her shoulder—that time her milk hit the floor. "Ugh! As if."

"I don't know you," I grumbled before taking a seat next to our lunchroom acquaintances, Morgan and Hailey. Daisy plopped onto the stool beside me, making a show of dropping her tray onto the table. Some of the spaghetti sauce splattered her shirt. "Shit."

"Well, stop pitching a fit." I twirled noodles around my fork.

"What's she pitching a fit about?" Hailey questioned.

"Wanting to sit at the popular's table."

"Of course." Hailey huffed. "Go on over there and sit next to Jenny."

Daisy guffawed, then clutched her chest. "Are you crazy? I'm not going over there by myself. And I most certainly would not sit next to Jenny."

"Then suck it up and be normal, would you?" I shoved the watery spaghetti into my mouth, wondering how in the world something so red could have so little taste. I watched the kids at the coveted table by the window, noting how their smiles all seemed forced and how they all wore going-out clothes to school. Nobody had time for that. I preferred a T-shirt and jeans coupled with a pair of Converse. Comfort over style any day. To be honest, most people in the school didn't even like the self-proclaimed cool kids who oddly enough seemed to have been bred from parents who were also once cool kids. I thought popularity was kind of like a tragic disease, one I had no interest in catching. Teenage politics were the bane of my existence.

Daisy droned on and on about some guy at church she had a crush on while I subtly searched the overcrowded cafeteria for Elias. But I didn't see him, and a guy that dangerously sexy would most definitely stick out like a sore thumb.

"What's their deal?" Morgan thumbed toward the window where several girls from the popular's table stood with their faces plastered to the glass.

I shifted, leaning back until I could see around them. Three boys loitered outside with a cloud of smoke billowing around them. Daisy and Hailey hopped up and made a beeline to the window while I just sat, spinning spaghetti around my fork, watching.

Principal Davis came out of nowhere, clapping his hands to break the group up. He shook his head before heading to the emergency exit and slinging it open. "Boys!" he shouted. "Put those cigarettes out this instant and come inside!"

The smokes were tossed to the ground and stubbed out by three sets of boots, then the trio strutted into the cafeteria with smirks—except for Elias. His head was down, and his hands were shoved deep in his pockets. Principal Davis instructed them to follow him to his office, and he led them down the aisle that ran in front of my table.

My pulse thumped, beating in my temples. The smell of cigarettes and outside wafted off them as they passed. Elias looked up, his watercolor eyes landing right on mine. No smile. No smirk. Not even a flinch. Just a cold, hard stare that sucked every bit of oxygen from the room.

Adrenaline burst through me, then faded into a weak, sinking sensation the second the door to the lunchroom swung closed behind them.

The hum of conversation buzzed around me filled with *OMGs* and gasps, titters about how hot the three new boys were. Thomas and Ben made a show of strutting down the aisle with their chest puffed out to poke fun at the guys they knew were now their rivals, and I just sat there with spaghetti still twirled around my fork and my cheeks on fire. I didn't care about the commotion around me. Elias had looked right at me. Right. At. Me.

Dropping my fork to my plate, I took my tray and headed toward the trashcans. I felt foolish for the way my chest grew tighter with heartache. That boy may have been my entire world for two years, he very well may have occupied my dreams like some celebrity crush, but it was no excuse for my heart to break all over again from one, single, unacknowledged look. After all, it had been three years. People changed.

DADDY WAS in the yard throwing baseballs with Simon when I got home.

Fostering kids had been harder for our family than I'm sure my parents anticipated. Most of the time, families didn't get to keep the kids. Eight of my foster siblings had been picked up by their family over the course of my life—leaving us with empty hearts and a temporarily empty bedroom.

Simon was the only foster we had been able to adopt. He was legally my one, and only, little brother.

"Sissa!" Simon shouted before taking off across the yard, a cloud of dirt kicking up behind him.

Closing my car door, I crouched down, opening my arms wide to receive him when he slammed into me. He was all sweaty and little kid smelling. I brushed his blond hair away from his eyes and then kissed his damp forehead. "Missed you."

"Missed you," he said. "You know what happened today in Mrs. Richard's class, huh? We got a baby frog that Jimmy Hailes diddy caught for him. We put it in this little tank, and it swims around and around and jumps on rocks, and we're gonna catch it some flies to feed him. His name's Bullfrog David—I picked out Bullfrog, and Jeremy Keith picked out David after his pawpaw and—" he sucked in a quick breath, and I prepared myself for another five-minute tirade about his day of first grade.

Smiling, Daddy tucked the baseball mitt in the waist of his jeans. "Have a good day, baby?" He kissed my cheek while Simon continued talking about Bullfrog David.

"Yeah," I said.

Daddy narrowed his eyes. "You sure?"

"Yeah. I'm fine." Sweat prickled my skin. I was terrified he knew Elias was back.

He squeezed my shoulder. "Just seems like something's weighing on your mind."

Elias Black weighed on my soul.

"Nope." I reached for the door just as Daddy asked Simon if he wanted to throw a few more balls to which Simon agreed.

Inside, the savory smell of pot roast filled the entrance, and the tinker of dishes came from the kitchen.

"Momma? You already cooking?"

She stepped around the doorframe of the dining room, wiping her hands on Grandma's tattered apron. "I'm going down to the Jimmy Hale Mission to help them sort through donations tonight, so I started early." She smiled. "Did you have a good day?"

"Meh." I dropped my backpack underneath the coat rack.

"Oh, come on. It's your last year of high school, Sunny. Humor your old mama."

"It was boring," I said. "Well, except for the new language teacher that's super young." I rolled my eyes. "The guys were all excited about that."

"Oh," Mama snapped her fingers on her way back to the kitchen, and I followed. "That new girl. Real sweet. Pastor Fulmer told me I should ask her if she wants to come down to the Mission, you know, help her get to know some folks 'round here."

I leaned my hip against the counter and arched a brow while envisioning Miss Weaver in her low-cut dress, standing next to Momma in a button up and high-waisted jeans, the two of them doling out food to wayward strangers.

"She doesn't look like someone that would go down to help out at the Mission."

Momma frowned. "Sunny Ray!"

Groaning, I shoved off the counter. "That did not warrant both names, Momma."

"How many times have I told you not to judge a book by its cover?"

"Ten trillion. But seriously, the dress she had on today was so tight I could see the outline of her thong. Plus, she's probably got better things to do than go hang out at the Mission." I headed toward the stairs at the side of the room. "Like, you know, go on dates or watch reality TV."

"There's nothing better than helping those in need."

That was Momma's life mission, to help others. Sometimes I worried that I wouldn't grow up to be half as good of a person as she was. She radiated happiness and breathed charity. I did good to smile at strangers on the street. I definitely wasn't volunteering at a shelter anytime in the foreseeable future, much as I doubted Miss Weaver would.

On my way past her, I patted her shoulder and kissed her cheek. "You're right, Momma. You should ask Miss Weaver."

That pacified her, and she gave me a doting smile before I disappeared up the stairs to my room.

The walls were still Pepto-Bismol pink, and the same white, Victorian bed I'd had since I was six sat between the two windows. The same one Elias used to sleep in to keep the monsters away, though the sheets had changed from fairies to polka dots.

With a sigh, I went straight to my stereo, put "I'm Kissing You" on repeat, and then dropped my head against the curved bedrail and closed my eyes. The image of a soaked Elias standing in the doorway to Miss Weaver's room crept to mind. His sudden entrance was as close to a movie clip brought to life as I'd ever seen—complete with awestruck gasps and whispers from the girls in the class. And while there was no denying that Elias' looks were a thousand times over enough to stop any woman dead in her tracks, that wasn't why I couldn't get the idea of him out of my mind.

It was the endless list of questions surrounding him. Why was he back? How long he'd been here? But most of all, I wondered what had happened to *him*. The vacant expression he had when looked at me that afternoon haunted me the same way he had haunted my dreams.

By the third repeat of the song, I'd pulled the shoebox out from beneath my bed and rummaged through the years of notes from friends and one boy loosely described as my boyfriend. Tucked away at the very bottom were the letters from Elias.

I spent the better part of half of an hour poring over his notes, hating myself all over again for sending the last one I had.

I couldn't help but think if my life were Shakespeare's *Romeo and Juliet* that this would have been the point where I was found cold in a crypt, nearly dead, and Elias would plunge a dagger into his chest because he couldn't live without me. Instead, he wouldn't even speak to me.

I hurt him.

I hurt myself.

I ruined us.

I TRIED on four outfits the next morning, finally settling on a yellow sundress with a white pinstripes. I wore white wedges and put on more make-up than usual—powder, mascara, *and* eyeliner.

Thomas gawked at me during first period, which made me seriously regret my wardrobe decision.

There had to be a reason why I tried to impress a boy that wouldn't even speak to me. Talk about pathetic. . . I pulled at the neckline of my dress and slumped in my chair just as Daisy came bouncing into the room wearing knee socks, a pair of shorts, and a Van Halen T-shirt.

Her brows lowered when she sank into her seat and took inventory of my outfit. "Do you have church after school or something?"

"No." I crossed my arms over my chest with a huff.

"Is that—" she leaned over the edge of her desk. "Eyeliner?"

"I had a moment of weakness."

"You've worn eyeliner three times in your life. Once for a pageant in second grade—which you hated. The other time was when you went through a rebellious streak in sixth grade. And then there was the time when you were trying to get Brian Wheeler to kiss you."

Tossing my head back, I closed my eyes. "I was bored, all right?"

She moved across the aisle until her book fell to the floor, her desk was on two legs, and she was right in my face. "I know better, Sunny Ray Lower. It's that boy!"

"Stop!" I shoved her, and her chair clattered to the floor with a thud.

When the bell rung, Elias' seat remained vacant.

Miss Weaver stood behind her desk, wearing another tight dress. This one had a plunging neckline that show-cased impressive cleavage *without* her bending over. She called roll, then instructed us to open *The Great Gatsby* and read chapter one.

Jenny grumbled as she pulled her book from her backpack. "How is this teaching?"

Thomas snickered, and Miss Weaver simply cocked a warning brow at Jenny who then made a show of huffing and flinging her hair around until she finally opened the book.

Ten minutes into class, determined clomps echoed down the hallway, not from high heels or Principal Davis' dress shoes, but from boots. The back of my neck prickled with sweat as the door opened and his shadow appeared a fleeting moment before his body.

There went all the air again, sucked out of the room. Elias might as well be an oxygen-deprived vacuum.

"Do you have a tardy slip, Mr. Black?" Miss Weaver asked in an effort to sound stern, but really, the red splotches over her exposed chest did little to give her credibility.

Elias' presence even flustered the teacher. If a twenty-something-year-old professional couldn't control herself any better than that, I shouldn't feel too bad for the palpitations in my chest.

"No," he said.

"Why were you late?"

"Because my truck's a piece of shit." He crossed the room. The entire class turned to look at him. The guys snorted, and the good girls acted appalled. But for me, that same tingle I got at age six—when I heard him swear for the first time—shot down my spine.

"Mr. Black!" Miss Weaver gasped. "That language is unacceptable in the classroom."

He fell into his seat, stretching his tattooed arm over the desk and curling his fingers around its edge. "It slipped."

"Don't let your language slip again, or you'll be going to Mr. Davis' office."

Elias' jaw ticced like he bit back words.

While the rest of the class went back to their reading, I struggled to focus on Mr. Gatsby and Miss Buchanan. A few words into chapter one, my gaze drifted away from the pages and across the room.

Elias glanced up, his stare meeting mine as he leaned back in his seat without the slightest hint of a smile.

Panicked, I turned back to the book, rested my head in my hand, and focused on the print. Heat flushed my cheeks while I chastised myself for giving a crap about him.

He was a daydream that should never have been within reach.

When I flipped the page to Gatsby, who was just about to encounter Miss Buchanan for the first time, the pink stones in the moon ring glimmered in the sunlight streaming through the classroom windows, and I inhaled.

It was going to take a while to let go of missing someone for three years.

8

ELIAS

The door slammed closed behind me, and I stepped into the house that was about five degrees cooler than the blazing heat outside. The ancient, single window unit did little to cool the place.

Judah looked away from the TV. "What's up your ass?"

"Shut up." I glanced at the kitchen counter covered in dishes and open Captain Crunch boxes, then dropped my backpack to the floor and sank onto the couch. "Clean that shit up," I said.

"Jesus. Are you on your man period or something?" He snorted. "Is your mangina cramping?"

"Don't make me beat your ass." I swiped a hand through my hair. "Where's your brother?"

"Over at Doodle's house."

Doodle was a dealer. A shitty-ass dealer that lived in one of those metallic Airstream RVs from the 70s. His quote-unquote job was tie-dye artist, and his claim to fame was smoking a joint with Jimmy Hendrix backstage at Woodstock—which, if it were true, I couldn't deny was pretty, fucking epic.

"That guy's weird." Judah flipped the channel, stopping on some commercial with a Chihuahua in a sombrero prancing down a sidewalk. Judah cackled and turned up the volume.

"Yo quiero Taco Bell."

Judah doubled over, laughing so hard he could hardly breathe. "Shit. That talking Chihuahua never gets old." He wiped tears from his face.

I took a step toward him, narrowing my gaze on his bloodshot eyes. "Are you high?"

"Of course."

Sighing, I grabbed the Playboy from the coffee table and chucked it at him. "Idiot."

"I'm just celebrating. You should be too. The coach let all three of us on the team and gave us killer positions."

"Of course, he did."

All the high school coaches knew who the Black boys were. We were so dominant on the field that the schools would turn a blind eye to the stupid shit any of us pulled... most of the time, at least.

Judah thumbed through the magazine, turning it sideways to pull out the centerfold. "Real tits look better than fake ones."

Leaning over, I snatched Miss August away from him and dropped it on the floor. "Clean up the mess you made in the kitchen. Now."

"Fine."

Seconds later, dishes clattered while Judah bitched and moaned.

"Suck it up, buttercup," I shouted as I sorted through the pile of bills on the coffee table.

Power. Gas. Water.

Then I dropped them in my lap and let my head fall

back against the cushion. There were people who had it worse than me—a lot worse—but I sure as hell didn't have it easy.

Billie ran off with some trucker named Jethro two weeks after she got this shithole hovel, which was more than okay. It wasn't like she contributed to anything other than her own alcohol and cigarettes.

The problem was if the bills didn't get paid now, I was afraid someone would find out the three of us were without adult supervision. And I was not going to let my brother's go back into the foster system at sixteen. All I had to do for the next year was make sure I paid every damn bill on time and kept us out of trouble. Then I could get the courts to grant me custody of the two delinquents until they were legal. If they could just keep it together for two more years, they'd have scholarships for ball, and maybe just maybe we could break the vicious cycle of poverty our family seemed to be stuck in.

The aluminum door rattled when someone pounded a fist on it.

I dropped the bills on the table and moved to the door. When I checked the peephole, I swore under my breath at the sight of the brown brim of a sheriff hat. "Judah, wanna tell me why the sheriff is on our porch?"

"What?" He skirted out of the kitchen and into the living room, suds falling from his hands to the stained carpet. "I didn't do nothing. I swear."

"Fuck. If Doodle got Atlas in trouble, I swear to. . ." I glanced at the safe deposit box sticking out from underneath the sofa and panic tensed my chest.

Arching my brows, I pointed at the metal case. "Hide that in the air return in the hall."

He didn't argue that. Just took it and ran out of the room.

The sheriff knocked again.

I waited until I heard the grate click shut, then I swung the door open and nearly fell back a step when my eyes landed on a much older looking Mr. Lower. He had been a cop when I lived with them. Not the Sheriff.

He removed his hat and nodded. "Elias."

"Hey." His cruiser was alone in the yard, which put me at ease. A little. I cleared my throat. "Hey, Mr. Lower."

He glanced over my shoulder into the house. "Your aunt at home?"

"Uh. No, sir. She's at work."

"Mmm." He paused, fiddling with the brim of his hat. "Can I have a word with you real quick?" He jerked his chin toward the house. I didn't have a choice but to open the door wider and let him through.

Judah was back at the sink scrubbing a skillet. He shot an uneasy look at me while Mr. Lower regarded his surroundings. His gaze stopped on the Playboy spread open on the floor where I'd dropped it.

He nudged it with the toe of his boot. "You been all right?"

"Yeah. Can't complain."

"Glad to be back in Fort Morgan?"

I shrugged. "I guess. It's better than Mississippi."

"Mmm." I hated when he made that noise. From my time at their house, I'd learned it meant he had something important he wanted to get off his chest. And that something was usually not anything I wanted to hear.

"Sunny," he started and a slow pressure built in my chest. "She's my little girl, and it's my job to make sure she has the best path laid out for her." His gaze met mine for the first time since he had arrived. A hint of regret swam in his old eyes but mostly just a warning. "I don't know how to say this to you, Elias."

I knew exactly why he was here. Finding a boy in his daughter's bed didn't sit well with him. At all. I'd never live that one down.

"You want me to stay away from her, huh?" I asked still holding his stare.

He finally looked away and gave a curt nod. "I don't doubt you care about her, but you got yourself a real unsavory reputation. You and your brothers. Sunny's still young and going through a little bit of a defiant streak, so I'm sure she'd love to ruffle my feathers, but she's impressionable. I don't want her to think. . ." His Ebenezer Scrooge brows pinched together. "Well, I don't want her to think that this is normal." He held out his arms, waving around at the shit-hole I lived in the way Vanna White would a prize on *The Price is Right*. "I want better for her. You should, too."

His thin lips pressed into a hard line. "Now I hate to say this 'cause it's gonna come out sounding all kinds of judgmental and mean, but not all things in life are fair. I remember what it's like to be a teenage boy, thinking you're in love and all. But you ain't right for her."

My fingers pulled into fists at my sides, my jaw tensed, and the rush of blood to my face set my cheeks on fire. It wasn't the first time I'd had someone tell me I wasn't good enough, but it was the first time it had sunk in.

My maw had come from a family similar to the Lower's. Good Christians with a nice house who sat around the table eating Sunday dinner. I'd seen the pictures. I'd listened to my maw tell me stories about growing up in a good home while tears built in her eyes.

My paw had swept her off her feet with his good looks and charm, and then swept her right into meth and living out of motels. Swept her so far away from the lifestyle she once had that it seemed more akin to something out of a Grimm's Fairy Tale. Almost too good to be true.

"Son?" Mr. Lower's voice snatched me away from my derailed thoughts. "Did you hear me?"

"Yes, sir. I heard you."

"Good. Now, you take care of yourself. Stay outta trouble." He placed his hat back on his head, straightening it out before he ducked through the front door.

I swallowed when it banged closed.

"The hell?" Judah turned from the sink. "He just waltzes in here and says some crap like that, then tells you to stay out of trouble?" He pointed a butter knife at the door. "Screw him. Cops are dicks!"

I didn't budge from my spot in the middle of the room. I just stared at the place Mr. Lower had stood while I listened to the gravel crunch under the tires of his cop car.

My vision throbbed with each hard beat of my heart. The blood that rushed through my ears drowned out everything except the words repeating in my head—*She's too good for you*. All that anger grew like the pressure building behind a bullet in the milliseconds after a trigger has been pulled. Then bam it all exploded.

My fist went straight through the sheetrock in front of me. A poof of powder billowed into the air. Drywall crumbled onto the floor when I pulled my hand away from the hole. Crimson blood welled from my dust-covered knuckles.

"Dude," Judah placed a hand on my shoulder, and I shrugged out of it. "He's not right."

"Sure he is." I shook off the throbbing in my hand, snatched the bills from the table, and went to go grab that stupid metal box out of the air return.

I popped the lock, pulled out a plastic baggie with a ten

scribbled on it in Sharpie, then crammed it in my pocket. "I'm going to meet Ben."

And then, I left to go deal drugs, so I could pay my bills and continue to be not good enough for anyone.

THE NEXT DAY, I came into class late. Again.

I kept my eyes trained on the floor when I placed my tardy pass on Miss Weaver's desk and then crossed the room to take my seat.

I made it thirty minutes into class before I glanced over at Sunny. The first two days, I wasn't sure she even recognized me. Honestly, the way she looked at me left me unsure if I should even talk to her and now.

Well now. . .

I wanted to tell her I never forgot her. That I still cared about her and always would—that I couldn't be upset with her for breaking up with me. She did the right thing, but I'd love her regardless. But there was no point.

She looked up from her desk. Our eyes locked, and my chest begged to explode. She pinched her bottom lip beneath her teeth, and then, I finally redirected my attention to my forearm. I traced over the tribal sun lost amongst the myriad of ink.

She was so fucking beautiful and bright. Happy. Perfect.

I didn't want to ruin her, even if it meant killing the only bit of hope I had clung to for the past three years.

After all, any idiot knows the sun and the moon were never meant to share the same sky.

9

SUNNY

The rest of the week went on much the same. Elias didn't speak to me, and I didn't speak to him.

It turned out that the other two guys who had gotten in trouble for smoking during lunch where his brothers, Judah and Atlas. The three of them sat together at the end of the loners' table every day for lunch—even though Jenny and Valeria invited them to the populars' table on a daily basis.

New kids with good looks had an automatic free trial with that group.

Meanwhile, as they turned down invitation after invitation, the rumors about the hot-as-hell brothers ran rampant. There were whispers that they dealt drugs. Some people said they belonged to a secret gang. Gun runners. Satanist. All of it, of course, was ridiculous.

They were just boys who didn't give a shit about anything. Not popularity. Not the clothes they wore. Not the people they used to care about.

Just boys.

Friday afternoons always seemed to have a buzz

surrounding them. The class would sit, people's eyes glancing at the clock every few minutes. When the dismissal bell finally rang, students bolted out.

I tended to wait until the mass exodus had fled through the doors before I left my seat and trudged into the chaotic hallway. Two of the football player shoved each other against the lockers, laughing like idiots and nearly knocking some poor freshman over. In turn, it caused me to screw up the combination on my lock.

Daisy popped around my open door. "You're coming tonight, right?"

I rolled my eyes and shoved my science book inside my backpack. She had taken it upon herself to agree to a double date with two meatheads from the football team. "No."

"Oh, come on. I only said yes because I knew you'd say no."

"So you understand why I'm not going?" I patted her shoulder and did my best fake grin. "Great."

"You do realize Brandon is like *the* guy. He's athletic. He makes good grades. Daddy even thinks he's a golden boy. He has the preacher's stamp of approval, Sunny. That's one step down from a blessing by the pope."

"So," I gave her a sarcastic grin, "you go out with him."

"He's too good. I need 'em a little rough around the edges. Like Ben."

"Then go out with Ben. Tell Brandon I've got the plague or something."

She banged her head on the wall of lockers. "You're impossible."

"You don't need me to go on your date with you."

"Yes, I do." She stepped in front of me, grabbing my shoulders. "You're the Thelma to my Louise."

"I'm pretty sure Thelma and Louise didn't go on double dates."

"Look, a hot guy likes you. Just once. If you hate it, fart or something, and I'm sure he'll never ask you out again."

"Wow."

Daisy started blabbing about how I needed to give the guy a chance, something about my dad would like him. Blah. Blah. Blah. I went back to my locker, grabbing my copy of *Gatsby* and my gym clothes before slamming the door with a bang.

When I turned to walk off, Daisy had her arms crossed over her chest. "Besides, you still owe me for letting you use my address to send those letters to Elias."

She was never going to give up. "Fine," I said on my way through the exit that had "Hammerhead Pride" painted above the doorway.

Elias and his brothers were in the parking lot. Smoking. A group of girls circled them like a pack of giggling hyenas. I bit at my lip when Elias glanced in my direction, determined to hold his stare. He squinted when he lifted a cigarette to his mouth and took a deep drag. I'd always found smoking repulsive—until I saw him do it. The smoke seemed to crawl through his lips like a belly dancer, teasing and taunting. The bad-boy look on Elias was undeniably, thigh-clenchingly sexy.

"Earth to Sunny," Daisy said. "Are you gonna just stand there or get in the car?"

I broke the stare and climbed in just as Daisy settled behind the wheel, pulling her hair into a ponytail. "Why do you look sunburned?"

"It's just. . .hot," I said, cranking the AC up to full blast.

It was too hot.

LATER THAT NIGHT, I found myself closer than I wanted to Brandon McClure in one of the rickety booths of Captain Ahab's, a crappy seafood restaurant that reeked of grease and crab legs.

This craphole was popular since every Friday a local band played live music, and underagers didn't get a big, fat X marked across the back of their hands.

Daisy was all smiles being on dates with football players.

In her mind, this rendezvous would slingshot us up the social ladder. I had no intentions of being slingshot anywhere, and besides, her date was a known virginity collector. I took this little excursion at face value. Ben wanted another specimen to add to his pinup board, and he had just brought Brandon along for the ride—just like Daisy had me.

The waitress came by to clear the table and then placed a pitcher of beer in the middle. Brandon poured drinks.

When he passed one to me, I just stared at it. "It's okay. I'm DD," he said.

By the time Daisy and Ben had chugged half of their drinks, I still hadn't touched mine.

"What," Brandon laughed. "Don't tell me you don't drink?"

"Beer tastes like week-old piss."

"She likes vodka," Daisy said, reaching for the pitcher to pour herself another.

Brandon grinned, dimples popping. "So, you aren't as innocent as you look then."

"I'm not screwing you if that's what you're getting at."

"Hey!" Brandon held up his hands, palms out. "I wasn't suggesting that."

I deadpanned him. "You're a guy."

"Sunny!" Daisy gave me a stern look. "Stop being. . .you."

I flipped the bird to everyone at that table.

"Watch out, McClure. You got a live one." Ben placed his arm around Daisy, then whispered something in her ear that caused her cheeks to blush, even underneath the pound of foundation she wore.

I knew Daisy better than anyone, and she was the epitome of a hopeless romantic. I was ninety-five percent sure she was planning their wedding at that very second.

Ben—aside from his sexual conquest and his appreciation of beer—was a good guy. And that was the problem.

Girls expect the bad boy to break their heart which is why we don't let them into anything more than our shirts or beds. It's the good ones like Ben and Brandon and the person Elias *used to be* who are dangerous because you trust them.

You invite the Trojan horse right through the walls of your heart, and once someone gets in, there's no salvaging the havoc they'll eventually reek.

WITHIN AN HOUR, the pitcher was empty, and Daisy had taken it upon herself to finish the beer I had never touched while Brandon and Ben had gone to the front to pay.

"He's so hot," she slurred. Her cheeks flushed, and her hair was a mess. "I'm going to screw him." She gave a curt nod before grabbing my empty glass, turning it up, and patting the bottom in a desperate bid to savor any remaining alcohol.

"Do *not* sleep with him!" I snatched the glass from her hand and placed it at the end of the table.

"Um. Hello? Dear friend. Ben's a super-hot football player."

"Exactly why you should *not* sleep with him."

She rolled her eyes so hard her head actually followed suit, lulling to the side on a groan. "You need to loosen up."

"And let my best friend make a tragic mistake?" I shook my head. "Don't think so."

"Having sex—"

"Correction, giving up your virginity."

"Whatever. Giving your V-card to a hot guy isn't tragic, Sunny." She blew an exhausted breath through her lips. "Being hung up on one guy your entire life is." The second those words left her mouth, her eyes widened.

She had reached the level of intoxication where the brain-to-mouth filter was definitely broken. I pushed my back against the booth, pretending her comment didn't slice me right open.

"I'm," she mumbled. "I'm sorry. I didn't mean it. I..."

"It's fine." I shrugged a shoulder then grabbed the straw paper from the table, balling it up and tossing it to the floor.

"Sunny?"

"It's fine, Daisy. You're right. You wanna sleep with Ben— like half the girls in the senior class, go right ahead. It's not disgusting at all." My chest was tight, and my skin grew hotter by the second. She was right. I was pathetic. *I* was the hopeless romantic, not her.

I held too tightly to a boy I had kissed once. A boy I'd said I love you to when I didn't understand the concept—I still didn't. Heck, I wasn't sure half of the adults in my life understood what it meant because it sure as hell wasn't the bliss Hollywood portrayed.

I was hung up on the idea of almost when Elias and I were so far from almost anything it was laughable.

Yet I couldn't let go of him.

"Shhh. No more mention of the V-card." Daisy slapped the table. "Here they come."

"Party at Mussafer's house!" Ben pumped his fist in the air, Daisy clapped, and Brandon shrugged.

Bless him. He was as disinterested as I was which meant heart-throb Brandon was starting to earn some major points with me.

Ben gripped Brandon's shoulders and shook him. "Let's go, homie."

The two guys went ahead of us into the gravel parking lot. I leaned in by Daisy. "Did he seriously just say homie? You did hear that, right?"

"Yeah."

"And you still want to. . .whatever it is you want to do with him?"

Daisy gave me a playful shove before we loaded into Brandon's Land Rover and headed out to the island.

BRANDON SHOWED HIS PASS, and the guard who looked old enough to have fought in the first World War waved him through.

The tires thumped over the tiny, two-lane bridge that led onto Ono Island.

Daisy wiggled in the seat beside me, eyes wide as she peered through the window at the massive houses hidden behind palm trees and boats.

Brandon and Joey Mussafer where two of three kids from the island who attended Robertsdale. The rest of the kids here went to Lockhart Private school. The problem with Lockhart was, while their education was top-notch, their sports teams sucked. Hence the reason Brandon and Joey ended up at a public school.

Football was everything in Alabama. Players—good players—were treated like royalty. They were handed grades if needed, they didn't get arrested for spray painting the cows out at Dallas Farms, and most importantly, their house parties never had the cops called on them.

We wound around the road, past the water tower, finally pulling through an open wrought iron gate, the intricate kind you would imagine Michael Jackson had in front of Neverland Ranch. When the house came into view, Daisy gasped. "Holy. Hell. That thing is huge!" She wedged herself between the front two seats. "Is your house like this, Brandon?"

"Kinda."

She slapped at my thigh like *see, Sunny.* "Damn. What's it like to be loaded?"

He shook his head and parked behind a string of luxury SUVs.

The melody of Garth Brooke's "Low Places" rang into the night sky when we climbed out.

On our way toward the side of the house, Ben wrapped his arm around Daisy's waist. She glanced over at me, about to burst from excitement.

"So I've noticed, you and Daisy aren't much alike." Brandon laughed, shoving his hands in his jean pockets.

"I mean, in some ways. I'm definitely the cynic though."

The second we rounded the house, the chorus to the infamous honky-tonk song hit, banjos twanging. The illuminated pool deck erupted with voices singing along while alcohol-induced woo-hoos intermittently drowned out the lyrics.

I had been to plenty of parties, but parties at Robertsdale where usually in the middle of some field or in a backyard littered with garden gnomes and plastic flamingos. This party—with its guest toll close to one-hundred, five kegs set up in front of the DJ table, and pristine, white lounge chairs that looked like they belonged to the Hilton, all sat behind a house that was bigger than the church— could have easily passed as the background to an MTV music video.

Daisy spun around like the girl from *The Sound of Music* to take in the lavish surroundings. "This is insane."

Ben slapped Brandon on the back so hard Brandon stumbled forward a step. "I'm going to get a beer. Want one?"

"Nah. DD." Brandon flashed his keys. "Remember?"

"Mr. Responsible." Ben grabbed Daisy, dragging her behind him. And then I was alone with Brandon.

I kept wringing my hands, uncertain where to put them. I swayed in time with the beat of the music while taking inventory of the faces, few of whom I recognized.

"So." Brandon's hands were in his pockets again.

For the first time since he had started at our school freshman year, he seemed uneasy. The air of confidence that usually radiated from him had dulled. If I didn't know him, I would never have pegged him for the popular jock all the girls fantasized about.

"So?" I echoed.

He rubbed a hand over the back of his neck and tapped his foot against a cooler. "You want a drink?"

"I'm fine."

He took my hand, awkwardly attempting to thread his fingers through mine as he maneuvered me across the pool deck covered with dancing party goers. A random drunk wobbled in front of us before losing his footing and nearly crashing into me.

Brandon shoved him out of the way, telling him to watch out for *his girl* then he placed his arm around my shoulders and pulled me close to his side like he needed to protect me.

Daisy was right. Brandon was nice, and for a moment, I wondered why I had been so opposed to a date with him in the first place. This was fine. Actually, it was almost more than fine.

We stopped at the edge of the patio that overlooked the bay. I leaned against the railing, and Brandon moved beside me, elbows on the banister, chin slightly tucked while he crossed one jean-clad leg in front of the other.

That careless stance was something a lot of girls would call effortlessly masculine, but to me, it just looked like he was trying too hard. Sometimes I wished I wasn't as jaded as I was.

"So, Sunny. What are you about?"

I arched a brow. "About?"

"Yeah. Like, what's important to you?"

I wasn't prepared for such a deep, probing question, especially not from a jock. Suddenly, I felt guilty for judging him. For doing exactly what all those kids I hated did. "I mean," I rubbed my hand over my arm. "Family. Friends. Stuff like that."

"For some reason, I think there's a lot more to you than that, Sunny Lower." With a smirk, he moved in front of me, trapping me between him and the railing. His hand swept along my jaw. Naturally, I leaned into the soft touch. The affection.

"You're really pretty," he said.

"Thanks."

I told myself to let what happened happen. That if Brandon McClure attempted to kiss me, I should go with it.

"Atlas!" Someone shouted, and my attention swung over Brandon's shoulder.

Elias and his brothers were making their way across the back deck, stopping to talk to a group of private school kids.

Mine and Elias' eyes locked while Brandon's fingers crept down my neck. Brandon mumbled something about my lips and how he wanted to kiss me, but the sound of his voice was drowned out by the drumming of my pulse in my ears.

When a redhead came sauntering up with two beers, handing one to Elias', his eyes didn't move away from me, in fact, his gaze seemed to grow more intense when he raised the drink to his lips and took a sip.

The girl's hands crept over his chest, and my heart pounded faster.

When she leaned in close to his face, his eyes burned straight through me.

Their hands touched. He passed something off to her.

My jaw tensed.

"You okay?" Brandon shifted on his feet which blocked my view of Elias.

"Huh. Oh. Yeah. Fine, I'm just. . . ." My pulse still thrummed. "Just. I just—"

"Shit," Brandon's lips thinned into a hard line. "I made you uncomfortable?"

"Oh. No. I just. . ." Swallowing, I craned my neck to sneak another glimpse of Elias, but he had been swallowed up by the horde of people.

Brandon turned to see what had caught my attention.

"I thought I saw someone. Sorry, I'm just—My head's in a weird place."

Brandon nodded like he understood, but there was no way he did. "Yeah. I get ya."

"You know. I think I do want a drink," I said.

"Yeah? Come on?" We walked over to one of at least fifteen coolers, and he popped the lid, fishing through the ice until he found a miniature bottle of wine.

Holding it up, he smiled. "This should work for that refined palate of yours."

I took the drink, twisted the cap, and took a swig.

It was sweet and dry, not as tasty as vodka but much better than beer. "You know, you're not as bad as I thought."

Brandon dipped his chin on a laugh. "Wow. Not as bad as you thought."

"I didn't mean it like that. I just..."

Ben and Daisy walked past, Ben glanced over his shoulder and made a slight thrusting motion as they headed to the open back door.

"You expected me to be like Ben?"

"I mean. Sorta."

"I'm just as much like Ben as you are Daisy."

I took another sip of wine, letting the warm buzz from the alcohol creep down my arms to my fingers.

His eyes narrowed. "So, why don't you ever date?"

"I don't know. I just. . . don't." Another sip. "Why don't you? Well, I mean since Valeria?"

"I just haven't found the right person."

Okay. I got why girls were a little hung up on him.

He was nice. He was cute. An absolute good guy.

He closed the space between us, and I was surrounded by the too-clean smell of his cologne. It wasn't masculine or sexy, just fresh.

He looked down like he wanted to kiss me. Part of me wanted to let him, just to remember what it felt like to have a boy's lips on mine. To feel wanted when the one guy I cared for wouldn't so much as speak to me. But most of all, I think I wanted him to kiss me in the hopes that Elias would see.

I placed my hands on his shoulders and pushed up on my toes.

Just when I was about to close my eyes, someone shouted behind me. "Lockhart High fucking rules!"

I turned my attention to the house in time to see a naked guy jump from the balcony into the pool. A wall of chlorinated water rained down on the people standing at the side.

A girl screamed, cussing Naked Boy out as he swam to the wall. Laughing, he reached up and grabbed her ankle, yanking her into the pool with a splash.

"That guy's such an asshole," Brandon mumbled.

"Funny though."

I watched the girl trudge to the shallow end while yelling about her Calvin Kleins as she scooted past Elias.

"You sure you're okay?" Brandon asked, dragging my attention away from the boy who used to be my world.

"Yeah."

I decided it was better that I didn't kiss Brandon. It would have been for all the wrong reasons.

"Hey, McClure! Get your ass over here."

Brandon shook his head. "I guess we should go see what Mussafer wants, huh?"

"Sure."

BY ELEVEN THIRTY, all the kegs were floated, and an unexpected thunderstorm had forced the party inside.

And I officially understood what the term "lit" meant.

The tingly warmth that ran through my veins from those little bottles of wine was a new experience for me. Beer made me sleepy. Liquor made me loud. Wine? Wine made me giddy. My jaw ached from smiling, and God was I chatty.

I stole another mini-wine from a cooler. The seal to the gold twist-off top cracked.

"Whoa there!" Brandon closed his hand around mine

and pulled me toward him, forcing my blurry vision to his face. "You're gonna make yourself sick."

I snort-laughed. "I'm good."

Actually, I felt so amazing, I needed to hug him. I threw myself at his hard chest, looping both arms around his neck and practically hanging from his body like he was a tree and I was a sloth. "I like you, Brandon McClure."

Laughing, he turned his head to the side. "Whew. That's some stout wine. But I like you, too."

Several girls lurking in the background gave me death glares.

My vision doubled, and I tried to decide which Brandon to focus on. "You're just..." I hiccupped. "Happy."

"Yep. And you're more than wasted." He wrangled the bottle from me, then winked. "Trust me on this."

The glass clinked against an empty fifth of whiskey when he tossed it into the overflowing trashcan.

Brandon was headed out of the kitchen when some Lockhart guy intercepted him. Brandon smiled and glanced over the guy's shoulder at me. His brow creased, he shook his head, then swiped one of his large hands over his face.

The room tilted and swayed.

"Hey, Sunny," Brandon called. "Give me just a minute, okay?"

Closing my eyes, I nodded and slumped against the wall.

A sudden hot flash zapped through me, and my stomach lurched, my head spun like I was on a horrible merry-go-round. I needed to sit, but people were passed out on the sofas. One guy had an assortment of colorful condoms stuck to his face. Another had crude drawings of the male genital on his cheek.

The deep bass of the music thumped through me as I stumbled toward the back door. Some girl I didn't know grabbed me, asking over and over if I was okay while sweat pricked its way across my brow and upper lip. Nodding, I broke free from her grip and slipped outside.

Water stood on the worn grooves of the porch, and a slight shower misted down from thick, storm clouds. I leaned on the side of the house and took a deep breath. While there was little relief to be found in the dense air, there was plenty in the near silence and the pitter-patter of the raind. I sunk to the cool decking, pulling my knees to my chest while wishing the world wasn't bobbing like a buoy in the middle of the ocean, and more than thankful that Brandon had taken that last drink.

A low groan of thunder rumbled in the distance followed by a dull flash of lightning, but I couldn't be bothered to move. The suction of the sliding glass door opening and closing sounded beside me, followed by footfalls and the once familiar scent of leather and spice.

"Shit," he mumbled before I heard the flint of a lighter catch once, twice, three times. "What are you doing out here?"

I rolled my head to the side and focused as hard as I could on bringing the two figures into one. Elias' gray shirt was speckled with raindrops and when he went to drag his hand through his hair, the hem of his shirt lifted. Thanks to how dangerously low his jeans sat on his hips, I could just make out the deep indention of that *V* that made girls stupid.

I recalled what it was like to fall asleep on him that night in my room. How close we used to be. Even drunk, that thought caused my chest to ache. I wanted things to be the way they were, but they couldn't.

He snapped his fingers. "You awake down there?"

"Aren't you supposed to be ignoring me?"

A stream of smoke blew through his lips, mixing with the drizzle and drifting into the night. "You're drunk."

"Maybe. But I still know you've been ignoring me. You know, if it's over that letter—I didn't write that because I wanted to. My dad made me. You should've known that."

"I'm not discussing this with you, Sunny."

"Come on. Are we fucking twelve?"

His lips kicked up in an amused smirk. "So, I see you've got yourself a mouth on you now, huh?"

Glaring, I flipped him a bird. "You're a dick."

"Maybe."

He stood there, taking slow drags and watching me like a caged animal at the zoo.

The light mist transitioned into a slight downpour, fat droplets splatting against the deck. "You never even fought for me."

"Oh, give me a break. I came back. I saw you at the carnival. You kissed some guy. Why the hell would I fight for you, huh?" He flicked his cigarette over the railing, the bright-red cherry streaking through the air. "We were just kids anyway."

If words were weapons, that was a spear straight to my heart.

Just kids. Another way to say it didn't matter.

I forced a laugh to hide the hurt. "Yeah. Right. Just kids."

With a sigh, he moved toward me then held out his hand. "Come on."

"Go away."

"Get up, Sunny."

"I'm fine."

There was a pause, but his boots were still planted firmly beside my leg, a puddle forming around their soles. "Look, I'm not leaving you out here. Just get up."

"I said I'm fine." My nostrils flared. "Like you care anyway." I couldn't control the butthurt bitch inside no matter how much I wished I could.

"Jesus."

"Just so you know, the guy who kissed me—not the guy *I* kissed—was James Leroy. And I shoved him away. I wasn't on a date with him. God." I pushed to my feet way too fast and staggered to the side. I swatted his hand away when Elias went to catch me. "Still, no reason to act like I don't exist," I mumbled.

The muscles in his jaw ticced, and he inched his way closer to me until my back was flat against the rough brick of the house, and his nose was almost touching mine. "Stop it. Sunny." His jilted words heated my lips, and it took everything inside of my weakening soul not to kiss him. "It's best this way."

"Best this way?" I laughed. "Wow."

"You don't belong with me. All right? So, there's no point revisiting the past."

"Oh my God, Elias, get over yourself. . ."

He shoved away from me.

I took a step and stumbled.

"I'm not talking to you when you're this drunk," he said. "Where's that Brandon guy?"

Even through the alcohol, I caught the hint of disdain that laced his tone.

"That *Brandon* guy?"

"Yeah, your boyfriend."

"No, no, no." I swayed to the side, and Elias reached out to steady me. His warm hand felt so right. So good against my skin. "He's not my"—hiccup—"boyfriend."

"Okay, whatever he is. Where is he?"

My mouth filled with the dreaded hot spit that warned

me vomiting was inevitable. "He'ssomewherewith—Idon't-know." The words caught in my throat like molasses, sticky and strung together.

The next thing I knew, Elias rushed me to the side of the porch and pulled my hair back while I threw up over the rail. My stomach went into spasms. I chocked and coughed while tears poured down my cheeks. And then the bottom fell out of the sky. Cold, stinging rain pelted down, but I couldn't move. I couldn't stop being sick.

"It's okay," Elias said beside my ear while sweeping the damp strands of hair away from my cheek. "You're all right. Okay? You're good. Just get it out." Elias stayed right with me, and for a moment, it was the way it used to be, then everything kind of just went black.

"Oh, God," I groaned, rolling onto my side in the hopes it would dull the pounding in my temples.

I tossed and turned, fighting to find sleep again, but the early morning sunlight had already begun to creep through my shades and reflect off the godawful-pink walls. "Enough with the light already."

When I opened my eyes, instead of staring at my closet door, I stared at Elias. His head had dropped to his shoulder; one knee was pulled to his chest, and his other leg stretched out in front of him. Boots still on.

With each beat, my pulse raced faster, harder. I struggled through the wine fog to remember what had happened the night before, but only managed to gather flashes.

Elias and some random guy shoving me in a car.

My head in his lap.

Him dragging me up the stairs to my room.

Jesus, if my parents had walked out of their room and

caught him carting my drunk carcass up those stairs, he would have been in a morgue instead of my floor. We both may have been.

The bedsprings creaked when I shifted my weight, and Elias' eyes shot open. His hands went to the floor preparing for a sudden bolt. Then he glanced at my closed bedroom door, and his palm went to his heart, the strain on his face dissipating.

"Definitely don't need that shit," he whispered, then somewhat grinned. "How do you feel this morning?"

"Like death."

"Yep. Figured as much." He interlocked his fingers and raised his arms over his head, the stretch causing his biceps to flex.

It was strange seeing him in front of my closet all grown up with a five-o clock shadow and tattoos. Strange and tempting and devastating at all the same time. I wanted to bury my face in his chest and breathe in his scent. I wanted to right all the wrong, make him unable to ignore me.

A million questions swirled in my head, but out of them all, the most pressing slipped through my lips in a barely audible plea for an I love you: "Why did you stay?"

"To make sure you were safe." He rolled a shoulder like it was nothing, but it was everything in that moment. Because he still cared. Just like when I thought he hated me as a child, he cared.

My breath snagged in my throat. I wanted to say so many things: I miss you. I love you. Please. . . But all that came out was a garbled, "Thanks."

"Sure thing."

When he stood, I sat up, squinting as I fought the throbbing in my skull. "Wait! Don't leave."

"So. . ." He glanced at his watch. "It's almost six, and I'm not trying to get shot today." He moved to the window and flipped the lock.

The old, wooden frame groaned when he lifted the sash.

"I don't like this."

"It is what it is, Sunny." He wouldn't even look at me now.

"Bullshit!"

"Don't start. Not this morning. I barely got any sleep," he said, and tears stung my eyes. "I just wanna go home before your dad catches me and—" His gaze met mine, and his expression softened to one I remembered all too well. One that said I care, and you mean something.

He moved away from the window, stopping at the side of my bed. "This isn't easy."

"Then why are you doing it?" I whispered.

"Because I'm no good for you, and I know it. Because I care too much about you."

"What the hell?" My throat burned, begging to cry or scream, wanting anything that showed the turmoil churning inside me. "What are you talking about?"

"You and me, Sunny. We're from two different worlds, all right? I don't belong in your world. And you sure as shit don't need to be drug into mine."

His lips pressed into a thin, hard line as he studied my face. I fought the burning in my chest when he tucked a piece of hair behind my ear.

"In another life though. In another life, I would've done better, and you'd be mine. I promise."

Pots and pans clanged in the kitchen below.

The stench of burnt coffee wafted underneath the door, and a wrinkle creased his brow, his eyes searching mine before he pressed his lips to my forehead. "It's because I love you that I can't be selfish."

My vision swam behind tears, and I grappled for a word, any word. Something, but my chest was so tight everything I tried to say remained lodged in my throat. He stepped to the window and threw his legs, one after the other, over the ledge. I closed my eyes, so I didn't have to watch him leave, and I pretended that come Monday, he would change his mind.

After he left through my window, just like Peter Pan, I sat in my bed, just like Wendy. The warm August breeze puffed the sheer curtains for a good half an hour, and I cried off and on before I went to the bathroom and headed down the stairs.

Momma was at the sink washing dishes, and I kissed her cheek on my way to the cabinet to grab a coffee mug, the one with a cat's face painted on it and a tiny chip in the handle.

"Need help?" I asked even though I felt like I may pass out at any second. Pushing through a hangover was a rite of passage that I was determined to conquer that particular day.

She smiled. "No, honey. Thank you."

After I poured myself a cup—half filled with milk—I flopped down at the table across from Daddy who was hidden behind the newspaper.

Simon sprinted into the kitchen, circling around the table while singing the Barney song before darting back into the hallway.

Sometimes I envied him for being that age. Life was so much less complicated at seven.

The crinkle of the newspaper caught my attention just before Daddy cleared his throat. "I hear Elias is at your school." He peered over the Sports section.

The rim of the mug was to my lips, and I hoped it hid

the shock I felt taking over my face. The first sip of coffee scalded my tongue, but I swallowed it anyway. "Oh. Uh. Yeah."

"Weren't gonna tell me?" He straightened in the chair, laid the paper down, then clasped his hands over it.

"Well, I mean. Why would I? It's just a guy a used to be friends with."

That comment did not amuse my daddy. He took an uneasy, halfway ashamed breath. "You two have a. . .history." The way he said that word made it sound dirty and wrong.

Momma turned on the faucet and started to scrub the sink. Her way of ignoring or avoiding I guessed.

"I haven't talked to him in three years, Daddy." *Liar! He was in your room less than an hour ago.*

Daddy stared straight at me until I feared he would call bullshit. "Mmm."

"So, I just figured it didn't matter. You know?"

I hoped my face wasn't as flushed as it felt, that he didn't notice my pulse thumping in my neck. Most of all, I prayed he wouldn't see through the lie, because it did matter.

It was the most important matter ever to exist in my life.

"I don't want you getting mixed up with that boy, Sunny. You hear me? He's bad news."

I focused on the ironically mocking quote painted on the wall behind him: *The fondest memories are made when gathered around the table.* I wanted to ask him why he cared. Why, if he thought Elias was so awful, did he open his home up to foster kids. Most foster children were from similar situations. Most of all, I wanted to call him a hypocrite. But the best thing I could do was make him believe I didn't care.

Nodding, I took a sip of my coffee then said, "Okay."

I heard the nearly silent breath Momma released just before Simon looped back through the kitchen.

Daddy took his cup to the sink and gave my mother a soft kiss, his hand sweeping over her cinched waist before he grabbed his gun from the counter and secured it in his holster.

Maybe he believed I'd stay away from *that boy,* or maybe I just believed that boy intended to stay away from me, and that's why Daddy was so easily convinced.

I, however, had no intentions on staying away. At all.

I FELL asleep in church that Sunday.

Well, nodded off would be more appropriate. Daisy's dad just had this monotone voice, like the teacher from *Ferris Bueller's Day off. Bueller. Bueller. Bueller.* It was enough to make anyone take a nap.

Luckily, Daisy nudged me in the ribs, and my eyes popped open before she leaned over and whispered, "Just so you know, I didn't have sex with Ben the other night."

I kept my eyes trained on the pulpit. "O-kay."

"I mean, we fooled around but nothing serious, you know? More or less dry humping."

Closing my eyes, I shook my head. "You realize that's your father up there"—I nodded toward the altar—"talking about Sodom and Gomora?"

"Yeah, the immorality thing is what made me think about Ben."

I facepalmed at that. "You've got issues."

Momma leaned around Simon and Bobby, shooting us both the kind of I-mean-business-stare that could make a serial killer's blood run cold. She snapped her fingers, frowning when she pointed at Pastor Fulmer. Sighing, I settled back on the pew. I took one of the gray donation envelopes and a pen from the hymnal shelf, checking to make sure Momma's attention was back on the sermon. I scribbled out: *You're going to hell* and passed it to Daisy while I stifled a giggle.

She shrugged her shoulders like she couldn't care less.

When she passed the note back to me, it said: *That's where all the cool kids go anyway. According to Kurt Cobain.*

She crossed herself in honor of the late rock god. That girl was concerned about popularity even in the afterlife. Oddly enough, the message finished on a hellfire and brimstone take away: We're all going to hell unless we repent.

"Hey," Daisy said as we filed down the faded-red carpet that lined the aisle. "We don't have to go eat with your parents, do we?

"No."

"Good."

A group of kids from school stood in a semi-circle by the exit with Ben and Brandon in the middle. Brandon smiled at me, but Ben didn't even glance in our direction. I did my obligatory wave at Brandon and then shifted my narrowed gaze at Ben who was making googly eyes at some blonde from Lockhart.

Daisy's shoulders sagged.

"Ugh." I shoved open the heavy, wooden door, squinting against the sunshine when I stepped outside. "Guys are such dicks."

The lady who ran the Meals on Wheels service, gasped then clucked her tongue disapprovingly.

"Like that old bat hasn't said worse things." Daisy leaned into me on our way to my car. "Mother said she was a stripper back in the sixties."

I glanced over my shoulder, trying to imagine the gray-haired lady in the floral-print dress swinging around a pole.

"No. Way." I opened my car door and let the trapped heat roll out before climbing in and cranking the engine.

Daisy placed her bare feet on the dash and hitched up her dress to the top of her thighs. "Alabama needs to learn the damn seasons." She cranked up the air conditioner to full blast.

"It's not officially fall," I said.

"Yeah, and I'm not officially a citizen of hell yet, either. This heat is stupid." She huffed. "So, you didn't tell me how your date went."

"You mean the one you forced upon me?" I shifted the gear into drive. "And don't roll your eyes. You know I didn't want to go on that date."

"Was it that bad?"

"No."

"Exactly!"

"But I'm just not into him like that." Mussafer's Z71 came barreling through the parking lot, an engine snorkel sticking up from the hood. I had to slam on my brakes to keep from T-boning him. "Shit."

"You're crazy! How can you not be into Brandon McClure?"

"I'm just. . . " *Elias. Elias. Elias.* "Not."

She sighed like she was either put out or disappointed, then skipped the CD to song number two, cocking a brow when the beat started. "This is your anthem."

By the time I pulled into my drive, Daisy had played "Losing My Religion" three times. Definitely not my theme song but probably hers.

We got snacks from the pantry, went straight to my room, closed my door, and then piled on my bed and turned on *American Pie*.

Halfway through the movie and a box of Crunch and

Munch, Daisy rolled onto her side. "What do you think it is about band camp?"

"Huh?"

She helped herself to a fistful of the caramel-coated snack and crammed it in her mouth. "Seems like everyone gets freaky at band camp. I mean, I thought band people were like. I don't know, not focused on sex or something. They're all quiet and sit right at the front of the class."

I blinked a few times. I loved Daisy, but sometimes she was ridiculous. "Wow. Judgey Mc Judgerson?"

"Come on, Sunny. In all these movies the band geeks get knocked up. Doing stuff with their flutes on their girl-friends." She zoned out for a second, then shoveled more food in her mouth. "I heard that Betty Minkle did something with a trombone that you just don't want to know."

I didn't want to know about Betty Minkle—or anyone for that matter—doing anything with a trombone aside from playing it. Shaking my head, I used my hands as earmuffs. "Nope. Do not want to hear."

Daisy pried my hands away from my head and pushed my arms down to my sides. I gave her a menacing look, hoping she understood I'd shove her right off the bed if she so much as breathed a word about what happened with that trombone.

"How are you supposed to make a guy like you?"

"I don't think you make them like you, Daisy. I think it just happens." She had this forlorn glaze to her eyes.

"Okay," I exhaled. "Spill. What happened when you disappeared with Ben?"

She grabbed the remote and paused the movie before staring down at the near-empty bowl between the two of us. "So we ended up in one of the spare rooms. Of course. . ." She sighed. "On this crazy, extravagant bed with a canopy. It was really romantic." Her eyes met mine, and she kind of just shrugged her shoulder.

"And?" I rolled my hand through the air like a director, telling the crew to keep rolling even though the scene was going down the toilet because nothing about hooking up at a party was romantic.

"So. Okay. Don't tell anyone."

"Who am I gonna tell?"

"I don't know. Hailey or Morgan?"

I glared at her.

"Fine. So anyway, we were making out and fooling around, and I went to. . ." Tilting her head a little, she made a fist then bobbed her head up and down. "You know."

"Oh. Gross. You sucked his dick, Daisy? You put Virgin Collector Ben's genitals in your mouth?"

"Yeah, and I guess I drank too much because halfway through I had to get up and run to the toilet to vomit."

"You didn't?"

She covered her face with her hands while nodding.

"Wow." I laughed so hard I fell over on the bed, spilling what was left of the Crunch and Munch. "Just. Wow. So, he may have been ignoring you this morning because he made you throw up. Ah-mazing!"

"It's not. Really it's not." She grabbed a pillow from my bed and threw it at me. "I'm never gonna live that down."

"Oh, surely he's not gonna go around telling people you threw up from sucking him off."

"He's a guy, Sunny. He would totally go around bragging about that." She puffed her chest out, curling her arms inward and flexing her lack of muscles while she made a menacing glare. "Yeah, dude. I'm so hung that I made the preacher's daughter gag."

My eyes went wide. "Oh, shit."

Ben would most certainly do something like that. Without a doubt.

"Anyway, I totally blew any chances with him."

I blinked a few times before snatching the pillow from her grip and whacking her in the face with it. "Are you kidding? You're worried that you blew it with him?"

"It's *Ben Jones*, Sunny!" The emphasis she placed on his name made it sound like he was some incredible guy. Not a pervy jock with a jacked-up pickup.

There was no showing her the proverbial light on the matter of Ben Jones. I patted her back and nodded like I finally understood. "Okay. Okay. I get it, but it'll blow over. He'll ask you out again."

"So how was your kiss with Brandon?"

I chewed at my lip, my stomach knotting while I thought about how that night ended with me over the balcony railing.

"Hello?" She waved her hands around in a tizzy. "Was it great or what?"

"We didn't kiss.

Her face scrunched. "Huh? Not even a goodnight peck? That's lame."

"He didn't exactly take me home." I paused. Daisy glared. "Elias did."

"Oh." She crawled onto her knees. "My." Then grabbed my shoulders and moved in close to my face. "God. He was there? And he took you home instead of the guy you were on a date with?" She clutched her chest. "Super scandalous."

"It wasn't like that." I diverted my attention to a loose thread on my comforter and twirled it around my finger. "I got sick then blacked out. When I woke up, he was over there." I pointed to my half-open closet with dirty clothes spilling out.

"He stayed the night? That's brave. Very brave." Her eyes narrowed. "You didn't. . .you know?"

"No. Definitely not." My finger swelled around the tightening thread, the skin changing to a weird, purplish-red. I thought about how Elias looked at me like he hated and loved me all at the same time before I finally unwound the string.

"So what are you gonna do?" Daisy pointed the remote at the TV, and the movie resumed.

"About what?"

"This little love triangle you've developed."

"It's not a love triangle."

"Sure it's not." She smirked. "You've got the high school heartthrob chasing you and the tatted up bad boy sneaking in your window. If that's not a love triangle, I don't know what is."

I rolled my eyes.

"You really should read more romance novels. You'd understand things like this much better."

THAT MONDAY I'm pretty sure Elias made an effort not to look at me.

When Miss Weaver called me to the front of the class to go over the answers to a pop quiz, he kept his head down on his desk. He passed me in the hallway without so much as a glance. And maybe I deserved that. After all, I didn't fight for us either. By the time the third-period bell rang, I'd swung between anger and sadness and why-did-I-cares a million times.

I followed the herd into the congested hallway. Lockers

banged, sneakers squeaked, a group of guys shouted douche canoe at the top of their lungs before shoving some poor kid into the restroom.

Daisy came strutting down the hall, the open flannel she had on over her Ramones T-shirt ruffled with each hard step and the pleated red skirt she was wearing was one-hundred percent too short.

"Okay," I said when she stopped in front of me. "I know you have questionable taste in clothing, Daisy, but. . ." My gaze dropped to the zebra-striped, patent leather pumps that finished off her ensemble. "You look like some grunge prostitute."

That insult must have gone in one ear and out the other because she grinned wide and bounced on the balls of her feet like she was about to explode. "Ben smiled at me. He's not mad at me for throwing up on him, I guess!"

I closed my eyes and shook my head once before turning the corner.

Elias stood by the stairwell at the end of the hall, and in front of him was Jenny, twirling her brown hair around her finger.

I stopped dead in my tracks, and Daisy bumped into me. "What are you—oh."

One of the twins came barreling down the stairwell, jumping from the fifth step and knocking Elias' books out of his hand.

"Judah!" Elias shouted before grabbing his textbook from the floor and whacking his brother with it.

Judah waved a dismissive hand through the air and took off down another hallway, shouting about Lockhart being a bunch of pussies.

"She is such an attention whore," Daisy said.

"It doesn't matter."

"You're jealous."

"Nope."

But I still watched them. Watching the way Jenny kept shifting her weight from foot to foot. And I was okay, really, until he smiled at her because it was the kind of smile that lit up his entire face.

I swallowed while forcing my gaze back to Daisy. "Not at all."

I gritted my teeth when I ducked into history class. Stupid puppy love wasn't supposed to feel like some devastating force of nature tearing through your body, but what I felt for Elias was nowhere close to puppy love. No, it was much more destructive. It was a Romeo and Juliet type love. Tragic. Heartbreaking. And never meant to be.

I stomped past Mr. Brunner in his tacky, brown suit he wore every damn Monday.

Like a true teenage, lovesick, heartbroken rebel I tossed my books on my desk and threw myself into my chair so hard the legs scraped the floor.

Daisy slid into the desk beside me, eyes wide. "Yeah. Okay. You're totally fine, Sun. Totes."

I flipped her the bird, and one of the goody-goodies behind me gasped.

Jenny's seat in front of me remained empty, and with every second that ticked by, a little more of my heart was torn out. I couldn't help but imagine Elias kissing her. I hated how that made my insides feel like a ship sinking inch by inch. The rest of the class funneled in. The low buzz of chit-chat filled the small room, and finally, just before the late bell rang, Jenny strutted in like a damn peacock.

My blood pressure spiked like a volcanic eruption, washing heat over my face and chest and down my arms to my fingers which gripped my pen so tight I was surprised it didn't snap like a twig. Someone had highjacked my body, because, I was *not* that girl.

I was not the girl who envied Jenny Smith—until Elias gave her my damn smile.

Mr. Brunner closed the door before turning his back to the class. The marker tapped on the whiteboard while he jotted out details on the Louisiana Purchase in his awful chicken scratch.

Jenny made this dramatic exhale—way too loud and long. The kind of sigh that wants to be noticed. Then she flipped her hair behind her back, the brown strands landing right on my desk. I swatted it away then flipped to the first blank page in my notebook, scribbling the subject and date in the top righthand corner.

Her fingers curled around the back of her chair, those stupid bangle bracelets she always wore jingling together. "So..." she said.

Closing my eyes, I forced every ounce of emotion from my face before I glanced up. Jenny was turned sideways in her seat, smiling at me like she and I were the best of friends. I arched my brows with a what-do-you-want fake grin.

"Are you still friends with Elias?" she batted her eyes.

"No."

"Too bad. He's cute." She rolled her lip underneath her bleached teeth and coyly shrugged a shoulder. "Like really cute."

I let out a laugh that wasn't really a laugh.

"But, I guess that's what happens. Isn't it?"

"What?"

"You know what." God her smile made me want to scream.

Before I could respond, Daisy had leaned across the

aisle, putting her desk on two legs. "She knows what, Jenny?"

Jenny's eyes slid over me like I was some rabies-infested cat she wouldn't touch with a ten-foot-pole. "Everyone knows you got caught with him in your bed. It was all the talk during Momma's Bible study a few years ago. Naughty by the way." She winked, and my heart ignited into this fiery ball of twisted hate and embarrassment.

"Go fuck yourself, Jenny!" Daisy said.

"Such a dirty mouth for a preacher's daughter."

"In case you haven't heard, preacher's kids are basically the spawn of the devil." Daisy cocked a grin.

With a sarcastic smile, I spun my finger in the air giving her the nonverbal turn-the-fuck-around.

Jenny smirked, crossing one leg over the other all prim and proper. "Mmm. And from what I hear, the devil's spawn should really work on her gag reflex." With that, she faced the front again, flicking her stupid hair over her stupid shoulder.

Daisy's nostrils flared. "I swear," she whisper-shouted, "I'm gonna get ahold of the prayer request roster at Daddy's church and put something so awful on there about you, Jenny Smith..."

"All right class. Let's settle down now." Mr. Brunner shuffled to his desk for the attendance sheet.

And for the rest of class, I fumed.

AFTER HISTORY, Daisy had theatre, which meant she was on the opposite side of the school. It also meant that I would pass Elias at precisely 1:45 on my way to pre-cal and trig, so I waited for the hallways to thin out until the thuds from the sneakers of people rushing to class echoed down the hall.

I was going to be late, but as long as I didn't have to see Elias, it did not matter.

I closed my locker and turned around, nearly running right into Brandon's torso. "Shit," I whispered, clutching my biology book to my chest. "You scared me."

"Sorry." He leaned against the red, aluminum wall then ran his fingers through his hair. "Look, did I piss you off the other night or something?"

"No."

"You sure?"

"Yeah," I said. "I'm sure." I started down the hall toward a group of girls who had their hands cupped in front of their mouths and their eyes locked on me—on us, really.

The skinny brunette in the middle, Valerie, was Brandon's ex-girlfriend, so I could only imagine the poison spewing from her lips simply because he walked beside me. Their polished lips twisted in self-righteous smirks when we passed.

"I just. I mean, you just left without saying goodbye or anything. I figured you were mad."

"What? No." I was still distracted by the muffled whispers from those girls. Or maybe more distracted by the fact that I cared about the muffled whispers. "I, uh, I got sick, and a friend took me home."

"Oh God. You did? I'm so sorry." He swept a hand through his hair. "I didn't think I was gone that long."

"It's fine. Don't worry about it." I stopped outside my next class. "Actually, be glad you didn't witness it. It was pretty disgusting. Total *Exorcist* stuff."

He laughed. "Thanks for going with me."

"Yeah. Thanks for taking me. I had fun."

He shot me his Mr. Good Guy grin, then kissed me on the forehead. "See you later, Sunny."

I watched him jog down the hall, not realizing I was smiling until I stepped into the room and Mrs. Blanchard called me out: "Take your seat, lovebird."

Crap. Maybe Daisy was right.

Maybe I was in a love triangle after all.

10

SUNNY

Monday turned into Tuesday which faded into Friday. One week rolled into two. Then three. And Elias had successfully ignored me. Poof. Like I didn't even exist.

I was no longer hurt over the entire situation. No, I had graduated all the way up to being totally and utterly pissed.

"Whoa," Daisy said before snagging the eyeliner from my hand. "What are you doing?"

I frowned at my reflection in her makeup mirror. "I'm trying to do that cat-eye wing thing you do."

"Come here. Close your eyes." Daisy went about drawing delicate strokes over my eyelids, swearing underneath her breath a few times before she told me to look in the mirror. "It's so weird to see you with real makeup on."

"I wear real makeup."

Daisy snorted. "Yeah, right." Then she patted the top of her metallic, rolling makeup cart. "If you don't have to basically peel your skin off to remove it, it's not real makeup." She smeared some cotton-candy pink lipstick over her lips before grabbing the pair of combat boots she had gotten from the thrift store and lacing them up. "So," she said. "Has Brandon given you his letterman jacket yet?"

"No."

"He needs to pony up. I mean, it's almost been a month. Which, by the way, what are you doing for your one-month anniversary?"

I blinked a few times, confused. Brandon had kissed me twice. Innocent pecks that were extremely awkward. "We aren't dating, Daisy."

"Sure you are. It's like unspoken." Her face screwed up. "You guys are an item."

Both my brows raised. "Uh. . ." I opened one of her dresser drawers and rummaged for a T-shirt.

"It's totally official. Jenny's nose butt even asked me what was going on, and I gladly told her you were madly in love. How does everyone else know you two are a thing except you?"

"Because we haven't talked about it." I snagged one of those retro, baseball tees with a white body and navy blue, quarter-length sleeves and slipped it on.

Daisy shoved a pair of cut-off shorts at me. "You don't talk about these things, Sunny. They just happen."

They just happen?

I get the just happening thing with Daisy and Ben, they were all hands and mouths and passing notes between classes. Brandon and I were just. . . *something*.

Sure, I liked him. I was attracted to him. And when he kissed me, it wasn't awkward because it was gross. It was awkward because there was no spark, no breathless moment. No tongue.

I buttoned the shorts and tugged the hem of the shirt down before smoothing my hand over the well-worn fabric. Daisy stepped behind me, pulling on some white lace ensemble over her tight shirt and hip huggers. She glanced at our reflection. "We've arrived, Sunny. We've arrived."

Funny thing was, I was never trying to arrive anywhere.

"I'm not doing it!" I was near a full-blown panic attack as I glanced at the well-lit window of Pickle's Pit Stop from Daisy's car.

"Really? You're way hotter than I am." She flipped her visor down and glanced in the vanity mirror, fluffing her hair.

"And I'm also the sheriff's daughter!" I tossed my hands up in a total what-the-hell gesture. "No!"

Rolling her eyes, she threw open her door. "Fine."

The door slammed closed, and I plastered my hands over my eyes.

Daisy was seriously losing it. Total preacher's kid. When I pulled my hands away, she was trotting up to the counter with a case—*a case*—of Natty Lite. Although I had to give it to her, she swayed her hips like she was on a runway, her gaze dead set on the poor guy behind the register.

She tossed the beer on the counter. There was a moment where neither of them moved. All I envisioned was the guy asking for her ID and her running back out to the car and us peeling off, but after a short stare down, she smiled and flicked her hair over her shoulder, and the guy grabbed his little scan wand and rang her up.

She had a victorious smile when she Peg-Bundy walked out. Squealing, she tossed the case in the back seat. "I'm telling you, arrived, Sunny."

Thomas Radcliffe's house stood right in front of us. Tall

and white and quintessentially Southern with its wrap-around porch and sloping tin roof. Every light in the house was on, the windows filled with silhouettes of people dancing.

Daisy pointed toward an area that resembled a car dealership lot—Robertsdale High and a few Lockhart High decals hanging from the rear views. "And can you tell me why we parked on the street?"

"In case we need a quick getaway," I said.

"Wow. What kinda plans do you have for tonight?"

With a half roll of my eyes, I stepped onto the porch. Unintelligible rap lyrics blasted from inside, and we both stared at the door. Every party I had been to had party-goers meandering around outside. The door was usually open or at the very least ajar, so there was never the question of whether you knock or not.

"Do we ring the bell?" I asked.

Daisy held the beer to her chest and shrugged.

Just when I went to press the doorbell, the door swung open and two very drunk Lockhart guys stumbled out, laughing and sloshing beer everywhere. We took the opportunity to dart inside, and my hand immediately went to my nose to block out the smell of alcohol that seemed to envelop us.

The thump of bass rattled the frame of the laughably stereotypical cross stitch—*Home is where the heart is*—tacked over the doorway to the living room. Frilly curtains hung from the windows. Commemorative NASCAR plates decorated the walls. And teenagers slammed back beers and vodka-laced punch like it was an Olympic sport.

"Wow," Daisy mumbled. "This is not what I expected bad boy Thomas Radcliffe's house to look like. There's cross-stitch."

"Me either."

"I expected more. Flare?"

"I expected something that didn't look like my grandma's house."

"Ladies!" Ben swooped in like a stealthy hawk, wrapping his arms around us both. "Welcome to the party." He led us to the large, white Igloo cooler placed on the kitchen island where orange slices and pineapple chunks floated on top of a red concoction.

The pungent smell of vodka wafted up, and I shook my head. "No thanks. DD."

"Man, you and McClure are just alike." He laughed.

Daisy took a cup, gagging as soon as she tasted it. "God, I could set my saliva on fire now."

"Just Kool-Aid and some Aristocrat. Well. . ." Ben jerked his chin toward the empty bottles on the stove beside him. "Like two liters of Aristocrat."

"It is what it is." With that, Daisy tipped the drink back.

The music booming from the living room cut off just as someone's hand crept around my waist. "There you are," Brandon said.

He gave me a once over, his lips curving in a pleased smile. "That's cute. Very rocker-esque."

"Thanks." I debated whether I should kiss his cheek or hug him or just stand there.

"You know," Daisy said, already ladling more of that horrific drink into her cup. "I've always told Sunny she looks like a rock star and a pageant queen had a baby."

Brandon tilted his head like he needed to consider the comparison for a second. Then he nodded. "Totally see it." He motioned to my empty hands. "Not drinking tonight?"

"Uh. No. I'm good."

Laughing, he took a bottle of water from the fridge and

handed it to me. "And I bestow upon thee, the official I'm-the-designated-driver-drink." He kissed my cheek then pushed a strand of hair behind my ear.

The first staccato beats of drums and electric keyboard filled the room, and Brandon snapped along to the beginning notes of "Billie Jean."

"God, Thomas. You and this eighties shit," Ben shouted before grabbing Daisy's hand. Looking back, she tugged at the shoulders of her shirt while mouthing *the jacket* before Ben dragged her from the room.

Brandon was in full Jackson mode, hip thrust, hand flourish—everything. I couldn't help but laugh when he took my hand and yanked me to him. "Let's go dance."

"Oh," I placed my palms against his chest. "I don't. . ."

He rolled his eyes. "Don't tell me you're embarrassed. You don't look like the kinda girl who gets embarrassed easily." He tugged on my arm. "Besides, everyone else is shit-faced. We'll be the best dancers in there."

THE NIGHT WORE ON. The house filled with more people with each hour that passed. By eleven, a group of jocks sat at the kitchen table playing beer pong, the stoners had congregated on the back porch passing joint after joint, and the inside of Thomas' house was nothing but a wall of bodies. It seemed like every high school student from the surrounding tri-state area had shown up.

After enough beers, rival schools seemed to set their differences aside. On the weekends, we weren't Robertsdale or Lockhart students, we were teenagers trying to exercise rebellious independence via cheap booze and meaningful hookups.

I had somehow ended up on my fourth bottle of water

playing Never Have I Ever with a group of strangers while sandwiched between Daisy and Brandon.

"All right. All right." The emo girl from my history class —who as it turned out was very smiley when she wasn't at school—clapped her hands together. "Never have I ever hooked up with a friend. Like a friend-friend, not some friends with benefits crap."

Everyone glanced around for a second. Emo Girl took the first and only swig.

"Wow. Prudes," she whispered.

Some Lockhart guy with perfectly spiked blond hair stepped into the doorway. He caught the attention of every girl in that room, including Miss Emo. There aren't many guys I would refer to as pretty, but that guy, he was beautiful. Straight nose. Perfect jaw and full lips. All I could think was he may very well end up being Fort Morgan's first high-end fashion model.

Clearing his throat, he leaned against the wall outside the room, his pale blue eyes locked on Brandon. I bristled. Guys only looked at other guys with that cold expression if they intended to beat the crap out of them. I noticed Brandon glance at him from the corner of his eye then shift in his seat, rubbing his palms over the legs of his jeans.

After a second, Pretty Boy pushed off the wall and disappeared into another room.

"You okay?" I asked.

"Yeah."

"That guy was looking at you weird."

He wet his lips with his tongue. "He's pissed."

"Why?"

"Stupid misunderstanding."

I wanted to know what this stupid misunderstanding was. In my limited life experience, stupid misunderstandings between guys usually revolved around a girl. And seeing as how I had learned earlier in the night that Brandon and I were evidently a thing, I didn't want other people to think I was *that* girl. You know, the girl who thought a guy liked her when he was secretly banging some Lockhart guy's prissy, rich girlfriend.

"Like," I took a sip of water. "What kind of misunderstanding?"

Brandon glanced at the now empty doorway, and some of the tension that wrinkled his brow seemed to dissipate. "Nothing to worry about, babes."

Babes? Why was I smiling at that? "Okay." I nodded, pretending I didn't want to pry, that I didn't need more information.

The game that could have been retitled How Slutty Are You continued, neither me nor Daisy with our inexperience finding much to drink over. At some point between a question about toothbrushes and pornographic, one-hour photo development, Brandon was summoned to a game of beer pong.

"Never have I ever had a threesome." That voice was deep and Southern and almost identical to Elias'.

The girls in the room all went doe-eyed when Judah Black stepped into the room, his unruly, dark hair covering half his face.

With a smirk, he chugged his beer. "What? No one else has had a three-way?" He laughed. "Shame." His eyes locked on Daisy, and he winked before strutting off.

The little hitch to her breath didn't go unnoticed, and I turned toward her silently mouthing No.

"Come on," she nudged me. "I wouldn't. I'm totally into Ben, but you can't deny the appeal."

"Oh, I won't deny the appeal at all." Those Black boys had the entire female population of Robertsdale's attention.

From the kitchen, I heard Jenny's annoying, high-pitched squeal. "Judah Black's here everybody!" Daisy glanced sideways and gave an exasperated eye roll.

Emo Girl started with another round of questions, but I wasn't paying attention. If Judah was here, chances were that Elias was as well, albeit I hadn't heard Jenny announce his entrance like the emcee at a wrestling match.

Fifth bottle of water down, and I had to find a restroom. Of course, the one downstairs had a line six deep. "Shit," I mumbled.

"There's another one upstairs." A petite blond stood behind me, swaying. Her eyelids looked heavy. She bumped into the wall and said," Excuse me, sir." She was either drunk or stoned. Possibly both. But she was out of her head, that was for sure.

"Come on. I'll show you." Her sweaty palm landed on my forearm, and she yanked me around with a lot more force than I thought she would be able to muster.

"You from The Dale?" That's what the kids from Lockhart called the public school.

"Uh. Yeah."

"Cool. I'm Laurel."

"Sunny."

"Hey, we both have hippy names. Were your parents hippies?"

Laurel was not a hippy name. It was a rich-girl name. "Um. Don't think so."

We stopped in front of the stairwell. An electric-blue ski rope had been tied from one banister to another. Attached to the middle of the barrier was a piece of notebook paper that read: *Don't Go Upstairs or I'll kick your ass!*

Laurel scoffed at that. "Whatever, Radcliffe."

She crawled over the rope, slamming into the wall and slipping down a step before she burst into laughter. "I'm so messed up right now."

"I can see."

"You coming?" She started up the stairs on her hands and knees. I followed her because I had to pee, and I would never get rid of the guilt if she ended up drowning herself in the toilet, which, from the way she was struggling at the current moment, seemed plausible.

None of the lights were on upstairs, and the noise from the party somehow seemed far away. Laurel flipped the switch and then staggered down the hall to one of the last rooms on the left. Smiling, she placed her hand on the knob and pushed open the door. Just enough light spilled in from the hallway that I could make out two people on the bed.

Brandon's perfectly-styled brown hair and broad, bare shoulders were hard to miss. However, the girl pinned underneath him was completely blocked from my view.

My heart clanged. My ears smoldered. Even though I wasn't emotionally invested in Brandon, betrayal stung. Fast and deep. He, after all, was a good guy, and I was a good girl, and yet, here we were.

Did I shout at him? Leave without muttering a word? I had no idea what the appropriate protocol was. As for Laurel? Drunk Girl didn't even see the cheating asshole. She made a beeline to the bathroom connected to the room, not even inviting me inside before she slammed the door behind her.

That's when Brandon shoved away from the girl so fast, he nearly toppled off the bed. "Sunny!" he panted, snatching his shirt up and tugging it over his head as though that would make it all better. "Fuck. I."

I held up my hands and slowly backed toward the door. "It's fine. I mean, we weren't even. You know—"

"Don't. Hey!" he started.

I tried to slip into the hall, but he snagged hold of my arm and snatched me back into the dark room. "Don't say anything. Okay? Please?"

"Are you kidding me! You're in here. . ." I waved my free hand around in a frenzy. "In a bed with—" I looked at the bed just as a guy. Stop. Pause. A guy? Climbed to his feet.

My mouth dropped, my heart skipped vital beats as it all sank in. Then I closed my eyes and took a long, hard breath while the same guy who earlier had been staring at Brandon from the doorway slid past me without so much as a word.

When I glanced back at Brandon, his hands were plastered to his face, and he repeated "shit" over and over.

Each pound of my heart seemed harder than the last, and my mind was a complete fog of confusion. I kept thinking maybe I missed something. "I. . ." Whatever I was trying to say stuck in my throat.

The toilet flushed, and Laurel came stumbling into the bedroom, the bathroom light blaring from the now open doorway. She ran into the dresser and then the bedpost before ramming into the door frame.

"Where'd he come from?" She pointed at Brandon. "Is he your boyfriend?"

I glanced at a panicked Brandon, then at her. Even though I still wasn't one-hundred percent sure about what the hell was going on, I just needed her out of the room.

"Yep." I bobbed my head. "Yep. And we're just gonna, you know—hookup in here. Boyfriend-girlfriend kind of hookup. Like sex and stuff. So if you could just. . ." I grabbed her by the shoulders and shoved her out into the hall. "Thanks."

I closed the door, locked it, and turned back around. Brandon's gaze was glued to the floor, and his arms were wrapped around his body like he was trying to keep warm during a blizzard. *That was definitely a guy. In the bed with him. His shirt was off. They were absolutely lip to lip. Shit!*

"Hey." I made my voice soft. "Look. It's, uh. It's okay."

"It's not."

"I mean. . ." I thumbed toward the crumpled bedsheets. "Was that like, I don't know, curiosity or. . ." I immediately felt awful for the words pouring from my mouth like vomit, but I had never heard of a guy at our school being gay. Guys at Lockhart, sure. Two or three rumors had flown around about a theatre guy, but not a star athlete from Robertsdale. Not guys like Brandon McClure, all suave and muscular and swoon-worthy.

"Crap. I didn't mean it like. I don't know. I'm just. Confused? Mainly because we were kinda sorta dating or something and then. I don't know. I mean, it's fine and all, but I'm just."

Another hard breath. "I'm sorry," he whispered. "I'm so sorry. I like you. Fuck. I like you, Sunny. You're this great, pretty girl, and you're sweet, and you're. . . God, I'm so fucked. If the guys at school find out." He shook his head.

"No one's finding out." I touched his arm.

"It's not like I enjoy lying. You know? I just figured, maybe if I tried hard enough that I'd like girls. And you're pretty and sweet. Something's wrong with me, but I can't—." He choked on his words before his brows pinched together like he refused to give in. Like maybe if he just didn't admit it, it would all go away.

"Nothing's wrong with you. Don't say that."

"You don't understand. Football scouts won't look at me if they know. My parents. God, my parents would disown me." His voice nearly folded in on itself, and my heart sank in my chest swift and hard. "I'm sorry. I do like you. I just. I just. Please don't hate me." Filled with panic and shame, his eyes met mine.

I grabbed his face, placing my nose inches from his. "It's *okay*, Brandon." I didn't care. Not that we were supposedly dating and I had found him in a room with a guy, not that he was gay. I only cared that he was obviously torn up over it and terrified.

"Please, Sunny. Please, God, don't say anything. Not to Daisy or Ben."

"I wouldn't." I swept my fingers over his cheek. "I'm not mad at you. And I most certainly don't hate you."

"You're the first person to know."

And while I was shocked, I wasn't.

He was the All-American football player. The jock. The guy whose sexuality would never be questioned. The same guys who looked up to Brandon were the same ones who would most likely beat the mess out of him if they knew he was gay. It must have been torture feeling like no one actually knew who you were. "I'm glad I know," I said.

A heavy silence fell between us. Not awkward, just the kind of silence that bridges moments of disbelief and acceptance. The faint music from the party below shook the floor. No one down there had a clue that our entire worlds had just shifted. They were going on with their lives while ours teetered on the edge of this black hole of trust and hurt feelings.

I jerked my head toward the doorway. "Come on, let's go back downstairs." Grabbing his hand, I laced my fingers through his, hoping it would provide some comfort. "You know, I hate to tell you this, but we've been up here for a hot minute. People are gonna assume we hooked up."

He laughed. "At this current moment, I gladly welcome that rumor."

"And just so you know. I'm a virgin, so you didn't go all the way. In case anyone asks."

"Duly noted."

We stopped just before the ski rope barricade. Brandon's jaw was tense, his hand sweaty in mine. "Hey." I placed my free hand on his cheek and turned his face toward mine. "It's fine." And then I leaned in, pressing my lips to his cheek. "I like you, Brandon McClure. Even more so now that I really know who you are."

When we stepped into the kitchen, Daisy and half the football team were gathered around the circular table. A bright-pink ping pong ball bounced across the surface and right into a solo cup in the middle. Daisy ordered Thomas to drink, and Ben patted Daisy's leg. "Good job, sexy lady."

Daisy gushed, and I shot a did-he-just-say-that look at Brandon. He leaned over and whispered, "I really struggle to see what girls see in him."

"Don't worry. I struggle to see it, too."

Ben glanced at us standing in the doorway, and he pushed to his feet. He took Brandon by the shoulders in a proud Dad grasp and cleared his throat. "Back from the boom-boom room upstairs," he shouted. "May I present to you, Sunny and Brandon!" The room erupted in whistles and claps. My face heated when Elias shouldered his way through a group of girls and grabbed a beer from the counter. I tried not to watch him. I tried not to worry whether he'd just heard Ben's stupid announcement.

Ben pretended to hold a mic to Brandon's face. "How was it?"

Brandon slapped his hand away. "Why are you such a dick?" Shaking his head, he pulled out a chair for me.

The game went on, most everyone making Thomas drink when they rang the cup. People filtered in and out of the room. I noticed every time Elias made an appearance. And I couldn't ignore the way Jenny usually trailed behind him like a fly on manure. Out of the corner of my eye, I caught Jenny flirtatiously flip her hair behind her shoulders when Elias handed her a drink. My jaw tensed. If Elias ignoring me wasn't painful enough, Elias ignoring me while paying attention to Jenny obliterated my heart. Ben tossed the ball, rang the cup, and pointed at Thomas to drink.

Brandon nudged my ribs with his elbow. "Who do you keep watching?"

"No one." I shifted my attention to the table.

"Come on, Sunny. We're beyond lying to each other, aren't we?" Brandon draped his heavy arm around my shoulder. A crease formed between his brows when he glanced back in the direction I'd been staring. "Ah, the guy with the tats?"

I took a sip of water.

Brandon leaned in close to my ear. "He keeps watching you."

I frowned even though his breath tickled my face.

"Don't believe me? Trust me for a second."

"What?"

Brandon's eyes crinkled at the corner with a smile. "Trust me." That look—had I not known he wasn't into me like that, may have been just enough to make me forget about Elias for two seconds. His eyes locked with mine, his face inching closer and closer while his hand crept up my neck and into my hair. And then his lips pressed to mine. Our lips didn't part. There was no electric crackle smoldering between us, but to anyone else that innocent kiss between friends would appear to be much more.

Ben whistled, and Thomas yelled for us to get a room.

The second Brandon pulled away, Elias slammed his fist on the counter, causing a few empty beer cans to topple to the floor before he stormed through the open back door.

Brandon smirked. "Still think he wasn't watching?"

11

SUNNY

I had half an hour to get home before curfew, and I couldn't find Daisy.

I searched throughout the house, kicking empty cups and cans out of my way. Two guys carted Thomas' unconscious body into the kitchen, snickering while they laid him across the table and folded his hands over his chest like a corpse in a coffin.

"Daisy?" I shouted, stepping in a pile of something that could have been puke. "God, I bet Thomas' parents are going to freak out—Daisy?"

"Five minutes," she called from upstairs.

"You guys could stay." Brandon crossed the room, the schlepp of his shoes peeling from the sticky floor caused my skin to crawl.

"I think I'll pass."

He chuckled. "Suit yourself."

Brandon collected some of the cans from the floor and placed them around Thomas like a chalk outline. The other guys joined in, surrounding Thomas with a teetering pyramid of Budweiser.

"Daisy?" I tapped my foot. "I'm going to the car. Come on!"

A door opened, and seconds later she appeared at the top of the stairs in nothing but Ben's T-shirt and a gleeful smile. "I'm gonna stay."

I deadpanned her.

"I'll be fine. I texted mom and told her we were staying at your house instead."

"Thanks for volunteering me to lie for you."

"It's what best friends are for, right?"

I shook my head, aware she was making a mistake—one she would most likely regret within a month, but I also knew when Daisy had her mind made up, it was a done deal. She'd be another notch on Ben's belt, and I'd end up hating him for breaking my best friend's heart.

With a sigh, I grabbed my keys from the counter. "Poor life choices, Daisy. Poor life choices."

"Love you," she sang before disappearing back into the room.

I waved at Brandon on my way out.

The single-note hum of the cicadas mixed with the gravel crunching beneath my feet in a weird Southern symphony. The sliver of a moon hung high in the sky, providing very little light. There's something eerie about walking through an open field alone in the dark. Something that makes you feel incredibly vulnerable. My imagination ran wild, picturing a Michael Meyers-like figure stalking behind me, butcher knife raised and gleaming under the moonlight. By the time I reached the street, I was almost in a jog.

I was about three feet away from my car when I heard Elias call my name. All I could see was the glow of a burning cigarette moving through the air, washing his face in a faint, red light when he took a drag. He blew a stream of smoke through his lips, tossed the cigarette onto the asphalt, and stepped between me and my car.

"What are you doing?" I asked, my poor heart not sure whether to beat or stall.

"I don't know."

I stood there for a moment, watching him watch me. Wanting him to say something, anything that would make the desperate pain in my chest give up.

"You going home?" he asked, his words slurring just enough to tell me he was a little drunk.

"Yeah."

"Alone?"

My jaw tensed. I could have said yes and left it at that, but every time he ignored me, it physically hurt and for some dumb reason, knowing I couldn't have Elias made the love I harbored toward him root more deeply in my soul. I dug my fist into my hip. "Not that it's any of your business, but yes."

Stroking his hand over his jaw, he opened my car door and then stepped to the side like he was waiting for me to climb in so he could shut it. I hesitated, waiting for him to tell me not to go. Waiting for him to kiss me. Waiting for anything other than goodbye. "Did you need something?"

He took a deep breath, interlocking his hands behind his head and curling his elbows in toward his face, his eyes closed. "I don't like you kissing him."

My heart skipped critical beats, but I somehow managed to hold up my chin and push my shoulders back like I couldn't have cared less. "Well, that's too bad." I went to climb into the driver's seat, but he grabbed my arm. "Let go, Elias." *Please don't let go.*

"Do you love him?"

"What?"

He inched closer to my face, the smell of cigarettes and beer heavy on his breath. "I said. Do you love him?"

One, two, three seconds ticked by, our gazes locked, our lips mere centimeters from one another. "What difference does it make?" I managed.

"Because your mine."

His warm, parted lips met mine and, suddenly, I was breathless. That kiss felt like being born and dying all at the same time. A supernova heating and growing brighter and brighter until finally its mass was too much for the meager universe and it exploded, sending tiny fragments of stars and suns and moons hurdling into outer space. His hands cupped my cheeks, tilting my head back until it hit the hood of my car. The kiss deepened while bits and pieces of our souls bled together. When his tongue brushed mine, I no longer knew who was breathing for who because there was no end to him or me. Just us. And when he finally broke the kiss, it felt like my entire world collapsed a little.

His forehead pressed to mine. "God, I fucking miss you." Every word filled with conviction, as though I were a priest and he was a sinner. "Just give me tonight. Please?"

My fingertips raked over his stubble and into his thick hair. I didn't want to give him one night, I wanted to hand him every night I had left in my life, but sometimes we must settle. After all, we're only supposed to live in the moment, and that moment right there, on the side of Highway 180, was one I hoped lasted forever.

12

ELIAS

S unny stopped at a pay phone to ask her mom if she could stay at Daisy's house. I only hoped Mrs. Lower wouldn't call to check up on her.

By the time she pulled onto the gravel drive, I had sobered up a good bit. I wondered what in the hell I would do if her dad drove by and saw her car. Terrified because after kissing her, I would never be able to stay away. God, I was selfish as hell.

When the headlights of Sunny's car bounced over the front of my crappy house, I sank down in the seat a little. She had probably never even been to the poor-side of town before.

She went to park, and I pointed through the window. "You might wanna go around back."

"Why?"

"You want your dad to see your car here if he drives by?"

She whipped the wheel around so fast my cheek smacked the glass. After she had parked by the back door, we sat there, the engine idling and the radio playing some commercial for acne medication. I reached over and cut the ignition. When I opened my door, the headlights went out, plunging us into darkness as we walked toward the back steps.

"Watch out for that first one." I pointed at the stairs. "It wobbles."

My pulse sounded like war drums in my ears, warning me of the impending moral battle that lay ahead if I took her inside. But I'd worry about that tomorrow because at ten past midnight, I sure as shit wasn't letting her go.

The unoiled hinges to the screen door creaked. I moved inside, holding it open. Sunny took two quick steps into the kitchen, then froze. "I can't see."

I flipped the switch. The fluorescent bulbs hummed before flickering to life. The TV in Judah's room was on. I could barely make out the canned laughter floating down the hallway.

"Where's your aunt?" she asked.

"She doesn't live here."

"Oh." She paused. "So, it's just you and your brothers."

"Yep."

"How do you afford to—"

"Don't ask. Just. . .don't ask." Her dad was right; she was good. I was bad.

Selling a spot of weed here and there was the only way I could make bills and cover food. I was seventeen and still in high school. I'd tried jobs at fast food restaurants and grocery stores, but the five-fifteen per hour pay wasn't enough to cover squat. Not even when I worked fifty hours a week over the summer.

I didn't want to follow in the footsteps of my parents, and while I had every intention of veering far from that path once I graduated high school, for now, I was stuck doing things I was ashamed of. Stuff that made me the type of guy she had no business hanging around.

"You want some water?" I asked. Before she could answer, I'd grabbed two bottles from the fridge.

Once I handed one to her, she unscrewed the cap and took a sip, her eyes trained on the floor. I wondered what she was thinking. But instead of asking, I chugged my water.

It was just us in that tiny kitchen with the linoleum peeling up at the baseboards. Us and the sound of Judah's TV and the random sputter of a car passing on the highway. It's funny how awkward it can be when the moments you spend your time daydreaming about become reality.

Sunny rubbed a hand over her arm, her teeth going to town on her lip. Even though I didn't bring her here with bad intentions, I worried that's what she'd think. After all, I heard the rumors. Rumors I did little to stop since I had found that usually works in my favor. When people never know the truth, they never know what to believe. People generally don't mess with someone whose actions they have no way to anticipate.

"You know, if you changed your mind about staying, you don't have to."

"I want to."

"Okay." I started through the living room, and she followed without question.

I flipped the switch to my bedroom, suddenly all too aware of the Sports Illustrated and Call of Duty posters that decorated my walls when I kicked off my boots. Sunny stood in the doorway, one hand rested on the frame like she wasn't sure whether it was safe to enter or not. Even though tension had my muscles coiled tight like springs ready to pop, I had to act normal. Unaffected. The way girls expected guys like me to act.

My hands had a slight tremor when I peeled off my shirt. "You gonna come in?" I asked when I laid back on the bed still in my jeans.

"Yeah. . ."

My heart nearly shot clean out of my chest when she crawled across the end of the bed and laid down beside me so close we were almost touching. That candy and vanilla scent that seemed to emanate from her enveloped me, lighting up every hormone in my teenage body like the Las Vegas strip.

I rolled onto my stomach to hide the hard-on developing against my will, and she glanced at me with those doe-like, blue eyes that begged me to love her. *But she was too good for that.*

"I like your room," she said.

"It's pretty boring."

"But it's yours."

I folded an arm underneath my head, then took the tiny, blond wisps of hair that framed her face and twirled them around one of my fingers. I'd be lying if I said I didn't want to have sex with Sunny. I sat in Miss Weaver's class, shifting in my seat more times than I could count, thinking about this very situation. It always started with her in my bed, and me slowly taking her clothes off, running my hands over her waist and tits. Really making her mine. But the truth was, as I studied her face, the slight slope of her nose, the perfect bow of her lips, every curve and angle of her face, the random freckle that dotted her cheek, I understood, for a fleeting, rational moment, that with some girls there's so much more than sex. Everything about Sunny was soft and peaceful. Like standing alone on a shore and watching the sunrise over the water, and it almost felt wrong to taint that.

So there was the dilemma. My brain and dick begged me

to screw her, but my heart didn't want to ruin her, and I was fucking terrified there was no differentiating between the two.

I wet my lips, trying my damnedest not to kiss her, because although she was mine—she belonged to someone else.

"I really have missed you," I said.

"You promise?"

"Yes." It was then that I decided I'd allow myself one night. One night to hold her, to pretend this was right. One night to let myself grieve, and let her go. So I kissed her, slow and soft so I could memorize how full her lips were against mine.

Her hand went to the back of my neck, and she tugged me closer. Closer until I had caged her in with my arms. She kissed me deeper until the natural progression of teenage hormones had led me to shift most of my weight between her thighs.

One more minute, I thought. Just a few more seconds and I would push myself away. Everything in my life had been shit before Sunny. Shit after her. But when I was with her, it was always perfect and calm. She was my peace, a home for a boy who never really understood what that word meant until her. How the hell was I supposed to stop that?

My muscles went lax, and I kissed her harder until there was no her mouth or my mouth, just our mouths. She felt too right even though every bit of us together like this was wrong.

I took her bottom lip between my teeth before slamming my mouth back over hers. Her hands moved down my back to my hips before sliding around to my fly. She fumbled with the button, and I could hardly breathe at that point.

She was a good girl, I thought. She deserved better than this, so I placed my hand over hers.

She froze, and I said every curse word known to man plus a few new ones.

"I just— I—I—just." Exhaling, she shoved me away, then sat up fast, and moved to the edge of the bed. "I just, um. I need to go."

When she went to stand, I caught her arm and pulled her back. "Wait."

"What? I need to go."

"Just wait a second, okay?" I sat up and moved across the bed until I was next to her. "What's going on?"

"I don't know."

"Sunny?"

"I don't know, Elias. You ignore me one day, then tell me I'm yours. And then I'm here in your bed, and you're kissing me like. . .like. . ." Her breath caught, and my chest went tight. I would never forgive myself if I made her cry. "I don't know what I'm doing. Okay?" She released a hard sigh. "I just thought you wanted me to. . ."

Placing my fingers on her chin, I turned her head and forced her to look at me. "That's not what I want from you."

She frowned at something I thought would make her smile, and the thought that maybe she wasn't such a good girl, after all, broke my heart a little.

"Then why am I here?" she asked.

She was there because I was jealous and a little drunk, and because I wanted things I couldn't have. I didn't have a clue how to begin to explain that. "I just want time with you, Sunny. That's all. Just a little bit of time where we can pretend nothing's changed."

Sunny's eyes closed, and her chin fell to her chest. I watched her shoulders rise and fall, rise and fall.

"Hey," I said. "Have you ever been to a three-ring circus?"

A short laugh slipped through her lips. "Yes. When I was five Daddy took me to Barnum and Bailey's."

"Damn. I never went to the circus. Guess I missed out on that, huh?" Smiling, I laid back and stretched my arm across the pillow. "Your turn."

She narrowed her eyes, and for a moment, I felt foolish. She'd forgotten the game we had played as children every night before we fell asleep.

"Have you ever. . ." She chewed on her lip before a sudden, pleased smile reached her eyes. "Have you ever ridden a wooden roller coaster?"

"Of course, I—"

She placed a finger over my lips. "I wasn't finished." Then she laid her head on my chest. "Have you ever ridden a wooden rollercoaster after you've eaten a hot dog and not thrown up?" She pulled her hand away from my mouth and trailed her fingers down my throat and across to my arm.

All I could think is that I wanted to kiss her again. "Um, no. I have a strict no eating hot dogs before rollercoaster rule I have yet to break."

"Wuss."

"Please." I shoved her arm. "Have you had chicken and waffles?"

"Gross! No."

"And you call yourself a Southerner?" I rolled my eyes, and she laughed.

God, I loved how soft and flirty her laugh was.

We went on and on with stupid questions just like we used to, while she traced the pattern of tattoos on my arm. It was almost as though nothing had changed. And then finally, when my eyes were so heavy I could barely keep them open—but was damn determined because I needed every second I could steal from her—she asked: "Have you ever wanted something you couldn't have? Like really wanted it until it ate you up inside?"

I turned on the pillow to face her. There were eight-thousand ways I could have answered that, but all that came out was a hoarse, "Of course."

Silence.

She snuggled against my neck, her fingers once again sweeping across my throat. "What was it?" she whispered.

"That's against the rules?"

"What is?"

"Asking two questions."

Her eyes searched mine. "We don't have rules, Elias."

She was right. I brushed a hand through her hair. "You, Sunny Ray."

She swallowed. I swallowed.

There was a long pause, where the only sounds were the low hum of the window unit kicking on and the muffled noise of the TV down the hall.

"That's not true," she whispered. "I am something you can have." Her lips pressed to mine in a featherlight kiss.

"Don't do this to me," I mumbled against her mouth, even though my hand was now tangled in her thick hair.

"No, don't you do this to me." Another kiss. This time her lips parted, and I couldn't help but open my mouth and fist her hair a little.

"I'm trying not to do anything to you."

"Stop trying." She grabbed my face, kissing me hard and angry, like she wanted to hate me but just couldn't.

And for a second, I did stop trying.

I grasped her hips and dragged her on top of me. I let my fingers slip underneath the hem of her shirt, teasing her warm skin.

Sunny rolled her hips just enough to force a groan from me and cause my fingers to twitch on her sides. The slightest friction could nearly drive me over the edge, but with her, it shouldn't have surprised me.

A soft ah pressed through her lips, and I slammed my eyes closed, using every ounce of restraint I possessed not to move, not to roll on top of her and do all the things to her bad boys are known for. My breathing went all uneven like I'd just ran fifteen miles uphill. I kept wetting my lips with my tongue, every now and then unintelligibly mumbling her name while pretending there wasn't a layer of clothes separating us and that I was inside her.

I swallowed the groan sitting at the back of my throat when she did send me over the edge, hoping to God she wouldn't notice the wet spot that most likely soaked through my jeans. Guys like me aren't supposed to get off that easily.

She tensed, and the slight rock to her hips ceased. Her head fell back, and her lips parted on a hard, moan-laced exhale. My heart pounded in my chest, and when her eyes finally met mine, she looked mortified.

She swallowed, then swept a hand through her hair before sliding off me. "Um. . ." She shimmied to the edge of the bed.

"Come here."

She glanced over her shoulder at me, her lip pinched between her teeth, then she reluctantly laid back, stiff as a bored, and I fell asleep beside her, wondering what kind of girl she'd grown into.

13

SUNNY

I debated on stopping at Pickle's Pit Stop Quick Mart to buy a pack of cigarettes, even though I didn't smoke.

It seemed like that was what everyone in high school did when they had some life-altering event on their mind. And I had totally, absolutely, positively dry humped Elias Black until I got off and then, as soon as his lungs fell into the rhythm of sleep, I left.

I just—left. I was terrified and embarrassed at the stupid, uncontrolled sounds I had made, not to mention that I lied to my parents about staying at Daisy's who lied to her parents about staying at my house.

It was a roundtrip shitshow.

By the time I parked in front of Thomas Radcliffe's house, the midnight blue of the sky had faded from a faint yellow to a pumpkin orange where the sun just began to rise. A low fog crawled out onto the fields, and the early morning birds' songs echoed in the trees.

I rang the doorbell, then pounded on the door a few times, finally crossing my arms and taking a step back when I heard the clatter of about a hundred beer cans topple to the floor. Heavy footfalls came from inside followed by a low groan. The lock clicked, and the door swung open to Thomas stumbling away while one last Budweiser rolled from the kitchen table to the floor.

"Not even gonna see who it is?" I asked.

He swatted his hand through the air before turning to go up the stairs. I closed the door behind me, nearly choking on the sour smell of beer that filled the air.

"What the. . . Dude!" Thomas' voice bellowed down the stairwell. "Not in my fucking bed. How many times do I have to tell you?"

There was unintelligible grumbling. Something whacked a wall.

"Hey!" Brandon's deep voice startled me, and I jumped, holding my chest as I spun around. He was sprawled out on the couch with a Coca-Cola bear Christmas blanket thrown over him. He lifted his head, squinting against the sun that shined through the bay windows. "I thought you left?"

"I did." I chewed at my lip. "I just, uh, came back for Daisy."

Scrubbing over his face, he sat up with a groan. "You look," he halfway arched a brow, "distressed?"

"No."

He smiled. "Quick answer." Then he glanced at the watch I never saw him take off. He wore it at school, at ball practice, during games, and evidently when he slept. "It's barely six in the morning."

"And?"

"Something happened," he said.

I was running on no sleep, and with each passing second, I felt guiltier about just leaving Elias. Honestly, the more I thought about, I worried I looked a little like a whore. Trying to fish his dick out, then dry humping him and leaving. God, I was turning into Daisy.

Brandon patted the spot on the couch beside him, and I begrudgingly took a seat. "Spill."

I frowned at him. "I mean, I like you, and we're definitely friends, but do you move this fast with everyone?"

He laughed.

"I'm serious. I feel like we've gone from casually hanging out a few times to picking scabs and becoming blood brothers"—I snapped my fingers—"like that?"

"All right. I can't force you to divulge information."

I stared off at the Dale Earnhardt commemorative plate in a display case. Thomas was still grumbling about someone screwing in his bed.

I needed to get Daisy before our parents figured out we weren't where we said we'd be. "Do you know where Daisy is?"

Brandon pointed toward the stairs. "My guess. She's in Thomas' room with Ben."

Tossing my head back, I groaned. Poor life choices all around.

Something tumbled down the steps before a thud dragged my attention away from Brandon. Daisy's heels landed haphazardly at the bottom of the stairs before she shuffled down, holding to the rail for dear life. Her gaze went from me to Brandon whose arm was still draped around me. "You two are cute," she said, pleased.

Brandon squeezed me a little. "We are, aren't we?"

Ben strutted into the hall, flipping a bird—I guessed at Thomas—before he slid down the banister. He gripped Daisy's waist and tugged her in for an aggressive, sloppy kiss, and then smacked her on the butt. "Call you later, Dais."

"Hey, dipshit!" Brandon called. "You gotta help us clean this mess."

"Man. Thomas has got it." Ben gave a dismissive wave. Seconds later, the door banged shut behind him.

"God, he's a dick," Brandon mumbled.

"He's gotta go to some lunch thing for his dad," Daisy said, starry-eyed. "Isn't that great? He's all close with his family and stuff."

"Uh, yeah." Brandon scrunched his face in a weird smirk while bobbing his head. "Sure, he is."

"We'll help." I went to the kitchen, grabbed a trash bag from the pantry, and waved it up and down to open it.

"You don't have to do that." Brandon knelt on the floor and shoveled cans into the bag.

"Yeah, Sunny. You *really* don't."

I scowled at Daisy, and she tossed up her hands, shaking her head. "Fine. You're too nice. You realize that, right?"

Too good for Elias. Too nice in general.

WE PICKED up Krispy Kreme donuts on the way to Daisy's. Since the shop was less than a mile away from her house, it stood to reason that an early morning donut run would stave off any questions about why we had decided to come over to her house so early.

We polished off half a dozen and then disappeared to her room.

"Ben's not as bad as you think, Sunny."

I looked up from the *Cosmo* article on skin care, and my lips shrank into my mouth. "Mm-hmm. Sure thing, *Dais*."

"He's not. You're not giving him a fair chance."

"I take it you slept with him?"

"No."

I grabbed the highlighter I'd been using for quizzes and chucked it at her. "Liar."

The pink pen rolled across the floor after she swatted it away. "I didn't. Everything but." She crossed her heart. "My hymen is still fully intact."

"I'm proud of you." Even though I was skeptical, I wanted to believe she at least tried to hold out.

"So. . ." She popped open the magazine, took the highlighter, and started on a quiz. "You and Brandon looked cozy this morning. Gonna tell me what happened when you two disappeared last night?" She waggled her brows.

I rolled a shoulder.

"Really? You guys were up there. In a room. Together. And nothing happened?"

"No."

"Jesus. What is he, gay or something?"

My pulse skipped, and I swallowed. "I mean. No." I drew a crisscross pattern over my thigh.

I hated lying, especially to Daisy, but all I could think about was the panic and fear that twisted Brandon's face last night. I had worried that maybe that drunk girl had seen something. I felt the need to protect him. "He just knows I want to wait. He respects that."

"He's such a good guy. You know, Brandon was considered the most unattainable guy at school." She had no idea how true that statement was. "And now he's all about you. He's a much better choice than Elias." She bubbled in a response, then crossed it out, and circled a different answer.

My chest tightened. I opened my mouth to tell Daisy what had happened, to tell her I didn't actually want to date Brandon and that my heart was completely hung up on Elias.

She glanced up from the floor and frowned. "I need to

tell you something." Shoving the magazine aside, she sat up, and her expression crumpled. "It's about Elias."

My stomach turned. From Daisy's tone, I knew whatever it was, I wouldn't like it.

"So, you know how Thomas' upstairs bathroom is a Jack and Jill?" She paused like I should nod, but I had no idea what kind of bathroom Thomas' bedroom had. "Well," she continued. "People kept coming in there last night, you know, since the toilet downstairs was flooded? And I overheard Jenny's loud mouth bragging to Valerie about him almost screwing her in her car."

My brows lifted. My ears smoldered. "Who? Elias?"

"Yeah. Evidently, she went out to her car, and he followed her, and one thing led to another from what I heard. And they all but banged in the backseat of her stupid Volvo."

Acid crawled up my throat. He kissed me—after he almost had sex with Jenny. I went back to his house and made out with him. I tried to take his pants off. Maybe that was why he stopped me. He'd already gotten his for the night.

Closing my eyes, I shook my head.

"Sunny?" Daisy touched my arm. "I'm sorry. I didn't want to tell you, but I couldn't *not* tell you. I just didn't want you making any decisions about Brandon because you maybe still had a thing for Elias. You don't want to give up a good guy for one who's evidently a dick."

"Yep." I opened my eyes, my stomach slipping around itself like a snake. I would never admit to her what I'd done the night before. Ever. "And you know what. Ben's doesn't sound so bad after all."

14

SUNNY

I was helping Momma do the dishes after Sunday dinner, still fuming over Jenny Smith, when the doorbell rang.

Simon shouted, "I'll get it," then dropped the broom in the middle of the floor before scurrying out.

A few seconds later, Daddy greeted someone. "Sunny?" he said. "You've got a visitor." I heard Daddy tell whoever it was to come inside and then the front door closed.

Momma glanced at me, and I shrugged while placing the last of the plates on the drying rack and wiping the suds from my hands.

Brandon stood in the entranceway with one hand in his pocket and a bouquet of white lilies in the other. My steps faltered. I didn't know what he was doing here, and from the approving grin plastered to my dad's face when he turned around, Brandon had just opened a whole new can of worms for me.

Simon bounced on the balls of his feet, rattling off questions about football and tugging on Brandon's shirt.

"Hey. . ." Brandon put his arm around me in the most

awkward hug in human history, then handed me the flowers. "I just, uh, saw those and thought of you."

"Thanks." I took a sniff. It seemed like that was the
appropriate thing to do even though lilies smell like nothing
aside from a funeral parlor.

Momma came sashaying into the entrance way, wiping
her hands on her apron. "Well, Brandon McClure, to what
do we owe this pleasure?"

Now both my parents were beaming. I wanted to groan.

"Simon," she said. "Come help me finish up in the
kitchen, baby."

"Aw, Momma."

Brandon ruffled Simon's hair. "I'll tell you all about football later."

That satisfied Simon enough that he took my mother's
hand and followed her into the kitchen.

"I'll go help your mother. You two kids have a seat."
Daddy walked off, whistling.

Brandon and I stood there, staring at one another for a
second before he finally cleared his throat. "I hope you like
lilies."

"Oh." I nodded, remembering I had flowers in my hand.
"I do. Thank you. That's— It's really sweet of you to bring
them to me."

"It's what boyfriends do." His lips shrank into his mouth,
and he shoved his free hand into his pocket, rocking back on
his heels.

My brow furrowed with confusion. Last night I caught
him making out with a guy, but now he was bringing me
flowers and calling himself my boyfriend. "Brandon, I—"

"I need to talk to you," he whispered, shifting his eyes
toward the front door. "Not in here."

"Oh. Okay. Let me just. . ." I backed toward the kitchen,

trying to read Brandon's expression, but all I could gather was that something not so great was going on. "Let me just go put these in water, and I'll be right back."

Momma already had one of the crystal vases down from the cabinet. "Those are just lovely, Sunny," she said, taking the bouquet and cutting the ribbon from the stems. "I can't believe you didn't tell me you two were talking. His parents are just lovely." She fussed with the arrangement for a moment before nodding with approval.

"We're gonna go out for a minute if that's okay?"

"Well, I think that's all right." She glanced at the clock. "It's only half past seven, what do you think, David?"

Daddy carted the dustpan to the trash. "I think it's fine. Where are you going?"

Where were we going? I had no idea, but I had to think of something to say. "Oh, just the beach."

"Be back by nine."

Simon made kissy faces at me before I ducked back into the hall and followed Brandon out to his car.

The second Brandon pulled onto the highway, he exhaled. "I'm sorry I just showed up, but you're the only person I can talk to about this. And I couldn't chance calling you and having someone overhear."

"It's okay."

"That guy." He paused to draw in a breath, but when he released it, he remained silent.

Worry constricted my chest as I watched him shake his head over and over. "The one from last night?" I asked.

"Yeah, his name's Travis. I was over at his house, hanging out. Playing Madden and uh, you know, it was nothing. Actually, it was stupid. We kissed in his room, and I guess his kid brother saw from his treehouse."

The streetlight flickered over the interior when we

passed under it. Brandon's fist pounded the steering wheel and I jumped.

"Okay?" I said, letting him know I was still there.

"His brother told his friends. The kid doesn't know my name, so it's just going around that Travis is gay." Brandon's jaw ticced, and his nostrils flared. "Mussaffer was talking about it after church, all the guys from the team were laughing, saying they were gonna beat his ass."

The only sound was the hum of the tires over the pavement. I didn't know what to say.

"They were calling him a fag and all kinds of shit." He choked on the words, then took a hard left onto the highway that ran alongside the beach.

My stomach sank as I recalled a headline from the news a few weeks prior where a guy in Birmingham had nearly been beaten to death after he left a gay club. The guys who jumped him didn't even know him. As much as I wanted to believe the kids I went to school with wouldn't be so cruel, I couldn't. Fear and hate do a lot of crazy things to people.

"Did you tell Travis they know?" I asked.

"Yeah. Yeah. He said he's not worried."

"You don't think he'd ever tell?"

"No." Brandon shook his head. "That'd be admitting he's gay, wouldn't it? And that wouldn't be safe. Not here."

I felt helpless, and I hated it. Brandon was a good person, but for a gay teen in small-town Alabama, it didn't matter how good you were. And that broke my heart.

We parked by the skeleton of the pavilion. The headlights shined over the dunes, attracting gnats and moths while the engine idled. Brandon sat, gripping the steering wheel and staring through the windshield while I simply watched him.

Momma always said life breaks everyone, but watching

Brandon, I thought maybe it wasn't life but hate that broke people.

I placed my hand on his shoulder in a silent *I'm here*.

"I need to get out," he said.

"Let's take a walk."

With a nod, he cut the engine.

I followed him onto the sand-dusted boardwalk. The moon that night was swollen and low, casting a silver haze over the dunes. We slipped out of our shoes when we hit the beach and walked in silence past the high-tide line and right to the water. Brandon stood in the surf with his hands in his pockets. The ocean shimmered under the moonlight. Waves rolled in and out, crashing around my feet.

In the dark, Brandon was nothing but a silhouette against the expansive sea. His shoulders sagged while he stared off, looking for answers he knew he'd never find. "What sucks the most," he said, "is that I laughed. I forced myself to laugh when they made fun of him and called him all those names. I said he was sick because I was scared." Exhaling, he faced me. "I said the person I was falling for was sick."

The muscles in his jaw tensed. Tears built in his eyes, and a dull ache formed in my chest. I didn't know how to fix this. I worried that Brandon's life would always be a myriad of lies and regrets, pretending to hate the things that he loved and love the things that hated him.

I rubbed a hand over his arm. "It's okay."

"It's not okay. It's never going to be okay because I'll never be able to be myself. I'm scared shitless, Sunny. Every day, I worry someone's going to find out. You know, *you* think a guy's attractive and you look at him a little too long, it's not a big deal. But me? I've gotten into the habit of counting to two and forcing myself to look away, so no one suspects. I have posters of swimsuit models in my room. Playboys under my bed just so I look the part. You know, the part of the straight guy. I thought maybe if I dated a girl I could make myself be straight. After all, I've heard people say it's a choice for so long I thought, hell, maybe it was. Maybe I was just fucked up and chose to be gay. So, I dated Valerie. And when she told me she loved me, I felt like shit for leading her on. I played with her heart to try to protect myself. That's messed up."

Waves crashed around us. "It's not."

"It is. Because I would've done it to you. I would've kept on dating you as long as you would've let me, knowing it would go nowhere. Had you actually liked me, I would have hurt you, Sunny. I don't want to hurt people, especially not good people. But I'm so fucking scared if I don't keep up an act, people will find out."

As hard as he fought it, a few tears eventually rolled down his cheek. I wrapped my arms around Brandon and laid my head on his shoulder. "No one will find out. I promise."

My father had forbidden me from being with the person I loved, and society had forbidden Brandon from loving the person he wanted to.

Life didn't seem fair. To be honest, the older I got, the uglier life seemed.

15

ELIAS

Bam Bam came running down the dark beach, sand kicking up from his feet. The long chain that hung from his jeans jingled. "Sorry I'm late, man." He panted when he leaned over his knees to catch his breath. "Practice ran over." He looked like a typical stoner. Baggy jeans. Chain wallet. A tie-dyed Phish T-shirt, and he was in a band that played nothing but Led Zepplin covers.

"It's fine."

He traded me a twenty for a little plastic baggie. Bam Bam nodded toward the wooden lounge chairs dotting the shore. "Sit over there and take a hit with me?"

Some customers thought it was customary to smoke a bowl with the dealer. Some of them were paranoid and wanted the supplier to take the first toke to make sure it wasn't laced. Bam Bam was one of the paranoid ones.

"Sure, man," I said, heading across the sand.

As soon as my ass hit the wooden chair, Bam Bam passed me a pipe along with a lighter. I flicked the flint, and he watched intently as I moved the flame over the buds. I took a deep drag, held it for a second, then coughed while I gave him the bowl with the weed still smoldering.

"Good hit?" He grinned, placed the pipe to his lips, and pulled so hard his cheeks hollowed out.

When he tried to pass it back to me, I shook my head. "I'm good."

"All right. I'll be in touch with you later this week." He strolled toward the pavilion with a cloud of pungent smoke billowing behind him.

The weed hit my system, and my heart rate kicked up just as that euphoric buzz crackled throughout my body. Folding my hands behind my head, I laid back on the lounge and closed my eyes. The muggy air wrapped around me, while the crashing waves morphed into some form of ancient music. I figured the ocean was one of the few things man hadn't managed to totally screw up yet. Sure, there was the odd oil rig here and there, and the beaches were covered with hotels and condominiums, but when you sat right at the water's edge and looked out, it had to be the same as it was thousands of years ago. Just sky and ocean and things that were so much bigger than me.

When I finally opened my eyes, the pale moon was overhead. My hand instinctively reached for the necklace tucked safely under the collar of my shirt. I skimmed my fingertip over the tiny metal prongs of the sun's rays, wondering what she was doing. Hoping she wasn't with him.

I'd be lying if I said it didn't kill me that she was dating someone, but I think it hurt more because that guy was the polar opposite of me. A rich kid her father would no doubt approve of. I loved Sunny, so I should have been happy she was with the kind of guy she deserved. But God, I fucking hated it. I hated that he could touch her and hold her. He went to dinner with her family and took her to parties. But what I hated more was that I had kissed her when she belonged to someone else. And I didn't want to be that guy, but more than anything, I didn't want him to be the guy who had her.

Groaning, I pushed up from the chair and started down the beach. When I reached the alcove area I used to bring Sunny, I decided God must really hate me. There she stood in the surf, wrapped up in the good-enough-guy's arms.

I stopped dead in my tracks and watched, partly because I was a masochistic bastard and partly because I hoped she would turn around and see me. I wanted her reaction, but she was too consumed with Brandon to notice me.

My chest tightened, my jaw clenched, and I fought the wave of emotions pummeling through me when I headed toward the boardwalk. That spot was sacred to me. It was mine, and then it was ours. But now it was theirs.

Something about her being there with him crippled me. It was an accidental fuck you.

BRIGHT and early the next morning I had six o'clock practice. *Six a.m. practice!* I almost wanted to knock Judah and Atlas in the head for talking me into walking onto the team.

The locker room smelled of bleach and stale piss, which did nothing but aggravate me further. "Why the hell are we practicing so early?"

Judah sat on the bench to lace up his cleats. "Coach said we're less likely to keel over from heat stroke when it's not a hundred degrees out."

Atlas pulled his practice jersey on and then laid down on one of the benches against the cinderblock wall. "I'm tired."

"Shouldn't stay up all night fucking then," Judah chuckled.

"Come on, Judah," I said. "What girl's gonna go for Atlas?"

"Valerie Beoudreax." Atlas smirked while pretending to grope a pair of tits.

Those two had a one-track mind. I thumbed toward the exit on my way to take a piss. "Get out on the field."

The door to the locker room swung open when I was at the sink. "I don't know, man." Ben dropped his duffel bag to the floor. "I'd hate to beat the guy up and then find out he's not gay."

"He's gay. Look at him." That was Thomas.

The hand dryer drowned out their conversation which I was fine with. I hated self-entitled pricks. Who cared if some Lockhart guy was gay?

Brandon shot a quick glance at me when I moved past him. For a second, I expected him to stop me. Confront me. Maybe it's because I wanted a reason to hit him. Just once.

Thomas balled his shirt up and chucked it at Brandon. "He's sick, man. You want some queer rubbing up on your junk during a game? I don't want him grinding his dick in my ass crack during a tackle. Besides, he—"

The door closed behind me, and I squinted against the sun peeking up over the tree line. The sprinkler heads spun around with a click, click, click, as I made my way past the baseball grounds to the football field. A few of the guys tossed the ball around while the underclassman dragged out the red blocking pads, grumbling when they threw them onto the lawn.

Thirty minutes into practice, my sweat-slicked arms were covered in grass clippings.

Coach blew his whistle. "Let's go. Scrimmage! One on

one. Ball on the twenty-five. Offense going that way." He pointed toward the far end zone.

We formed a small huddle. As the middle lineman, it was my job to tell the dumbass defense what to do. Coach crossed his chest then pointed at his eye to signal our call. I pulled out my mouth guard. "Cross stunt left. Cross stunt left," I called, and then we fell into alignment.

Brandon-fucking-McClure. Middle linebacker and the asshole that stole my girl was crouched about ten feet in front of me. Our eyes locked, and all I could see was him and her on the beach, his lips on hers at that party. And it didn't matter how nice he was, I hated him for being all the things I could never be.

"Blue fifty-two. Blue fifty-two. Set. Hike."

The ball snapped, and I lunged forward. My heels dug into the turf as I picked up speed. Lowering my head, I drove my helmet right into Brandon's chest and wrapped my arms around the back of his thighs, picking him up. I drove his ass into the ground.

"Hu-ugh!" Brandon hit the field with a thud.

Adrenaline buzzed through me as I hopped to my feet, fist clenched at my side. Brandon drew his legs to his chest on a grunt and rolled onto his side.

"Black!" Coach shouted. "What the hell are you doin', son?"

Turning toward the sideline, I yanked out my mouthpiece. "Sorry, Coach. Wrong call."

The second Brandon was up, his helmet was off, and he was in my face. Cheeks red and eyes wide. "What the fuck was that, huh?" His palms smacked against my pads, shoving me a step back.

Shit, that boiled my blood. "Sorry, man." I pushed him. "Didn't think you were such a pussy."

He went to throw a punch, and I ducked just as Judah snatched me by the arm and pulled me back. "What the hell, dude? Calm down before you get kicked off the team."

Out of the corner of my eye, I saw Ben grab Brandon.

"All right. All right." Coach stepped onto the field. "Enough!" He pointed his clipboard in my direction. "I don't care how much of a beast you are, Black. You pull some dumb shit like that again and you're suspended for a game. You hear?"

"Yeah, Coach."

I pulled on my helmet. As shitty as it was, I didn't feel any better than I did before I laid his ass out.

16

SUNNY

There were already whispers about Travis circulating Robertsdale's hallways Monday morning. News like that makes its way around a little country town faster than a chicken on a June Bug.

Daisy followed me to my locker, blabbing about Ben and Brandon and a bunch of crap I couldn't have cared less about, but I had to look at her and nod my head like I was interested.

She stopped midstride, one side of her lip lifting in a half-snarl. "What the hell is on your locker?"

I turned, my heart near death when my eyes landed on a delicate silver necklace with a ring dangling, taped to the metal. My throat burned. My vision blurred. He had held onto that ring for nearly ten years, and now, after he tried to make me sloppy seconds, he was telling me nothing we had mattered. Like I had done something to him.

"Hel-lo?" Daisy sang. "What's with the necklace?"

Without a word, I snatched it off and crammed it in my jean pocket. "Something I lost."

"Uh." Daisy wedged herself between me and the wall of lockers. "Who would've known that was yours? I wouldn't know that was yours. I've never even seen it."

"An asshole." I forced a withdrawn smile before slamming the metal door.

"Why do I feel like you're totally hiding stuff from me?"

"Just don't, Daisy. Not today." I brushed past her.

"Jesus. Fine."

When Daisy and I walked into Miss Weaver's class, someone had written *Lockhart's full of queers* on the board in blue marker.

I dropped my books on my desk and marched up to the front to erase it.

"Ah, come on, Sunny," Thomas said. "That was my best handwriting."

"You're a dick!"

The class snickered. Thomas' cheeks reddened, and he sank a little in his seat. "I guess you're a gay rights activist or something?"

"No, I'm just not an asshole." I dropped the eraser and glared at Thomas on my way back to my desk.

Daisy's eyes were wide, her brow furrowed. "They're just being guys."

"No. They're being pricks."

I pulled out my notebook and pen, resting my head on my hand as I scribbled out the date. Students continued to trickle into the class. I made the mistake of glancing up from my desk when Elias walked into the room. He gave me a cold stare, and I shot one right back, my pulse ratcheting up with such fury I had to grip the edge of my desk to keep myself grounded.

Miss Weaver skirted in just as the bell rang, and I committed not to look at Elias for the rest of class. I tried to pay attention to the notes on *Gatsby*, the irony that betrayal was laced throughout that book was not lost on me.

Miss Weaver capped the whiteboard marker and turned to face the room. "Can anyone tell me what they felt was the greatest betrayal in the book?" She scanned the class and then smiled when she found someone willing to answer. "Elias?"

I heard the desk scrape the floor, but I refused to look over. "Gatsby spent all this time trying to get Daisy Buchanan to love him. That's all he wanted. He wasted his life chasing that girl. Every wrong decision he made was in an attempt to win her over. And in the end, Gatsby finds out she loved another man."

Daisy stuck her leg into the aisle between us, tapping the toe of her shoe against the floor as she cleared her throat. I glanced over, and she motioned her eyes toward Elias who shot a death glare in my direction. His defined jaw tensed.

I dropped my gaze to my paper while a slow heat burned over my chest.

"So, Daisy's betrayal of Gatsby?" Miss Weaver asked.

"No. Gatsby's betrayal of himself. He wasted his life on a girl who never really loved him even though she said she did."

My cheeks smoldered, and I began to bounce my leg underneath my desk.

"Very profound, Elias."

How dare he have the audacity to glare at me like I had done something to him. He ignored me. He told me I was too good. He messed around with Jenny Smith before he kissed me and took me home with him. I couldn't help myself. I raised my hand, my foot still twitching under my desk.

Miss Weaver called on me.

"I disagree. I think Gatsby's self-doubt made her question the way he felt about her. Maybe she just told Gatsby she loved Tom to see Gatsby's reaction." My heart drummed up to my throat, but I didn't dare look at Elias.

Daisy kept fake coughing which was enough to ensure me Elias was looking.

"Oh, very good point, Miss Lower."

"What a load of crap!" Elias laughed, and that time, I did look at him. Our eyes locked in a cold I-hate-that-I-ever-loved-you stare. "She promised Gatsby she'd wait on him, and she didn't!"

"Ahem." Miss Weaver took a step toward the class. "I love that you two are into this debate, but we should try to use our inside voices."

Closing my eyes, I inhaled to calm my shaking voice. "What was she supposed to do, Elias? At least she didn't give him a necklace back! Besides, I'm pretty sure Gatsby had some brunette on the side the whole time."

"If I were him, I'd have made it a blonde."

The class erupted in laughter. Miss Weaver tried to quiet everyone with a quick snap of her fingers. She glanced between Elias and me. "No need to yell."

"He thought he needed to obtain a certain social status to win her over. I guess he thought she was too good for him." That was a dig. A cold. Hard. Dig.

"And Tom was a fucking rich dick!" His voice boomed around the room. Half of the guys were about to topple out of their chairs from laughter. The girls were all whispering —except Daisy and Jenny and me.

Miss Weaver clapped her hands. "Elias! That's not appropriate language."

"I apologize, Miss Weaver. I come from a low social bracket. I hope you understand."

The bell rang, and I was the first one out of my seat and through the door.

I slung my locker open and shoved my books inside before yanking out my gym shoes. *A girl who never really loved him even though she said she did.* Those words cycled on repeat. I slammed my locker closed so hard the girl underneath me shot an annoyed glance before I stormed off.

Halfway down the hall, Daisy caught me by the arm. "Hey. What's going on?"

She had to be kidding. After all, she was the one who noticed him glaring at me and just had to bring it to my attention.

"Nothing." I jerked free from her hold and continued shouldering my way through the congested hallway.

"Bullshit. You're like warpath Sunny today. And that passive-aggressive stuff with Elias. What in the actual hell?"

"He's just an asshole." I stopped, and the person behind me bumped into me just as Jenny passed by with a tight-lipped smile. I shot her an impassive glare. "God, sometimes I wish I wasn't a nice person just so I could slap her."

"I mean, you did punch her in elementary school," she said.

"Not hard enough."

"Don't let her bother you. She's a whore. And besides, you've got Brandon."

Even if Brandon and I had been dating, it wouldn't have lessened the sting. Daisy shrugged like losing the love of my life to Jenny Smith wasn't a huge deal.

"It doesn't matter! I still care about him, Daisy!" My voice thundered off the lockers. The girls standing closest to us appeared shocked at my outburst.

Rolling her eyes, Daisy yanked me to a less occupied corner of the hallway, right by the boy's restroom. "Okay. But what are you gonna do? Do you want to hurt Brandon? I mean. . ." Daisy's words were lost amongst the bustle of the hallway and the cacophonous noise of my thoughts.

The door to the restroom opened, and Elias stepped out, shaking water from his hands.

My nostrils flared when our eyes met. "Hey!"

He took a few steps forward until his brooding expression was only inches from me. "What?" His lips barely moved.

For a second, I thought I would walk off, but then I channeled all the anger and embarrassment, how cheap it made me feel to know that I was only second choice. "So did you sleep with Jenny or did you get enough to hold you over until you could come hunt me down?"

Elias cocked a brow. "Really? We gonna do this here?"

I could handle indifference from most anyone, but not him. Not over this. "Do you know how that made me feel to find out you messed around with her?"

His jaw twitched. "Did it break your fucking heart, Sunny?" He moved in closer until our noses nearly touched. "Because how you feel right now is only a fraction of how I felt *watching* you kiss him. So, don't start this shit with me. All right?"

A heavy numbness infused my body, crumpling the part of my heart that only beat for him. Hurt welled inside me. "So what, Elias? Did you do it just to get back at me?"

Walking backward, he tossed both hands up, unfazed.

This was where we had gotten, I thought, to the point of getting even. Fine. If Elias Black wanted to play that game, I'd meet him inch for inch.

"You were right," I said pushing my shoulders back. "I am too good for you."

His eyes narrowed. His chest rose on a deep swell, telling

me the arrow I shot landed right in his heart. When he turned around without another word, I closed my eyes.

Bang! I jumped at the sound of his fist punching the lockers, the sudden movement nearly dislodging the tears that stung my eyes. *Breathe. Don't be that girl.* I pressed the heel of my hands against my eyes to stop the tears. The bell rang, and within seconds, the hallway fell silent.

I knew Daisy was still behind me, but I didn't want to look at her much less explain anything. "I'm fine. Go to class, Daisy."

Her footfalls echoed down the hall, and I stood alone, broken and angry that I had told him I was too good for him. If anything, that boy had always been too good for me.

AFTER SCHOOL, Daisy said we had to stop by Magpie's on the way home, rambling something about a surprise for Ben. Surprisingly, she didn't bring up the incident in the hallway until we were halfway down the parkway.

When she reached over and switched off the radio, I slouched in the seat. An interrogation was coming.

"So, that little thing with Elias this afternoon. It sounded like you two have been seeing each other. And I love you, but you and Brandon are kind of a thing, and that's just shitty."

"Brandon and I are," I exhaled and glanced out the window, staring at the Tweety Bird mud flaps of an eighteen-wheeler. "It's complicated."

"Care to enlighten me?"

I didn't want to explain anything right then, so I settled on: "We aren't serious. I mean, we haven't talked about it or anything."

"Whatever. So what happened with you and Elias to

cause that *Days of Our Lives* outburst?" That was a loaded question.

I didn't want to lie. I didn't want to tell the truth. The truth would then involve me outing Brandon, and half the truth would make her think I was a two-timing, dry-humping whore. I drew an invisible heart on the glass while debating about how much I should tell the girl I once told everything. "Elias unexpectedly kissed me Saturday."

"What do you mean unexpectedly?"

"Like, he came up to my car and just grabbed my face and kissed me."

"Okay." Daisy leaned over the steering wheel, craning her neck to check for traffic before whipping the car onto Highway 35. "Not gonna lie. That's kinda hot."

"Yeah. Well. Not when you find out it was evidently after he'd hooked up with Jenny."

Daisy stuck her tongue out and clutched at her throat while making a horrific gagging sound. "Sick. Okay, so you were totally validated in your little explosion today then."

"Thanks," I mumbled.

"God, what a dick though!" Daisy kept ranting about what an asshole Elias was, and I wanted the conversation to end, so I turned the volume up. Two beats into the song, Daisy turned it back down. "I mean, what's wrong with him? Seriously? That's disgusting. And what's going to happen when Brandon finds out?"

"He's not gonna find out."

Daisy raised both eyebrows. "You don't think anyone overheard you two in the hall today? Or at the very least took notice when he got about half an inch away from your face?"

"I don't know."

"You're Brandon McClure's unofficial girlfriend, and Elias is the unofficial bad boy every girl wants. People noticed."

I turned the radio up as far as it would go that time, and Daisy got the message.

THE BELL over the door jingled when we stepped inside Magpie's.

The smell of incense nearly knocked me over. Daisy coughed, swatting the thick smoke curling up from one of the burners away from her face.

Magpie sat behind the counter, puffing on a wooden pipe and staring through her John Lennon glasses. "What brings you two pretties in today?"

"I came to see Ziggy," Daisy said.

Magpie lifted one bushy eyebrow, her gaze shifting from me to Daisy. "You or the sheriff's girl?"

"Me."

"You eighteen?"

"Yes, ma'am."

My mouth dropped open, and Daisy placed a single finger underneath my chin to shut it. Daisy was six months away from being eighteen. God, she lied like it was her job.

Magpie cleared mucus from her throat before shouting for Ziggy, telling him he had a customer. Daisy led me around the maze of shelves and counters.

When we were out of Magpie's sight, I leaned over and whisper-hissed in her ear. "What are you doing? Who's Ziggy?"

"This guy."

"No shit. How do you know him?"

"He came into the church a few weeks ago when I was filing some paperwork for Dad. He has a few tattoos, and I started asking some questions. One thing led to another, and he told me he'd give me a piercing for half off."

"What?" I went all wide-eyed on her as it sank in that she was actually here—the preacher's daughter—to get something pierced. Not to mention, she had dragged me along, by proxy making me an accomplice.

"It's for Ben." A devious grin curled her lips.

There were three places a girl would get pierced for a guy. Two of them were more for her than him. I snatched her elbow and yanked her down an aisle full of Buddha figurines and coffee cups. "You are not getting your tongue pierced."

She smirked. "You think I should go for the nipples instead?"

"No." I facepalmed. "Your dad is gonna kill you, Daisy."

"He won't know."

I kind-of-sort-of laughed and decided that my best friend had officially lost her mind. We made our way back to the front of the store just as the door leading to the second floor creaked open. A guy with black rimmed, Buddy Holly glasses and a trench coat stood in the stairwell. Tattooed flames crawled up his neck and curled around his ears.

"You ready?" he said.

"Yep." Daisy snagged a random tongue ring and ducked under his arm.

I glanced at Magpie like she would do something, but she was busy with a crossword puzzle.

"Come on, Sunny."

I followed Daisy and Ziggy up the dingy stairwell and into an open room. The walls were covered in tattoo designs.

Ziggy pointed to what looked to be a dental chair as he moved to the side of the space, snapping on a pair of latex gloves. Daisy hopped into the seat with a pleased grin.

"You want something pierced?" Ziggy asked me as he sat on a rolling exam stool.

"Um. No. That's all right."

Shrugging, he rolled the chair to the far side of the room and grabbed a silver tray from something that resembled a metal fridge, then scooted next to Daisy.

It was hard for me to focus on anything aside from the three rings hung through his septum, at least until he held up the biggest needled I had ever seen in my life.

I glanced at Daisy in horror. "He's literally going to stab you with that thing."

"I'm not stabbing anyone," he said, his voice surprisingly monotone.

"It's fine. Relax." Daisy folded her hands over her chest while he tilted the chair back. She smiled like the idea of having the strongest muscle in the human body jabbed with a sharp object was the best thing in the world.

Tattoo Man grabbed what I could best describe as a pair of tongs, then glanced over the rim of his glasses. "You aren't gonna pass out, are you?"

"No." I wasn't going to faint because I was about to close my eyes and keep them shut until this was all over.

In a matter of seconds, Ziggy was done, and Daisy had a silver barbell dangling from her swollen tongue. On the way out to the parking lot, all I could think about was Pastor Fulmer discovering that I came with Daisy. Her mom would definitely tell my mom. God, I would be grounded for being involved, and Daddy would likely have Magpie shut down for piercing an underage preacher's daughter's tongue.

I glared at Daisy when I climbed in her car. "If your

parents find out, you better not dare tell them I came with you for emotional support."

17

ELIAS

Warm air blew from the AC unit. "Piece of shit." I pounded my fist over the grate, and the motor ticked a few times before cooler air whooshed out. I laid back on the couch, "Stars" playing in the background.

Groaning, I wiped my hand over my jaw. I hated the tight, jittery feeling in my chest that I couldn't seem to shake. I couldn't stand that every time I closed my eyes, I saw her and him on our beach. I liked having control, and I had none with Sunny—not with how she felt about me or how I felt about her. Out of habit, I reached for the ring on my necklace, pausing when I realized it was no longer there. Just like she wasn't.

Since moving home, I'd spent plenty of time wondering what it was about Sunny Lower I'd never been able to quite let go of, but some things are just beyond simple explanation. The earth is round and the moon changes the tides. That's just how it is.

And I just loved Sunny. It was a shit feeling to realize the love of my life didn't love me anymore.

Judah came out from his room clutching a crumpled Cheeto's bag. He flopped down in the recliner and stuffed his mouth full of the disgusting puffs. "You laid McClure out because he's dipping his wick in your girl, huh?"

"Not my fault he doesn't know how to take a hit." I flipped the channel.

Judah snorted. "Did you feel better afterward?"

"What do you think?"

"I think if I were McClure and my girl was staring at you the way she does, I'd beat your ass."

"He couldn't beat my ass if he wanted to."

Judah wiped orange dust over his undershirt. "Still. I'd try. Hey!" Pointing at the TV, he sat up with crumbs falling out of his mouth. "Go back. That was the Yo quiero dog."

I chucked the remote at him and rolled over on the couch while he recited the commercial, laughing like an idiot. "God, I hope you get a scholarship for football because you aren't getting one for your brain."

"Suck my dick, Elias."

The back door opened and closed, but I didn't look up.

"Dude?" Judah said. "Is that blood?"

That made me flip over. Atlas stood between the kitchen and living room, his brow furrowed and his shirt covered in reddish-brown smears.

"Atlas?"

He sank to the couch, elbow to knee and hands combing through his hair. "Radcliffe is in some deep shit."

18

SUNNY

"I hate these bleachers." Daisy wiggled on the metal bench. "Why do we have an assembly on a Tuesday anyway?"

Assemblies, when they happened, occurred on Mondays. Pep Rallies took place on Fridays. "Maybe some D.A.R.E. presentation?" I said, even though I knew that wasn't true because my dad would have been ranting about it for days prior. Deep down, I knew it was something bad, and I wanted to live in that naïve world I had once frolicked in as a child. The one where nothing terrible happened and all the bad guys covered their faces with ski masks.

Daisy shot to her feet, waving her hand around, shouting for Ben.

Neither Ben or Brandon smiled when they maneuvered their way through the overcrowded gymnasium.

"Jesus, who died?" Daisy mumbled and scooted to the side to make room for the boys.

They plopped down. Brandon interlocked his hands behind his head then leaned over his spread knees. He looked like someone about to walk the green mile.

I stared at him, but he wouldn't look at me. "What's going on?"

He opened his mouth and twisted his tongue a few times like he was rolling the words around. Then he shook his head which only added to the vortex of anxiety swirling through my body.

I tugged on Brandon's sleeve, dipping my chin to look in his eyes. "Brandon?"

The ear-splitting screech of feedback from the speakers caused a unified groan.

Principal Davis stood center court in his navy suit, a grim frown on his face. The paper he held in his hand shook, and somehow, I knew what this assembly was about.

"Travis?" I whispered.

Brandon swallowed.

I covered my mouth before grabbing his sweaty hand and lacing our fingers together.

"Students of Robertsdale High. I'm very saddened to be holding this assembly." Principal Davis' voice echoed into the silent gym. He paused, scanning the crowd like he was looking at each of us. "As some of you may be aware, last night one of our students assaulted a young man from Lockhart." The room buzzed with whispers. "That student has been expelled.

I have been in the school system for thirty years, and while I understand the notion that kids will be kids and that there will be disagreements and rude remarks, what I refuse to understand is hate."

Brandon squeezed my hand. My heart raced, so I could only imagine what his did. I rested my head on his shoulder and held on tighter to his hand, hoping he understood that I cared.

"Rumors were circulating that the young man who was

assaulted was homosexual." More gasps and hushed whispers. Brandon tensed beside me, and I closed my eyes. Aside from me, he was alone in this. No one else understood the turmoil that must have been tearing up his insides like an F-5 tornado.

"Those rumors and some people's intolerance of differences is what allegedly led to the attack. The reason for this assembly today is for me to make clear that this school does not tolerate hate or discrimination. I will not tolerate it. You are dismissed."

AFTER SCHOOL, Brandon and I went to Coconut Larry's, a run-down burger joint on Gulf Shores Parkway. The fries tasted like fish, and the burgers were always undercooked.

We sat at one of the wobbly picnic tables out front. The traffic that whizzed by on the strip was completely ignorant to what had happened at our school, what had happened to Brandon and Travis, and how distraught and utterly helpless I felt.

A seagull perched on the empty table beside us, and I tossed a fry to it while Brandon stared absently at his plate. I wondered what went through his head. I worried how knowing your best friends so naively hated what you really were affected him, and I secretly hoped that someone would beat the absolute mess out of Thomas.

"It's not a choice."

I glanced up from my soda and nodded. "I know."

The seagull scampered to our table, cocking its head and staring at me with one eye.

"That's why you don't feed them. They won't go away." Brandon tossed a fry to the concrete, and the seagull scarfed it down. "I wouldn't choose this, you know." He traced his finger over a crack in the concrete tabletop.

"I know you wouldn't, Brandon." Maybe this was heartache, this tug, this I-would-trade-places-with-you-beat thumping in my chest. And if it were, I would never live to be twenty, because, God, it was painful.

"Have you seen him?" I asked.

"No." He took a sip of his drink, eyes down in thought.

I didn't know the extent to Travis' injuries, but it was enough that almost twenty-four hours later he remained hospitalized. And if that were Elias, I would want to be there. I grabbed my purse and pulled a twenty out, tossing it onto the table. "We should go."

"We?"

"Yes. *We.*" I stood, and the seagull scurried beneath an empty table. "I'll take you."

"Sunny, I don't know that's such a good—"

"Let someone say something!" I felt my nostrils flare. It wasn't fair that he had to be afraid to visit the person he loved in the hospital.

Brandon grabbed my hand, shaking his head as though he were trying to convince himself this wasn't a good idea.

"It's fine. I'm your girlfriend after all."

THE ANTISEPTIC SMELL of hospitals caused an involuntary sweat to break out on the back of my neck. It reminded me of being a terrified eight-year-old with blood streaming from her forehead when she had fallen off a jungle gym. Elias held one hand, and Momma held the other, while the doctor gave me stitches. *Everything* somehow came back to Elias.

I settled back in the plastic chair, watching strangers meander in and out of the waiting room with cups of coffee and peanut butter crackers from the vending machine. Some people wore stress on their face. Some managed to hide it in, but the constant bounce of their leg or wringing of their hands told a different story. I wondered what had happened to the person they cared about, and then I thought about Travis. Trying to comprehend why anyone would hurt another person over something as innate as love. *I hate you because of who you love.* It didn't make sense to me, and I hoped that kind of hate didn't make sense to a lot of people. I couldn't think about what would happen to Brandon if it did.

The automatic doors caught my attention when they swung open. Brandon's face was splotchy, and his eyes were bloodshot. He nodded toward the exit, and I stood up, meeting him at the elevators.

He looked fragile enough that even a hug may cause him to shatter like crystal.

I dragged the toe of my shoe over the tile while we waited. "Is he gonna be okay?"

"Yeah. Broken ribs. Punctured lung." He inhaled just as the doors opened, and we stepped in.

"I'm sorry."

"Would Thomas have done that to me if he knew? Ben? Would Ben do that?"

"They're your friends. They wouldn't—"

"They're Brandon McClure, the straight guy's friends. They aren't mine."

The floor indicator beeped a few times before I finally spoke. "It's bullshit."

"I don't even care anymore. I just want to make it through the year, so I can get signed to a team. People can beat my ass, call me all the names in the book. I just don't want my chance to play college ball taken away."

The elevator doors slid open to the stark-white lobby.

Brandon was one of the most genuine people I'd known, and I felt desperate to help him, the same way I felt desperate to love Elias. Why should both of us be forbidden to be with the person we felt was right for us? "All you need is an alibi," I said. "And I think I make a pretty good, doting girlfriend if I do say so myself."

He stopped midstride, his brow creasing while his eyes searched mine. "Why would you do that?"

"Because I like you." Inhaling, I swept my palm over his cheek. "And because I'm so hopelessly in love with a boy I can't have, I couldn't fall in love with someone else if I wanted to."

"Damn." Brandon opened my car door. "I guess that's one thing you and I have in common. Falling in love with people we can't have."

19

SUNNY

OCTOBER 1999

S ome places in the world have four definitive seasons. Fort Morgan, Alabama, does not.

In autumn, the temperature swings from unbearably hot to bearably cool, and the weather forecast is inaccurate eighty-four percent of the time. The night of our homecoming game, the weatherman got it wrong. He promised a low of seventy-one. It was sixty-three at best.

Much to my surprise, Daisy had spent the past month as Ben Jones' actual girlfriend, while I had spent the last month as Brandon McClure's pretend girlfriend. Thirty days of holding hands in the halls and going to parties together. Thirty days of dropping him off at Travis's house when we told everyone we were going on a date.

Bats dove in and out, catching insects buzzing around the stadium lights. An army of red and white helmets with a hammerhead emblazoned on the side hustled onto the field.

Daisy leaned over the chain link fence and whistled at Ben. He blew a kiss before bending into a stretch. "God, look at his ass."

"I'd rather not."

"Okay." She swatted me. "Look at your man's ass then."

Instead of looking at Brandon, I watched Elias lunge side to side in a stretch.

"What gives with you two anyway?" she asked.

"What do you mean?"

"You guys just seem more like friends. I swear, sometimes he seems more into Ben than you."

"That's not funny!"

Daisy nudged me in the ribs. "I'm just joking. Geez."

The cheerleaders lined up, tossing their red and white pompoms to the ground before slipping out of their jackets.

Brandon jogged over with his helmet tucked under his arm. "Hey, you." His eyes crinkled at the corner when he smiled, and I thought how I could absolutely-maybe love him in that way if he were straight and Elias didn't exist.

"Good luck." I leaned over the fence and gave him a peck on the cheek before he ran back to the team.

Daisy shook her head. "On the cheek? You kissed him on the cheek, Sunny?"

I thumbed towards the concession stand where my mom and dad stood talking to Pastor Fulmer. "Our parents are right there. Give me a break." That was a completely legitimate excuse.

Daisy gave a flippant glance over her shoulder, then rolled her eyes. "That's it. I'm convinced you and Brandon are worms."

"Worms?"

"Have you not been paying attention in Weber's class?" Groaning, she grabbed onto the fence. "Worms. They're all asexual and stuff."

"We are not worms."

"Really?" She cocked her head. "Have you had sex yet?"

I hesitated, thinking maybe I should lie, because wouldn't most seventeen-year-old couples have had sex a month into a relationship? But, damn, that was a lie I could never come back from. Not with my best friend. "Not yet," I said.

"Dear. Lord. Do him already, Sunny!"

Ozzy Osbourne's wicked laugh rang out from the speakers. People in the stands stomped their feet in time with the percussion, and the crowd screamed when the electric guitar riffs kicked in. Daisy and I fumbled through the stands to our seats, and instead of watching Brandon, I watched Elias, feeling like a complete fraud. . .even though I was doing the only thing I could do to protect my friend along with my heart. As long as everyone else believed I was Brandon's, people couldn't think he was gay. I couldn't want Elias. And I couldn't really be as broken as I felt on the inside.

A twinge of guilt worked its way to my core. Momma and Daddy liked Brandon. He had dinner with us most Sundays. He had taught Simon how to hit a baseball when it wasn't on a tee. Whenever we had our inevitable fake break-up, it would gut my family.

The entire game, I cheered for Brandon while watching Elias. I had almost found the games to be some twisted form of a remedy for a broken heart. I could watch the boy I loved without anyone knowing.

Elias tackled some guy from Kingston. He hopped up curling his arms inward in victory, and God help me, my heart went into those crazy-I-love-you beats, and I smiled.

"Brandon really laid that guy out." Daisy cupped her hands around her mouth and shouted.

I didn't even see Brandon tackle anyone.

Fifteen minutes after the game was over, the parking lot was teeming with students trying to flesh out their after-game plans.

Truck exhausts rumbled and the deep bass from "Ruff Ryders' Anthem" boomed into the night while cars took off through the exit.

Daisy hugged me before climbing into Ben's truck. "You sure you guys don't wanna come? It's just a few guys from the team."

"Yeah, I'm sure. Brandon promised we'd watch *The Craft*. I grabbed his hand and laced my fingers through them.

Ben leaned over Daisy's lap, pointing at Brandon. "You're turning into a grade-A wuss."

Brandon flipped him the bird. I laughed because I was supposed to, even though, out of the corner of my eye, I saw some girl follow Elias and his brothers into the parking lot. It sucked to be jealous of someone whose name you didn't even know.

"All right, love birds. Catch y'all later." Ben cranked his engine.

Daisy shut her door, and they pulled off, following the rest of the traffic through the open gates.

"We could've gone," Brandon said on the way to his SUV.

"It's fine."

"Seriously, Sunny." He opened the passenger door. "I'll go anywhere with you."

I almost wanted to swoon because he was just that nice. Patting his cheek, I smiled. "I know." Then I sank into the seat, and he shut the door.

Thirty minutes later, the headlights of his Land Rover

shined over a little wooden sign with the name of the house: Life's a Beach. All the houses on the island had those signs at the end of the drive like it was some rule rich people had to name their beach houses—even though these houses would never be rented out to a family trying to escape the harsh winters up north.

He shifted the gear into park and narrowed his eyes on me. I knew what was coming. "Is it Daniel Thigpin?" he said, trying to guess the name of my mystery, non-existent boyfriend.

"God, no, Brandon." I stepped out of the car. "Give me some credit," I said when I rounded the trunk.

"I wish you'd tell me."

"One day, I will."

He dragged the toe of his shoe over the pavement. "It's not Elias Black, is it?"

My heart thumped a little harder. There was a twinge of disdain to Brandon's voice when he said Elias' name, like out of all the people in the universe that was the last person he wanted it to be.

Just like everyone else. . .

"Sunny?" He kind-of-sort-of scowled, and I kind-of-sort-of panicked when I climbed behind the wheel without responding. "Please tell me it's not him," he said, grabbing ahold of the doorjamb.

"Nope. Definitely not Elias Black." I went to close the door, but he was still holding it. "What? It's not. Now go spend time with your man so I can spend time with mine."

I did that a lot—told Brandon I was going to see *that boy* whose name I refused to share. Why? Because had I divulged that every time I dropped him off at Travis' house, I went and sat at the beach alone, he never would have stayed. And I wanted one of us not to fall victim to Shakespeare's curse. I needed to believe that some star-crossed lovers could work out. Or maybe I just wanted to feel like a martyr.

"You're stubborn, you know it?" he said.

"So my mother has told me."

Brandon hugged me before jogging down the drive and disappearing behind a jungle of palm trees.

TEN MINUTES later I was the only car in the public beach parking lot, and I had two hours to kill.

Sighing, I grabbed Brandon's CD case from the floorboard and flipped through until I came to a Matchbox 20 CD. I put it in and skipped to the last song, losing myself in the acoustic guitar and Rob Thomas' voice. I played it twice, made myself a little sadder, and I still had an hour and fifty minutes to spare.

When I opened the door, the little buzzer that let me know the keys were still in the ignition sounded. I reached back in, snatching them and slipping them inside my pocket on my way to the boardwalk. The familiar crash of the waves swirled around me. The wind rustled the sea oats that dotted the ever-growing dunes that towered over the railing of the boardwalk. That was the tallest I'd seen them since the last hurricane had swept through.

I didn't bother to take my sneakers off when I reached the sand. I just shoved my hands in the pockets of Brandon's varsity jacket and hunched my shoulders against the wind as I started down the deserted coastline.

The thing a lot of people didn't know about the beach was that it can be the loneliest place on earth. Most people came here when the days were blazing hot, and no matter what you did, you couldn't escape the scent of tanning oil or the sound of children splashing in the surf. Those nights are filled with families carrying flashlights, searching for crabs. Summer loves trying to find somewhere to seclude themselves.

But in October, when there's a bite to the air and summer was long gone, the only people that came out here had something on their mind. It was dark and empty. The endless sea and sky could make you feel so small if you let them.

I kicked at the white sand, and it caught in the moonlight like dull glitter.

Plopping down on one of the empty lounges, I placed my hands behind my head and stared up at the stars, wishing I'd paid more attention in science the semester we went over the constellations.

Freshman year I didn't think the pattern of the stars mattered, but too often we don't realize the significance of things. To me, it was just a bunch of broken planets and dying suns that didn't seem to make up a fish or a big dipper. I definitely never saw a dog. . . But now, lying on the warped, wooden chair, I realized that in a really poetic way, the heavens connected me to existence.

The same sky bearing down on me at that very moment was the same one overlooking Shakespeare when he had penned *Romeo and Juliet*. The same sky Cleopatra and Marc Antony had made promises under—the same sky Elias and I had made promises under.

Like ancient eyes, the stars had seen everything. And we all need something to connect us.

I glanced at my watch, then at the rings on my finger. I almost threw both away after Elias taped his to my locker, but the idea of tossing them out hurt more than the thought of keeping them. And some masochist part of me liked having the sun and moon together on my finger. When I looked down at those rings, it made me happy and unbearably sad at the same time.

But that was how mine and Elias' story had always gone. A little happy, and a lot of sad. So much to hope for because life was too long to let go of each other so soon.

BY THE TIME I started back to the parking lot, my fingers were numb from the cold, and my heart just a little more broken.

My shoe hit the first plank of the sand-covered boardwalk when I heard a girl shout Elias' name. I froze and gripped the worn, wooden rail before I glanced over my shoulder, watching two figures walk toward each other. I wondered if they would kiss or if he would make pretty promises to her, but it didn't matter.

I was the sun, and he was the moon, and while we may share the same sky during the early hours of dawn, we would never be close enough to matter.

20

ELIAS

We won our homecoming game against the rich-kid school from Daphne, the Kingstown Knights, and that was reason enough for Ben to throw a party at his house the next day. Which was reason enough for me to want to stay home, but a pipe at the house had just busted which jacked my water bill through the roof. And I needed some cash.

By the time my brothers and I pulled into the drive, the front yard was full of trucks, SUVs, and a few rundown clunkers.

"Ah, shit," I mumbled, yanking the keys from the ignition.

Judah and Atlas grabbed the cooler from the back and started toward the double-story house. A group of girls was gathered on the front porch, smoking cigarettes while trying to look prissy by cocking their hips to the side and continuously flipping their hair.

"Hey Elias," one of them called when we stepped to the gate at the side of the house. I was pretty sure that was the girl who bought a dime bag from me the night before on the beach, but I couldn't be sure, so I gave a half-ass wave.

"Dude," Judah said. "Bet you five bucks you could at least go up her shirt, and you just blew her off."

"Seriously, man," Atlas added.

"Why don't you two go talk to her then?" I said, rounding the bushes.

With a shrug of his shoulders, Judah spun around. Atlas followed suit. By the time I had my hand on the gate, I heard them both singing, "Ladies. Ladies."

WITHIN AN HOUR I'd sold the ounce I'd brought with me and pocketed two-hundred and fifty bucks. That was enough to cover the pipe, the water bill, and a Little Caesar's pizza.

I took a seat on a railroad tie that separated the lawn from for Mrs. Jones rose garden and stared straight ahead at the bonfire. One of the logs crackled as it collapsed, sending the flames roaring higher into the night sky.

Atlas fiddled with the massive CD player set up on the patio table, turning around after the distorted opening notes of "Pepper" came through. He grabbed a few twigs on his way across the yard, tossing them into the bonfire before he took a seat beside me and cracked open a beer. "I love the Butthole Surfers."

"That's the stupidest name for a band ever."

He glanced at my empty hands. "Since when did you become such a buzzkill?"

"It's called trying to be responsible, shithead."

Brandon took a seat across the fire from me. The heat and smoke warped my view as I watched him talk to some Lockhart guys.

Atlas snorted. "You hate him, don't you?"

"No."

But I did. God, I hated him for the simple fact he had the girl I always imagined would only ever be mine.

I snatched a dandelion from the grass and thumped the fuzzy white seeds. They haphazardly floated toward the heat of the fire. I watched a few of them incinerate in the flames and caught Sunny out of the corner of my eye. I tried my damnedest to focus on the blaze reaching toward the sky like red-hot fingers but failed miserably. Too much of her long legs showed between the top of her laced Doc Martens and the hem of her too-short jean skirt. Her hips swayed in beat with the slow rhythm of the song. My jaw tensed at the sight of the black bra clearly visible through her tight, white shirt. *What the hell was she trying to do?* Sunny had never been a girl who needed to feel noticed. Then again, there were a lot of things she'd never been. . .like his.

I grumbled under my breath when she bent over to dust off a chair. As hard as I tried, I couldn't help but look. Atlas whistled under his breath, and I whacked him. "Stop being a perv."

"You were looking!"

"Shut up."

Before Sunny could sit down, Brandon grabbed onto her waist and pulled her into his lap, that damn skirt riding up her thighs. She squealed, and I threw the dandelion to the ground.

"Still don't hate him?" Atlas asked.

"He had no loyalties to me."

"So you hate her?" He tipped his beer back.

"Don't you have some girls to go screw around with or something? Jesus!"

I listened to the lyrics while I stared through the bonfire at the way Brandon's fingers curled around Sunny's side. It ate me up from the inside out. I may not have thought Butthole Surfers was a good name for a band, and most of the lyrics made no sense, but the chorus? That chorus resonated with me because Sunny had no idea how she looked through my eyes, curled up in his lap. She looked right at me, and I gave her the coldest stare I could muster.

Atlas crushed his beer in his hand and pushed to his feet. "She watches you all the damn time."

"I know."

"Why don't you do something about it?"

"It's better this way." I told myself that at least once a day, but I had yet to believe it.

"Whatever you say, dude."

Judah stumbled over, dragging the cooler behind him. "You two fart-knockers gonna do the Jell-O wrestling?" He thumbed over his shoulder where two underclassmen were busy carting a plastic baby pool across the lawn.

"Whose genius idea was that?" I asked.

Judah grinned. "Mine."

"Of course, it would be."

"Dude, think about it." He hooked an arm around my shoulders. "Girls covered in sticky goodness. Epic."

"What girl is going to roll around in that crap?"

"Ah, by midnight, someone will be in that pool."

Jenny's hyena-like laugh floated over the music. Judah grinned. "Like Jenny Smith. Speaking of which, I heard you hooked up with her at Radcliffe's party?"

"I didn't touch her at Radcliffe's party." I glanced back to the bonfire, watching the tiny orange embers intertwine with the smoke. I regretted letting Sunny believe anything happened between Jenny and me, but I did stupid things when I was hurt. And Sunny had already annihilated me by that point. My initial reaction was to hit right back, and I figured Jenny would be an obvious blow to Sunny's ego.

"Dude, why didn't you bang the bottom outta her?"

I glared at my brother. He didn't get it. He couldn't. He'd never loved anyone. "Because I have standards."

"Like McClure's girl?" Judah smirked, and I pulled my arm back like I would hit him, then I dropped it.

Someone changed the music. The song started off low enough that I couldn't help but make out Sunny's boisterous laugh. She threw her head back, nearly toppling off Brandon's lap. He caught her, and it was too much.

I snagged a beer from the cooler and crossed the yard, wedging myself between a group of girls who had been staring at me and giggling. If she could pretend she hadn't lost anything, so could I.

By eleven the stereo had been converted into a karaoke machine, and Ben's backyard was trashed. Someone had taken a piss in the rose bushes, the back-porch swing had collapsed after fifteen girls climbed on it to have their picture taken, and the garden gnome by the back gate had been decapitated.

I stood a few feet away from the baby pool, watching a drunk girl flail around, screaming she that she was making a snow angel. I nudged Judah with my elbow. "Is that what you guys had in mind?"

"Not exactly."

I jumped when someone grabbed hold of my shoulder. "Hey," Atlas said. "I was out at the car, and Sunny came up asking me for weed."

My heart pounded. "Please tell me you didn't fucking sell her any?"

"She's the sheriff's daughter! I'm not touching that."

I quickly glanced around the yard, but couldn't place my eyes on her see-through shirt. "Where is she?"

"I don't know, man. She was by McClure's truck. It looked like they were leaving."

Judah leaned in, face all serious. "You don't think she's gonna snitch on us to her dad?"

"No." I half rolled my eyes. "Stop smoking so much. You're paranoid." He shoved me, and I pushed him right back. "Don't fucking start with me!" I warned. I stared off at the smoldering bonfire, wondering what the hell had gotten into Sunny. Maybe that good guy I thought she was better off with hadn't been so good for her after all.

"Give me a smoke." I wiggled my fingers, feeling the itch for a hit of nicotine.

Judah reluctantly pulled a pack of Marlboros from his back pocket, placing a single cigarette along with a red lighter in my waiting palm. "Those aren't cheap, dildo."

Lighting it, I took a seat on the porch steps, puffing and puffing and thinking. I had the thing smoked down to the filter by the time the door to the upstairs porch creaked open.

"Where did Brandon go?" Daisy asked.

"He went home." Sunny didn't sound too disappointed at that, and I caught myself fighting a smile.

"Wait. Did he leave you?"

"No."

I felt like a shithead for eavesdropping, so I pushed up. "He said he had to—uh—go back and get things ready."

Ready? That caused me to pause.

"Oh. So is tonight *the* night?" There was an excited lilt to Daisy's voice, like Sunny giving it up to him was a milestone instead of a betrayal.

Only, I was the lone person who would use the word betrayal to define her sleeping with her boyfriend, because I was the guy she promised all her firsts to. My fingers pulled into fists. My skin crawled at the thought of her and Brandon in bed together. I took one final drag from my cigarette, that last pull burning my fingers. Just before I turned to throw it to the ground, Sunny stepped onto the top stair.

"Were you. . ." Her eyes met mine and went wide. "Listening?" She crossed her arms over her chest, tapping her foot while she waited, I guessed, for me to respond.

I tossed my smoke down then shoved my shoulders back. The classic riff to "Jessie's Girl" echoed into the night. Maybe it was a combination of those lyrics and the condescending way she stared down at me from the porch, but something inside of me went on the fritz. It was like someone else was in complete control of my body. There is no way in hell I would have ever flipped Sunny the bird. But damned if I didn't.

She glared at me, jaw dropped and eyebrows pinched together in an angry scowl.

I took my keys from my pocket and headed to the side of the house.

"Hey, bro! Where you going?" Judah shouted.

"Home!"

I barely made it past the pool of Jell-O before Sunny shouted my name. Next thing I knew, she had me by the arm, jerking me around to face her. "What were you doing, Elias?"

"Fucking breathing. Is that okay with you?"

Her nostrils flared. "Why were you listening?"

I leaned down, placing my face inches from hers and

trying my hardest not to pull in her scent. If I did, I'd lose it. "I wasn't," I said.

"Bull."

She didn't budge, and neither did I.

"Why were you trying to buy weed from my brother?"

A wicked grin shaped her pretty lips. "Because I'm not as good as you or my daddy think."

"Oh, is that why you're dressed like this?" I looped a finger underneath her bra strap still on full display and popped it. "To prove a point? Or are you just trying to get fucked?"

There was a moment of silence that seemed to stretch on for ions before she clenched her jaw. "I hate you!" she said with icy precision.

Even though those words went straight through my chest like a machete, slicing and cutting, I managed a sick smirk that I hoped said I didn't care. "Ah, come on, Sunny. I can do better than have you hate me." I scooped her up. Her bare legs dangled over my arms, and damn, was I torn.

I didn't want to let her go, but I didn't want her to know how much I hurt. How much I still cared when she had stopped loving me long ago. So I carried her across the yard, staring right through her, swallowing the urge I had to tell her Brandon couldn't possibly care about her the way I did.

"Put me down, Elias!" she shouted, pounding her fists against my shoulder and kicking her legs like an angry mule.

My shins hit the plastic rim of the baby pool, and panic tore across her face.

"By the way," I whispered. "Good luck tonight." I winked, then dropped her into the Jell-O. The party erupted in loud brouhahas. Pink gelatin exploded into the air, splattering my shirt.

"See if Brandon can get you that wet," I said, giving her a hard stare before I strolled past the shocked partygoers and through the side gate. I wasn't sure whether to be concerned about the sick satisfaction I found in thinking I may have taken a little of the fun out of her and Brandon's special night.

21

ELIAS

Monday morning, Brandon came steamrolling through the halls, varsity jacket in place and his gaze honed in on me.

I stopped by the emergency exit to the stairwell with a smile, just waiting.

"What the hell, Black?" That was the most commanding I had ever heard his voice.

I glanced at the textbook in his hand and squared my shoulders. "Might wanna make sure you have both hands free."

He didn't drop the book, but he did grab me and pin me to the wall.

Laughing, I bit at my lip to stave off the sudden bout of heat that fired through my muscles. I didn't like being against the wall, but he had every right to be pissed at me.

"Why would you do that to her?" He dug the heel of his hand into my clavicle.

I didn't have an answer. At least not one I would admit to Golden Boy. People began to congregate around us, waiting for the inevitable alpha-male showdown prone to high school hallways.

"Let. Go of me," I said. It wasn't a plea or a request. It was a warning. I stood a good three inches taller than Brandon, and unlike him, I didn't grow up in a household were privilege maintained pride. I grew up where you scrapped to settle differences.

Brandon's brows pinched together, and he took shallow breath after shallow breath. He was scared, but the thing he most likely couldn't pick up on: I was terrified. If I knocked him out, Sunny would never forgive me—not that I expected much from her in the way of forgiveness, but this would be crossing new lines. It would be the guy she used to love hurting the guy she currently loved.

"McClure." I raised my chin. "Step back."

He swallowed, and the seconds ticked by, our eyes locked. "Even if she wasn't mine," he said, "she's too good for you."

My pulse spun up like a tornado, ripping and shredding every bit of control I had. I grabbed the collar of his jacket and yanked him eye level to me before I threw him on the ground. The words *too good* bounced around my skull like a loose cannon. My forearm was over his throat within a millisecond, my knee in his groin, and my nose to his.

"If I didn't think. . ." I choked on the words *she loved you*. They were like thorns ripping apart my throat. Some terrible poison threatening a slow death that I had to expel. As much as I wanted to punch him right in the face, I loved her more than I hated him. And I wanted him to know it.

"Elias!" Sunny stood at the end of the hall, shouting my name over and over like I was the villain in all of this.

I shoved Brandon into the floor one good time, then climbed to my feet and backed away step by step. He shot up, rubbing at the red mark on his throat, never breaking our stare down. Sunny sprinted down the hallway. The soles of her shoes skidded over the floor when she grabbed Brandon's shirt to keep from slipping right past him. Her brow creased. I saw her lips form: *Are you okay* before she cupped his cheeks and checked him over. Watching her love him like that was too much.

Balling my fist, I turned toward the emergency stairwell and shoved it open. The bustle from the hallway went silent when the door banged shut behind me, the stale aroma of cigarettes surrounded me, and my uneven breaths amplified in the enclosed space. I made it down three—maybe four steps before I sat, elbows on my knees and my head hung. Blood pulsed through my ears, adrenaline crackled through my veins like an angry wildfire, and I hated myself.

I started out in ratty clothes with dirty hair. I swore because I didn't know better, and I stole because my maw told me that's how we survived. Then the Lower's took me in, and I realized my parents had been wrong. I didn't have to take any more beatings or steal, and I understood that some people were just good.

Sunny was damn good, and as far as everyone else was concerned, I wasn't.

The problem was, I didn't grow up wanting to be the bad boy. Everyone knows he breaks the good girl's heart, and I never wanted to hurt her, but here I was. Hurting her. Hurting us.

The lock to the door clicked, the door closed, and then there were one, two, three footfalls.

"What's your deal?" Her voice didn't sound near as sweet laced with anger like that.

I rubbed over my arms, debating on whether to answer her.

Sunny took another step, her standing shadow towered over mine on the wall. "You could have hurt him." Jesus, she sounded sad. Heartbroken. And I felt worthless, but I still managed to roll my eyes because they had both hurt me in ways that don't heal.

It's better this way. I shoved to my feet.

When I went to brush past her, she snagged my hand. Her fingers almost threaded through mine, and damn, if such a simple touch didn't nearly bring me to my knees.

"Answer me," she whispered. The smell of candy and vanilla wrapped around me like a cocoon when she stepped closer. She took a few shallow breaths then wet her lips. "Why are you so mad at him?"

I couldn't help myself, I just wanted to touch her, so I brushed my knuckles over her soft cheek. I leaned down so close I could kiss her if I were a little less nice. I felt my brows pull together, my chest went all tight like my ribcage might just explode into shrapnel that would pierce us both. The answer was simple: "Because you used to be mine."

Her eyes slammed shut, then her chin fell to her chest. "I'm still yours." It came out so low I almost didn't hear her.

"What?"

She glanced up, and a few tears spilled down her cheeks. "I said, I'm still yours."

I moved back underneath the blinking stairwell lights. I didn't need to be any more messed up than I already was, so I refused to accept that answer. "Nah, Sunny," I said. "You're his."

You would think I had just slapped her from the way she looked at me. "Are you kidding me?" And there came the anger reddening her face. "What did you expect?" she said, her voice growing louder. "For me to just sit around and let you and everyone else tell me I was too good for you? And then you get pissed at me for dating someone?" Her face caved in on itself before she shoved me so hard I stumbled back against the wall. "Well, fuck you, Elias Black." She choked back a garbled word. "Just fuck you!"

She went to push me again, but I caught her by the wrists and held her there for a second, wishing this wasn't what had become of us. Wishing she wasn't the good girl who broke my heart. She attempted to jerk away from me just as the bell rang outside the door. The low hum from the hallway fell to a dead still.

"You were already his when I realized that, no matter how wrong I was for you, no one else would love you the way I do." My voice caught, but I refused to break in front of her. "So don't you fucking blame me! I'm trying to do the right thing here."

I let go of her, and she covered her face, furiously shaking her head.

Something on her finger glinted underneath the fluorescent lights. A solid lump formed in my throat when I noticed she had both rings—the sun and moon interlocked—on her finger.

"You asked me if I loved him." She dropped her hands to her sides and looked straight at me. "I don't."

Part of me believed that because had she truly loved him, she wouldn't have been standing in that stairwell with me. There was maybe an inch separating us, and I closed it with a single step. Chest to chest. Heart to heart. "Then why are you with him?" I asked.

"I don't think I can make you understand."

"Try." One syllable. One plea.

"I. . ." She gulped back a breath. Her bottom lip rolled underneath her teeth and, for a moment in that ratty, stale stairwell it felt like our entire world hung in the balance, teetering on the edge and ready to tumble over a cliff depending on what her next words were.

"I can't," she whispered.

"I don't have time for this bullshit, Sunny." I turned my back to her and moved toward the door.

"But I love you," she whispered.

Those words pressed down on me, and for a moment, I understood how the Greek Titan condemned to bear the weight of the world on his shoulders must have felt. For what greater punishment is there than to carry a love you can never have?

Given enough time, I was sure it would break me.

"I love you, Elias." She said it louder that time like she was begging me to love her—like she didn't know I always would.

I could have told her I still cared. Maybe I could have spun around and kissed her, but it wouldn't change anything. Except possibly dull some self-inflicted heartache or guilt she had.

"Did you hear me?" Her voice cracked. More tears fell down her pale cheeks.

Inhaling, I nodded and took another step away from her. "But I suggest you learn to love Brandon."

Then I left her in the stairwell.

22

SUNNY

The first floor of the high school consisted of an art room, a single wall of lockers, and restrooms hidden in the corner by the janitor's closet. Which is why I chose the last stall of that particular girl's restroom as my sanctuary for most of third period.

Elias' voice was cold and indifferent when he told me to love Brandon. Out of all the things he could have said in that moment, that was the cruelest.

I sat in the stall, and I cried until I thought I may throw up. I pounded my fist over the flimsy aluminum door, and I didn't have to apologize for losing my temper.

I allowed the aggravation over Elias and Brandon and my being too good for anything that was good for me to swell until it grew bigger and angrier, eventually catching fire, smoldering and choking my heart with thick black smoke. And then I cried some more because I realized I was eternally powerless when it came to the matters of my heart. No one can will themselves to unlove a person, and no one can be forced to love someone they don't.

Resolving that—while it may have felt like my world was

on a collision course with doom—I still had to finish the rest of the day. I wiped my eyes dry and forced myself to snap out of it. Two steps into the hallway, I tripped on my shoelace, nearly face planting into the bright-red bulletin board that hadn't been changed since last Spring.

"Shit." I bent to tie my shoe, and when I stood, I noticed *Brandon McClure's a fag* scribbled in thick black marker, right underneath the cut-out letters spelling *Hammerhead Pride*.

My heart sputtered. I slapped my hand over my chest to work out the hiccup while my eyes remained glued to those awful words. I blinked, thinking they may somehow disappear. But when I opened my eyes, there they were. Uninvited and accusing.

And then the fear set in. Someone knew.

My vision blurred. I crunched my teeth when I grabbed the corner of the paper and ripped it. I shredded those words until they were nothing but hateful confetti in my hands, and then I went to class and sat next to the boy I pretended to love in a way I loved Elias Black, wondering how we could keep this all together.

THE SUN HAD ALREADY BEGUN its slow descent behind the ocean when Brandon and I sat down at our usual table at Coconut Larry's. The waitress swooped by with our drinks, and Brandon placed our order, while I stared across the Parkway, watching the sea oats waver on the cooler than normal breeze.

"Hey. You okay?"

"Yeah. Fine." I rubbed over my arms while forcing a smile.

He shrugged out of his jacket. "You look cold," he said as he passed it over the table.

I slipped my arms through, quickly enveloped within his jacket's warmth and too-clean smell, and I fought the tightening sensation crawling up my throat. I didn't want to tell him what I saw on that bulletin board. I didn't *need* to tell him. Which meant I had a secret that felt like a barb buried deep in my heart.

The wrought iron gate surrounding the terrace squeaked, causing the pack of seagulls to scurry toward the opposite end of the patio. A group of guys from the basketball team lumbered toward an empty table.

The tall blond glanced at me while the waitress passed out menus. Seconds later, I heard a rumble of laughter. Brandon didn't seem to notice, but my ears burned. They could have been talking about anything in the world, but to me, they were laughing at Brandon, saying the cruel things I'd heard others say about Travis, and it filled my heart with anguish.

Our waitress placed a plastic basket of hushpuppies in the middle of the table. Brandon took one and broke it open, steam rising as he set it on his napkin to cool. "I didn't mean to piss you off today," he said.

"What?" I had to drag my attention away from the basketball guys.

"You seemed mad after the, uh, the incident in the hall."

I twisted my cup around a few times. "I wasn't mad at you."

"I just. . ." he rubbed over his neck. "The guys on the team were ragging me about Black dumping you in that pool. Not to mention, you're one of my best friends. I'm sick of him hurting you."

"He hasn't hurt me, Brandon."

"Come on, Sunny."

"Getting tossed into some gross Jell-O didn't hurt me. It just made me mad."

His face looked a little confused, and then he did this half laugh. "Look, I know Elias is the guy. Okay?"

I fell silent. My heart thump, thump, thumped in my ears, and my mouth went dry. I took a sip of water while Brandon's gaze bore through me. "I mean," I started, but I didn't know what to say.

"I should've known it. I mean, the way you two look at each other, but you kept telling me it wasn't him." The wind kicked up, blowing the straw paper across the table. Brandon caught it and balled up it. "I didn't want it to be him because I thought he was a dick. Elias and his brothers deal weed. He's rough, and you're. . .not."

"You don't even know him, though."

"He laid my ass out at football practice after that weekend after Radcliffe's party."

I took another gulp of water and swiped a finger through the ring of condensation.

Brandon folded his arms over the tabletop and leaned in. "Does he know we aren't really dating?"

"No."

"So," his lips pressed into a thin line. "He thinks you're screwing around on me with him?"

I buried my face in my hands. This was such a mess.

"Sunny? What's going on?"

Groaning, I tossed my head back. "Nothing's going on. I'm not seeing him."

"Then where have you been going when you drop me off at Travis's?"

"The beach. Look, it doesn't matter, okay. I just wanted to help you out, and I knew you would get all weird if I just went by myself, but I've been fine, and you're fine, and everything is just. Fine."

"Yeah, because the definition of fine is me and you pretending to date so I can see a guy and so you can go sit on the beach alone."

I snagged a piping hot hushpuppy and popped the whole thing in my mouth, burning my tongue just so I didn't have to talk for a second.

"He cares about you," he said.

I looked down at the gum stuck to the concrete.

"Are you listening to me? He cares about you, and he thinks we're dating."

I swallowed the dry bread thinking about how Elias had told me to love Brandon. "He doesn't care, Brandon. Trust me."

"Bullshit. When he had me pinned to the floor earlier, he told me, 'If I didn't think she loved you'. . . He didn't deck me because he thought it would hurt *you*."

I turned the rings on my finger, feeling my nostrils flare as I fought to keep my emotions in check.

"I may think he's a dick, but he loves you."

"It doesn't matter. My dad would kill me if I dated him."

A dull smile shaped his lips. "And you think my dad wouldn't kill me if he knew I was seeing Travis? You don't get to choose who you love, Sunny. It just happens."

The waitress scooted by, and Brandon reached across the table, squeezing my hand. "Maybe we should break up?"

My thoughts sped from heartache to worry over the message I had read earlier in the day, and I shook my head. "Don't be ridiculous."

"I thought you loved him?"

I stared at Brandon hard, upset he would question that. "I do."

"Then why are you hurting him by letting him think you're with me?"

"Because I don't want anyone to hurt you." Tears burned my eyes, and I fought them back. I was so sick of not knowing what was right anymore.

Brandon dipped his chin, and his hold on my hand grew tighter. "You're something special Sunny Lower. I sure hope you know that, and that's why I can't let you hurt yourself."

The waitress dropped our food off, and neither of us touched our plate of greasy fries and undercooked hamburger. We just sat, holding hands, maybe trying to figure out why things that should be so simple were so complicated.

23

ELIAS

eadlights streamed through the window. I kept my gaze aimed at the TV, watching some weirdo in a black shroud and a stupid white mask try to stab someone through the slit in a bathroom stall. "This is stupid," I mumbled.

"Bet you wouldn't think it was stupid if the guy was chasing you." Atlas shoved half his arm inside the family sized bag of potato chips and then crammed his mouth so full he looked like a chipmunk storing nuts for winter.

"I wouldn't run from that asshole," I said.

Someone knocked on the door. I glanced at Atlas, but he didn't budge. "Dude?" I said. "That's probably Doodle. You answer it."

With a roll of his eyes, he tossed the chips on the recliner and trudged across the room. "What's McClure doing here?"

That got my attention. The guy had some major balls if he was showing up at my house to start a fight. Atlas slid the latch back. The hinges creaked. From where I was on the couch, the open door blocked my view. "Is your brother here?"

"Which one?"

"Elias."

"Yeah." Atlas stepped to the side, and Brandon ducked inside, barely setting foot into the living room. I expected his face to be red, jaw tight, but he looked the way I felt— broken as shit.

He wet his lips and scratched over the back of his head a few times. "Can I talk to you?"

I held my hands palm up and shrugged.

"I'm not trying to start anything." Brandon shifted his weight on his feet. "I just need to talk to you. Alone."

"Man, I'm not trying to do this right now."

"Look, I get you don't like me, all right? I'm not a huge fan of you, either, if you can't tell. But Sunny means a lot to me, and I just. . ." He exhaled. "I'm just trying to make this right. Okay?"

He knew Sunny was my weakness, and he used it against me.

Atlas shuffled past, giving me an I-don't-know-man brow lift before resuming his spot on the recliner, chips in hand. A shrill scream broke the silence as the masked man sank a knife into a girl's chest.

Brandon glanced at the TV. "Scream?"

"Yeah."

"It's pretty lame," he said.

I stared at him, wondering why in the hell he would need to talk to me about Sunny, and then came the worry. "Wanna talk outside?"

With a nod, he stepped back through the door, and I pushed up from the couch. Cold, dry leaves crunched underneath my bare feet as I followed him down the steps and into the yard.

He stopped halfway down the drive, shoved his hands in his pockets, and stared at the ground.

"All right." My breath turned to fog in the cool night air. "What did you want?"

"Sorry about today in the hall."

I lifted a shoulder. "Shit happens. I shouldn't have fucked around with your girlfriend." That title felt like acid on my tongue.

"She's not my girlfriend."

I couldn't say I was disappointed. "What do you want me to say? Sorry?"

He glanced up, wiping a slow hand down his face. I knew distress when I saw it, and that guy was spinning in turmoil. But I wasn't surprised. Loving Sunny would do that to any guy.

"God," he said. "I love her, or I wouldn't be doing this." He moved toward me, and I clenched my fist, prepping for the brawl I felt coming. "And I hope you love her as much as I think you do because if not, I'm really screwing up here."

I fought the bewilderment tightening my face.

He took a hard breath like he was struggling. "She was never really my girlfriend. She uh. . . She basically pretended to date me to take some of the heat off me. When Travis got beat up, she was trying to make sure that didn't happen to me." He choked up a little. "Because she's a good person."

I paused. I had to be missing something—didn't I? Surely, I was. Before I even realized I'd said it, I mumbled, "What are you saying, man?"

"I'm saying," he hesitated, shaking his head and kicking at the gravel. "The guy Travis was seeing was me."

Shit. It fell silent with the exception of the crickets and the random whirr of a passing car on the highway.

Finally, Brandon kicked at the rocks again. "Can you say something? I'm not in the habit of outing myself to complete fucking strangers. And you not saying anything is freaking me out."

He was serious. "You uh, you must really care about her if you're telling me this."

"I do. And she really cares about you. That's the only reason I'm telling you. I just hope I can trust you."

Jesus, I felt guilty. I felt like a complete shithead for hating him when he obviously loved her. Stepping toward him, I rested my hand on his shoulder. "Don't worry about me. I've got your back. And my lips are sealed."

"Appreciate that, man." His expression tightened before he turned toward his car.

The interior light cut on, and I caught a small wave before he settled behind the wheel and cranked the engine.

Damn, that girl's heart was pure gold. And so was his.

24

SUNNY

I laid in bed that night listening to "The God of Wine" on repeat, staring at my ceiling and thinking about Elias and Brandon. At some point, I started to wonder why, at the age of seventeen, my life was already such a mess.

I had been dumped by my pretend boyfriend who was dating a guy, and I was in love with a boy who my now pretend ex-boyfriend swore was in love with me, too, but I couldn't see it.

The phone rang. Seconds later, Simon burst into my room with a toothy grin. "A boy's on the phone for you." Then he skirted back into the hall, his footfalls heavy on the stairs.

I grabbed the receiver. "Hello?"

"Hey."

I swallowed at the sound of Elias' voice, not near as cold or distant as it had been that afternoon. Part of me was hesitant, the other part curious. Hopelessly hopeful. "Hang on a sec." I covered the receiver with my hand and shouted at

Simon to hang up the line in the kitchen, then I waited for the click.

I twirled the phone cord around my finger, listening to Elias breathe for a second. "All right."

"Have you ever," A long breath rustled the line. "Have you ever loved someone who made an absolute ass outta himself because he didn't know how to handle watching you with someone else?"

Thump. Thump. Thump-thump. My heart went out of rhythm.

"I talked to Brandon," Elias said. "And he told me about Travis. About you."

"Oh..."

"I don't wanna do this over the phone. Can I come get you?"

"Yeah. Give me thirty minutes, and I'll meet you at the end of the drive."

SOME TEENAGERS GET a thrill from sneaking out of their house. Me, on the other hand, I was mortified. My parents would kill me if they caught me, but at some point, growing up, I realized that while nine times out of ten my parents knew what was best for me, there was always the one time they would be wrong.

Elias was where they were utterly and eternally wrong.

Every pop and creak of the stairs caused me to pause, and the back door had never seemed to groan so loudly. I just knew the soft suction of it shutting must have woken someone, so I waited on the porch, my stilted breaths drowning out the chirp of the crickets and the eerie whoop of the owls.

Once I was certain the house was still asleep, I took off through the yard only slowing down when I reached the end of the driveway.

Elias' truck was parked on the shoulder of the highway. Engine cut.

The interior light turned on when he opened his door and climbed out. I watched his silhouette move around the tailgate and lean against the side of the truck. I took several more steps, and then there we were, face to face on the side of the road.

He smelled like leather and spice and wind, and my heart—my heart felt like it wasn't even in my chest.

"Hey." I swallowed, shifting on my feet. There was so much hope in the silence because no words had yet been spoken. Our future was still to be determined so I could continue to imagine it ended with us instead of him and me.

"I'm sorry." Two simple words that sometimes mean everything.

"Me too," I said.

"I, uh." A line sunk between his brows, and he took a long breath like he was still trying to wrap his head around what to say. "I never even kissed Jenny. I just let you think that because I was pissed."

So we were both guilty of malice. "Even if you had kissed her, I had no right to be mad."

"Yes, you did." He kicked at the tall grass. "I've spent a lot of time thinking about you and me, and God, Sunny, there are eight-hundred reasons why I'm not good enough for you. But there's one really good reason why I am. I've spent over half of my life in love with you, and I know without a shadow of doubt, no matter what happens, I'll spend the rest of it loving you."

He pulled me up by my waist until I was on my tiptoes and my arms were around his neck. "That's gotta count for something," he whispered before his parted lips pressed against mine.

Our mouths moved together soft and perfect, and my entire body felt lighter like it could evaporate into some kind of beautiful mist. A car passed on the highway, it's horn blaring. Elias spun me around and pressed me against the cool paint of his truck, our mouths reconnected harder and deeper, unapologetically.

I was certain for a few minutes that the gravity of that kiss caused the small, miniscule part of the world surrounding us to still while the rest of the universe continued to spin. It made me dizzy and all too aware that the pain and heartache and boring days that tended to fade in and out of oblivion had been necessary just for me to finally understand what it meant to live for another person.

When Elias finally broke the kiss, he pressed his forehead to mine. "I love you, Sunny Ray."

"And I love you."

THE NEXT MORNING, I pulled into my parking spot under the molting oak tree. Daisy was leaned against her car, waiting. The moment I cut the engine, she yanked opened my car door.

"Why didn't you tell me you and Brandon broke up?" She threw her arms around my neck, and I went rigid.

The group of girls gliding past threw passing glances in our direction, already cupping their hands around their mouths and whispering. And there goes the gossip train. . .

"Are you okay?" she asked.

"I'm fine."

I managed to slip out of her hold, and I reached into the back seat to grab my backpack. "We just both decided we're better as friends."

"Seriously, Sunny." Daisy's face screwed up. "Who does that?"

"It's not a big deal." I slung my backpack over my shoulder on my way across the parking lot.

I was maybe a foot away from the double door entrance of the school, right in the middle of the mass of sleepy-eyed students, stumbling like zombies into the building when Daisy grabbed the strap to my backpack. "Hold up!" She jerked me back a few steps. "You don't think there's another girl, do you?"

"Um. No."

"There better not be!" Daisy gave a warning glare before maneuvering past the cheerleaders attempting to tack a spirit banner over one of the doorways.

On our way through the congested corridor, she babbled about how she and Ben had thought Brandon and I were good together, how maybe I should give it time and see if I felt differently. She told me how she had imagined he and I getting married and having babies while I shoved my backpack in my locker.

I never responded with anything but a few head shakes and nods, a shrug here and there, but that was the beauty of Daisy Fulmer's tirades—you never had to say a word.

Elias was already slouched down in his chair when we got to Miss Weaver's class.

Daisy was still talking when she took her seat.

I dropped my books on my desk and fished out the necklace from my pocket on my way to Elias, and then I placed it on top of the ripped cover of his language book. "Think you misplaced this," I said.

Smiling, he picked it up and looped it around his neck, fastening the clasp. I wanted to kiss him or tell him I loved him before I went back to my desk, but I couldn't. Because no one could know.

When I dropped into my chair, Daisy's mouth was open. A confused-shocked-maybe slightly-appalled expression wrinkled her forehead. "What." She thumbed toward the back of the room. "Was that?"

Ignoring her, I opened my notebook and scribbled the date.

Daisy swatted at my arm. "Psst. Hello? What are you doing?"

"Getting ready to take notes."

She rolled her eyes along with her neck. "Seriously? I can't believe you." She leaned farther across the aisle. "Are you seeing him?" she whisper-hissed.

I tapped my pen on the edge of the desk. "Daisy. Not now."

The bell rang, and Miss Weaver closed the door while Daisy stared at me like I was the fourth horseman of the apocalypse. Horrified and in complete disbelief. "Not now? Are you mental?"

"Aarons. Andrews. Benson. Black. . ." Miss Weaver called roll.

"If you're doing what I think you're doing, your daddy's gonna—"

"Daisy?" Miss Weaver stood at the front of the class with her fists buried in the feminine flare of her hips.

"Here," Daisy said, not even bothering to look away from me.

Miss Weaver snapped her fingers. "I wasn't checking if you were here. I was trying to get you to be quiet."

The class snickered.

"Oh. Well. Okay." Daisy's desk dropped to the floor with a thud, and she gave me one last, flustered glance before scribbling something in her notebook. Seconds later, she ripped out the page, and then passed the note to me.

You aren't getting out of this.

I leaned back in my chair with a sigh, determined to find a way to tell Daisy what had happened without outing Brandon and without lying. Which would prove to be difficult since Daisy didn't take anything at face value. I was convinced, at seventeen, that girl could already carry out successful interrogations for the F.B.I.

DAISY GOT CALLED to the principal's office after school for shoving her tongue down Ben's throat in the hallway, which meant I managed to "get out of it" until four o'clock.

The door to my bedroom slammed against the wall, and I glanced up from the calculus book spread open on my bed. Daisy crossed her arms with a hard huff. "Such bullshit," she said, kicking the door closed behind her. "How many people do you see groping each other in the halls, and I'm the one who gets written up over it."

"It's because you're the preacher's daughter."

"Oh, I know it is. I'm like Hester-fucking-Prin except instead of a scarlet *A* I have a scarlet *P* on my chest." She grumbled something under her breath before laying across the foot of my bed. "Now. Before you start explaining this entire Elias ordeal, I want you to know that it's not nice to lie to your best friend." She snatched my math book away, thumbing through the pages before tossing it to the floor. "We'll never use that crap."

"I was trying to do my homework."

"You'll get the book back when you tell me what's going on."

"I don't know why you're so shocked." I huffed. "You said Brandon and I were worms."

"Come on, I just meant you guys acted like," she frowned. "Friends."

"Exactly. We just liked hanging out, and it took a minute to realize there wasn't anything there."

"So, I take it the sex wasn't like whoa or anything?"

Closing my eyes, I sighed. "There was no sex, Daisy."

"Damn. Good looking guys are wasted on you."

I grabbed my pillow and whacked her with it. "There's more to life than sex, Daisy."

"I know that, *Sunny*." She knocked the cushion to the floor. "Geez. So, Brandon's okay with everything?"

"Did you see us sitting together at lunch today? Did we seem okay?"

She narrowed her gaze at me.

"And before you ask. He knows about Elias."

"And. . ." She threw up her hands and closed her eyes for a second. "He's still *talking* to you? What is this life? There is no way Ben would still be civil to me if we broke up and I started dating some other guy. Sunny, breakups are supposed to be tragic and like life-altering. If the fifteen times we've watched *Cruel Intentions* hasn't taught you that, I don't know what will."

Fighting a laugh, I smoothed my hand over Daisy's hair. "Life is not like the movies."

"Don't tell me that. I like to think everything ends with a good song and everyone's life going just the way they planned." She sulked for a minute, obviously more devastated about my "breakup" than I was. "So now that you're seeing the forbidden one, how are you gonna manage that?"

"I figured a preacher's daughter with a penchant for romance novels would be just the person to help me figure that out."

A wicked grin flashed over her face. "And you are in luck. Being sneaky is my area of expertise."

25

ELIAS

The inside of the dollar movie theatre smelled a little like the guy's locker room—sweaty and mildewed. The good thing was, after a while, I got used to it.

I sat on the top row with a tub of popcorn and two sodas. Cherry for Sunny because that used to be her favorite. The entire auditorium was empty except for a couple at the bottom, already lip-locked by the time the previews started. I bounced my leg and crammed a handful of popcorn in my mouth before checking my watch. *Seven ten.*

Part of me worried Sunny might not show. That somehow her parents had found out about her plan to have Daisy drop her off. Everyone in Fort Morgan knew Mr. Lower, and most of the women here were in a tight-knit, gossip circle. All it would take was one person to see us together, and we'd be screwed. So having Daisy drop Sunny off to meet me at the deserted dollar movies was about as risky of a date as we could take. I hated that we had to sneak around. All it did was remind me that the world didn't want us together, and that was a shitty feeling.

The loud ring of gunfire boomed through the speakers followed by the high-pitched squeal of tires peeling rounding a corner. There was a flash of Tommy Lee Jones and some actress I didn't recognize, and then Sunny came jogging up the stairs. Damn, I smiled.

"Hey."

Before she'd managed to sit all the way down, I had my hand at the back of her neck and my lips to hers. I could have kissed her for hours, hard and long, but I wanted so much from Sunny, and we only had a limited amount of time. "Hey," I said, then pulled away to offer her the bucket of popcorn.

She grabbed a handful and settled back in the seat, placing her feet on the back of the chair in front of us. It was so easy between us like we were picking up right where we had left off.

I shoved some of the stale snack into my mouth. "Where do your parents think you are?"

"The Haunted Hayride thing with Ben and Daisy. Which, I would never pay someone to scare me like that. One chainsaw and I'm done for." She tasted her drink. "Cherry Coke?" Then smiled with her eyes as she took another sip. "You remembered?"

"I've never forgotten a single thing about you." I hadn't. I couldn't. You don't forget things about people you love.

"Green," she blurted, the loud theatrical music in the background almost drowning out her soft voice.

I tilted my head. "What?"

"Your favorite color is green. You only eat PB and Js if the crust is cut off, and your favorite song—at least when you were eight—was 'Look Away'."

"God, I haven't heard that song in forever."

"I listened to it all the time when I'd read over your letters."

I couldn't decide if the tight feeling in my stomach was pride or guilt over that comment, but I was leaning toward a little of both. I watched her take another helping of popcorn. I noticed the way she shook her leg a little, and while I remembered that Sunny liked Cherry Coke, I wanted to know the things she'd come to like since me. "So what kinda music do you listen to now?" I asked.

Narrowing her gaze in thought, she tapped a finger on her chin.

"And if you say that group that sings the theme song to *Dawson's Creek*, I'm gonna to judge you."

Her mouth dropped open, and a hand went to her chest like she was appalled.

"Don't tell me you watch that?"

"Shut up." She shoved me. "And no. My favorite band is Foo Fighters."

"That's acceptable." I winked at her. "They're mine, too."

And then I kissed her again, her tongue cold with the taste of cherry soda. Our lips didn't part even when the harsh, discordant sounds that accompanied every horror film known to man filled the theatre. Sunny barely jumped with the sound of a single gunshot and subsequent scream sounded through the speakers.

I couldn't tell anyone one thing that happened in the one-hour and fifty-five-minute movie, except that, by the end of it, my lips were sore, and I had fallen a little more in love with Sunny Ray Lower, even though I hadn't thought that was possible.

26

ELIAS

It had been three weeks since Sunny and I had started seeing each other, and I quickly learned that two things sucked about having to date her in secret. One was obvious, we only had stolen moments. Minutes here, and minutes there. If we were lucky, we would get a few solid hours.

The second reason it sucked was that mundane life chores could easily turn into a small form of torture.

Sundays were my favored day to go shopping. If I timed it just right, I would get in and out of the Piggly Wiggly before church let out, making me one of few people in the store. That's how I preferred it. Nothing grated my nerves more than standing in line behind some lady with a thousand coupons.

"Why did you make me come with you?" Judah opened the freezer door, grabbed a few Totino's Pizzas, and tossed them into the shopping cart.

"Because I'm sick of you eating my food. And when we get home, I'm writing my name on my stuff. You can write your name on yours. So help me God, if you eat something that's mine, I'm going to punch you." I had come home to an empty fridge more times than I could count.

Judah gave me a blank stare. "Atlas eats your food."

"Atlas is always at Doodles. He eats Doodle's food."

"I forgot something," he said. "I'll be back."

Ignoring him, I turned the shopping cart down aisle two in search of instant oatmeal and Captain Crunch. When Judah came back, he dropped three boxes of cookies and an economy pack of condoms on top of the groceries.

I stared down at the prophylaxis with a cocked brow. "I'm not paying for your dick sleeve."

"Come on, we can share them."

Turning to glare at my idiotic brother, I headed down the hygiene aisle and plowed right in to someone else's buggy. "Sorry, I..."

Mrs. Lower stood behind the shopping cart, Sunny right beside her with pink cheeks. My eyes must have lingered on Sunny too long because Mrs. Lower cleared her throat.

"Elias?" Her gaze strayed from my face to the tattoos on my arm, and I noticed her swallow because only bad kids had tats. The thing was that every single piece of ink held meaning. I looked at my tattoos as a poetic expression, not rebellion. Society, however, only saw a delinquent instead of fucking Edgar Allen Poe.

"Hey, Mrs. Lower," I said, then nodded in a how-do-you-do-way to my girlfriend. "Sunny."

"How have you been? How's your aunt Billie?"

"Good." I couldn't help but glance at Sunny again. "Pretty good."

"This must be one of your brothers." She glanced at Judah.

"Yeah."

We stood there with one of those *I know I should talk to*

you, but I don't know what to say, and this is getting awkward moments.

Finally, Mrs. Lower said, "I've, uh. I've come to a few of the games. You boys are pretty good."

"Thanks."

She fidgeted with her coupon book while Sunny shuffled her feet over the grimy grocery store tile. "You should come to church sometimes. It would be good to have you there." In small-town Alabama, that phrase was the go-to when someone had no idea what else to say.

"Yeah. Maybe. Well," I moved the cart to the side. "It was good to see you."

"You too." And then she and Sunny started around the corner of the aisle, the wheel on their buggy squeaking. Sunny looked over her shoulder, and I mouthed *I love you*.

With a smile, she thumbed at her chest and held up two fingers before she disappeared behind the shelving.

"Sick!" Judah snarled his lip then yanked the buggy out of my grip and headed toward the checkout. "How long have you been dating? Two weeks?"

"Three."

"And already with the, *'I love yous'*? You're a puss."

I grabbed the condoms and chucked them at him. "Buy your turkey chokers and shut up."

Judah unloaded his crap onto the conveyer belt, grumbling beneath his breath.

"And make sure you don't come back until ten tonight. She's coming over, and we're watching movies, so I need the living room."

With a laugh, Judah shook his box of latex. "Don't worry. I'll be busy. *Not* watching movies."

LATER THAT NIGHT, I sat in my floor with VHS tapes scattered around me. "*Lost Boys, The Never Ending Story,* or *The Goonies*?"

"You really expect me to pick between those?" Sunny flopped down on the couch with a bowl of ice cream.

"Hard. I know." I picked up *Lost Boys* and noticed the reel of tape was all on the right. "This one hasn't been rewound. Atlas!" He was the laziest asshole on earth. "So, I feel that should take *Lost Boys* out of the pick."

"Yeah. I don't wanna wait five minutes for it to rewind." Sunny slipped a whipped cream-covered spoon into her mouth. "*The Goonies*?"

I shoved the cassette into the VCR and pressed play. When the previews started, I settled on the end of the couch, and Sunny automatically reclined against my me, clutching the bowl of ice cream to her chest.

Most teenagers wouldn't keep their clothes on for five minutes in a dark room without adult supervision. But Sunny and I weren't most teenagers. There was something deeper between us than sex and hormones—not to say I didn't think about undressing her all the time. The desire was there, but so was the need to simply be with her.

"This is my favorite," she said, staring at the TV while she lifted a spoonful of ice cream over her head and into my mouth.

An unexpected mixture of chocolate and cream and caramel-toffee-something exploded on my tongue. "Holy shit." I swallowed that insane goodness down. "What is that?"

"My special recipe." She took a bite herself. "And don't even ask. I'm not at liberty to divulge the ingredients."

Moments like that were what got me with Sunny. Just lying on the couch and eating ice cream. Moments that weren't monumental but meaningful—that's what brought me to my knees with her.

"It's damn good. No wonder it's your favorite," I said.

"Not the ice cream, weirdo. This." She sat up and faced me, pressing her chilled lips to mine. "Being here with you."

"Good, because I'm planning for you to be stuck with me for a long time. Think of it as a life sentence, if you will."

"I wouldn't have it any other way."

We made it halfway through the movie before we stopped paying attention to anything but each other. After all, we'd seen *The Goonies* a million times.

We kissed, and I would have stopped at that, but her mouth eventually found its way to my neck and ear, and that tightened the sexual tension. First, my shirt went, and then her sweater. My jeans followed by hers. Between kisses, there were touches. Hesitant hands slipping places they had never been. Whispered pleas of *more. Again. Oh, God.*

We were a train without brakes, barreling down tracks and picking up steam with every stoke of the fire.

Hands turned into mouths exploring the salty taste of skin, creeping lower and lower.

By the time the credits rolled across the screen, Sunny was on my fingers, and I was in her mouth, with my eyes closed and my teeth working my lip. My hips bucked. Her mouth was soft and warm, and more than I could take.

I was right there when the alarm on her watch went off, and she shot up, wiping her mouth.

"Shit." She glanced at the time, and I fought the tightening sensation in my groin. "Shit," she said again. "I've gotta. . ." She snatched her sweater from the floor and pulled it over her head, the static causing her hair to stick up. "I'm gonna be late. My dad'll kill me." Before I could sit up, she had shimmied her jeans over her hips and was fighting to

cram her feet in her shoes. "I'll see you at school Monday."
She reached for the door.

"Two more minutes." I swallowed. "Fucking please."

She hurried across the room and gave me one, quick,
sloppy kiss. "I can't."

Groaning, I tossed my head back on the couch.

"I love you." The door opened.

"I love you, too."

Then it closed.

The sneaking around bullshit blew. Literally.

THAT NEXT MONDAY, Sunny wasn't at school. I called her
house when I got home, but her dad answered, and I had to
pretend I had the wrong number and ask for Josh.

Before class on Tuesday, Daisy strutted over, straight-
faced as she placed both hands on my desk and leaned over
to whisper, "Mono."

"What?"

"Sunny's not here because she has mononucleosis."

The ominous way Daisy said it, I expected thunder and
lightning to sound. She stared at me like it was something
horrible, so I glanced around the room, but no one was
paying attention to us. "What the hell is that?"

"Some kissing disease you must have given her."

"I'm not sick."

She straightened up and rolled those damned eyes of
hers. "Well, you will be. It's evidently super contagious." She
made an X with her fingers and held them in front of her as
she backed away. "So, you just like, stay out of my breathing-
bubble area."

Having grown up without health insurance, I didn't
know much about illnesses except that if I got a sore throat,

whiskey and honey helped, and if my fever broke one-hundred-five, I could go to the ER because, at that temperature, they couldn't turn me away. I could have had the bubonic plague three times, and I would have never known, but this mono crap sounded terrible.

During study hall, I went to the library, pulled the *M* encyclopedia, and sat at one of the tables next to a group of freshmen girls. One of them giggled and cupped her hand around her mouth before she leaned over to her friend.

Ignoring them, I thumbed through the thin pages until I found *mononucleosis*, and what a fucking vile virus it was. What I gathered from my research was that Sunny would be sick for weeks—months even.

Sinking in the chair, I wiped a hand over my face. For some reason, it literally felt like it was us against the world —viruses included.

27

ELIAS

NOVEMBER 1999

A fter two weeks of not talking to Sunny, I went stircrazy.

Every time I called her house, her parents answered, and I couldn't waltz up to her front door with flowers. My only means of communication came from the notes Daisy smuggled back and forth through Sunny's schoolwork which she dropped off and picked up every Monday and Wednesday.

Those notes were the only way I found out Sunny's mom had a bad habit of leaving the back door unlocked. Three nights in a row, Mrs. Lower locked that door, but on the fourth night, when I tried the knob, it turned. I paused. Sweat slicked my palms as I fought against the knot twisting my gut before I cracked the door just enough to slip inside the dark house.

Of course, sneaking into the Sheriff's house to visit his daughter—whom I had been strictly told to stay away from —may not have been the best idea. But I was desperate to see her, kiss her, tell her I loved her.

The floorboards groaned when I reached the bottom of

the stairs, and I froze like a deer in headlights. A stairwell had never looked so long or ominous. Each step served as a possible, noisy alarm that would wake her parents. Mr. Lower would likely arrest me and send me to juvie for breaking and entering.

The second my weight landed on that first step, the wooden planks creaked. I swiped a hand over my face, thinking there had to be another way. The latticework outside Sunny's window had been torn down not long after Mr. Lower caught me in her room so there would be no scaling the proverbial castle wall. No. The stairwell was the only option. Shaking my head, I grabbed hold of the railing and shook it a little. It was sturdy, and the rungs were wide enough to place the toe of my boot between. As I shimmied my way up, I realized love makes people do stupid things.

When I bolted past the Lower's closed bedroom door, I realized love actually made *me* do crazy-stupid things.

I snuck into Sunny's room, locked the door, and then checked to make sure the latch caught—I wasn't going to make that mistake again. Sunny laid asleep amongst a mountain of pillows and crumpled tissues. I tiptoed across toward her bed. The mattress dipped under my weight when I sat down, and she opened her eyes.

"Hey," I whispered, sweeping some of her tangled hair away from her face.

"Hey." The hoarse sound of her voice sent a twinge of guilt for waking her through my core.

"How you feeling?"

"Like death."

I stroked my knuckles over her worrisomely heated cheek. "Jesus, you're hot."

"Thanks. But I prefer to be called beautiful." She gave a weak smirk.

"Noted." I glanced at the medicine bottles and cups that cluttered her nightstand. "Can you take some more Tylenol or something? Cause, I'm no doctor, but you have a fever."

"I think so. Check the notepad."

I took the spiral steno book, trailing my fingertip down the charted times she'd had medicine, then I checked the clock. "Yeah, you need more." I took the pill bottle, dumped two capsules into my palm, and then handed them to her along with a half-empty glass of water.

She sat up to swallow them down before she fell back against the pillow mountain. "I feel selfish that I asked you to come over here," she said. "You're gonna get sick."

"Nah. But even if I do, it's worth it." As ridiculous as that sounded, I meant it.

"You're crazy."

"Obviously." I waved my hand around her room. "I did just creep into your house even though your dad hates me."

"He doesn't hate you."

I gave her a sure-he-doesn't glare.

"He's just. I don't know." She sat up and coughed. The way her chest rattled made mine go tight.

I crawled into bed, positioned myself against the headboard, and stretched out my arm. "Come here." I pulled her warm body to mine and kissed her forehead. "I missed you."

"I missed you, too."

We laid in silence, tracing our fingertips over one another's arms. "Have you ever wondered if Jimi Hendrix ate peanut butter sandwiches?"

"No." She laughed, then coughed a little. "Why would I wonder that? Oh, wait. Against the ruled to ask two questions?"

"There are no rules in Have You Ever, Sunny Ray. I was just stalling that time." I kissed her cheek. "And to answer your question, I always like to think about famous people doing normal stuff. Like eating cheap sandwiches and having to put stamps on bills."

"I doubt they pay their own bills."

"They probably don't make their own peanut butter sandwiches either. Okay, your turn."

Her finger drew a zigzag over my chest. "Have you ever. . .wondered if maybe the world is just some tiny blood cell floating along in some giant's bloodstream?"

I felt my brows raise, and I placed my hand against her forehead again. "Do we need to take your temperature? That sounds like the fever is really getting to you."

She gave me a look. "I'm not that sick."

"Okay. Well, no. I can one-hundred percent, honestly say I have never thought about that."

Inhaling, I tried to come up with some Have You Ever question to top that one, and while I struggled, Sunny snuggled into the crook of my neck.

"Whatever it is about you that always makes me feel better, I sure do like it." She buried her nose in my shirt and took a deep breath. "And I like the way you smell familiar and good."

"Yeah?" I rested my chin on the top of her head. "I like the way you smell, too."

"What? Like dirty bedsheets."

"Nah, like the girl I'm madly in love with," I said.

"How lucky am I to be a girl who's madly in love with a boy who's madly in love with her?"

"I think we're the luckiest people in the world."

Sunny draped an arm over my stomach and, soon enough, the rise and fall of her chest fell into the rhythm of sleep.

I held her as the clock changed from eleven to twelve,

then twelve to one, believing I had unlocked the mysterious meaning of life that seemed to evade so many unfortunate souls. Possibly because of its simplicity.

Life was about stolen moments that harbored no real significance but made you feel alive.

The meaning was that uncomplicated.

28

SUNNY

DECEMBER 1999

The mono kept me down for a total of five long weeks.

During that time, Elias came over more nights than not, and somehow, he never got caught. Even more impressive, he never came down with mono. I told him he must be immune. Elias said he was hopeful his apparent insusceptibility meant he was a descendant from some mutant, subhuman species.

And he thought I was weird for the whole blood cell in a giant's body theory...

DAISY'S PARENTS went to some Man of the Cloth retreat in Atlanta the first week of December. As far as our parents knew, she and I had an epic girl's night planned, complete with a tub of chocolate chip cookie dough and *Pretty in Pink*.

Momma kissed my cheek and loaded me down with a two-liter of Coke and some face masks she thought Daisy and I would enjoy.

Maybe that's why the guilt ate me up inside. She wasn't

sending her only daughter off for a night full of gossip and chatter, she was sending her off to lose her virginity to the boy they would never approve of.

FORT MORGAN WAS such a small town. The only roads that had proper streetlamps were the Parkway and Highway 59 that led all the tourists down to the beach, and the glow from the Krispy Kreme was often compared to the Vegas lights.

The neon sign for Pickled Pig's Quick Stop flew past the window. Instead of pumping the brakes and taking a right into her subdivision, Daisy kept straight at a steady fifty miles an hour in a forty zone.

"Are you nervous?" Daisy asked, turning the radio down.

"Not really."

"Don't expect much the first time. To be honest, I had to ask Ben if we'd done it. It was over like that." She snapped her fingers.

"Wow. Sounds amazing." It didn't matter to me if it lasted one second or one hour, I just wanted to be as close as humanly possible to Elias Black. I wanted him on me, in me, and more importantly, I wanted there to never be anyone else that knew me like he would once tonight was over.

"You know." She tapped on the steering wheel. "This has come full circle. Here I am covering up your secret relationship with Elias. Again. Except this time, instead of love letters and phone calls, I'm dropping you off for a sleepover at his house. The mountain of lies is growing steep."

"It's what best friends do," I said. "Besides, don't act like telling your mom I was coming over wasn't a cover for you, too. So, you and Ben are welcome."

I pointed through the windshield. "It's the third drive on the left."

"The one with the crooked mailbox?"

Daisy's brakes squeaked when she slowed to turn into Elias' drive. The engine idled, shaking the hood while the headlights cast eerie shadows over the front of his tiny house.

Daisy leaned over the steering wheel and peered through the windshield with a somewhat horrified expression on her face. "This is uh. Nice."

"Give him a break. He pays for it himself."

"Is it clean?"

I shoved her door open. "Yes. It's clean. I swear, you'd think your daddy would have taught you to be less judgy."

Holding up one hand, she scoffed while I closed the door. "I'm not judging," she said.

"You totally were."

"So, if your mom calls, I'll just tell her you're in the bathroom and then call Elias on a three-way."

"You're so conniving, it's worrisome."

She drew an invisible *P* on her chest. "I've gotta earn that preacher's kid title before graduation." Smiling, she backed up, the red glow of the taillights reflecting off Elias' truck.

By the time I reached the first step of his porch, Elias was already waiting at the door. His lips were on mine before I'd made it inside, and he swatted blindly at the door until it clicked shut.

Hands and mouths and a lot of bumping into walls on the way to his bedroom. My chest was tight with excitement and fear and what ifs. Suddenly, I was terrified I would do something wrong, scared of how ridiculous it must look for two people to have their naked bodies tangled together. Worried I wouldn't be as good as other girls had been . . .but never once did I worry I was making a mistake. That was the one thing I was certain of. Nothing with Elias would ever be a mistake.

And no matter what happened, I wanted this with him. No one else.

The back of my legs bumped against the mattress, and my heart went into a crazy hiccup. Elias kissed me until I couldn't breathe, until I felt if I stayed in these clothes for a second longer, they would eat through my skin like acid rain.

I broke the kiss, sliding my hands from his shoulders to his chest and then to the hem of his navy-blue shirt. I lifted the material the way I imagined a collector would peel the protective shield off a fine piece of art. Slowly, inch by inch.

I tried to memorize each dip of his muscles and the hair that disappeared underneath the waist of his jeans. And once both our shirts were crumpled on the floor, we just stood there. Staring, touching. Using our fingertips and mouths as silent confessions of love.

"God," he whispered against my neck. "You're so beautiful." Beautiful meant so much more than hot or sexy.

Somewhere between the kisses and touches and our shoes and pants coming off, we ended up on the bed. Skin to skin.

That very new sensation quickly became my favorite— the way his warm body pressed against mine, how much closer I felt to him with nothing separating us that wasn't *us*. It was just he and I, and this moment that no one could take away.

Elias worked his mouth over my collarbone, and I lazily circled my fingertip around his sun tattoo.

"That was my first tat." His lips met mine. "For you."

"So, you did save some of your firsts for me?"

"I saved them all for you." He hovered over me, one expression after the other creeping onto his face slow like a lazy summer's night.

Certainly, he didn't mean sex. He must have given that away long ago to some girl in the back of his truck, because that's what bad boys did—only Elias wasn't really bad. "All?" I asked.

"Every. Last. One," he said, and I kissed him hard and long, breathing I love you against his lips.

His mouth eventually worked down my stomach to places only he had seen or touched. Each touch, each kiss built until my body felt like a fault line bearing the brunt of some incredible tension.

"Are you sure?" he mumbled against my throat.

"Yeah." I swallowed, trailing my fingers over his back. "I'm so sure."

I pretended to ignore when he grabbed a condom because it felt embarrassing. I closed my eyes, waiting for his weight to settle between my thighs.

More kisses and touches and just when he positioned himself between my legs, his brow creased. "I may not," he wet his lips. "You know, be very good at first."

"I may not either."

And then slowly, everything changed. It was nothing like I expected. It was clumsy and perfect. Passionate. A mess of tangled limbs and heavy breathes. Of feeling vulnerable and eternally connected because you can only give this part of yourself away once. We faded into each other in ways only people who love one another can. This was so much more than sex. It was two people who had long ago fallen in love with each other's souls finally falling in love with each other's bodies.

29

SUNNY

A my Grant's "I'll Be Home for Christmas" channeled through the speakers of the Piggly Wiggly. I had the pregnancy test buried under a pack of Soft Batch cookies and toilet tissue while I stood in the middle of the aisle trying to find a cashier who may not know I was Sheriff Lower's daughter.

The lady at register two had bottle-blonde hair and electric-blue eyeshadow. The black smock emblazed with the smiling pig ironically wearing a butcher's hat didn't conceal her massive, Dolly Parton chest. The little name tag tacked to her left boob read: Krystal.

Smiling, Krystal waved me over.

I tried to act nonchalant when I unloaded the basket, making a teepee out of the cookies and the tissues that I slipped the E.P.T under.

"Going to a Christmas party?" She popped her gum.

The toilet tissue toppled over on top of the test when she grabbed the cookies. The register beeped when she passed them over the scanner.

"No. No party," I said.

"Well, hey Sunny."

No! I closed my eyes and pretended that was not Miss Weaver's voice I heard behind me.

"You getting ready for Christmas?"

That was totally Miss Weaver. The cashier picked up the toilet paper, and I had to distract my language arts teacher from what was now alone on the conveyer belt, so I spun around with a forced smile plastered to my face,

"Hi, Miss Weaver. You look amazing! I like that snowman sweater. It's very festive." Sweat pricked over my forehead. "Like super, incredibly festive!" I giggled—like a nervous, little schoolgirl.

"Oh." She glanced down and thumped the silver bell hanging from the snowman's neck. "I'm going to a faculty Christmas party."

Beep. There went the tissues. The bag rustled when Krystal dropped them in.

"Cool." I nodded so hard I could have given myself a concussion. "So, um do all the teacher's go to that? You know, the faculty party?"

Her brows furrowed. I couldn't have been acting guiltier if I tried, so I shouldn't have been shocked when her gaze strayed behind me.

Beep.

Her eyes widened, and I knew she'd seen it. My cheeks heated, my neck, my ears.

"Total's gonna be fifteen-sixty-seven, hun." By the time the cashier had bagged that test, my entire body felt like it was engulfed in flames.

Krystal popped her gum again. I crammed a wadded-up twenty bucks I'd earned from making Honor Roll into her hand and snatched up the bag. I was already past register four before I heard her shout that I'd left my change.

"It's yours. Merry Christmas!"

A freezing drizzle filtered through the air, and I swore under my breath at Daisy for parking at the end of the lot. My fingers were frozen by the time I passed behind the cloud of exhaust puffing from her tailpipes. I slung open the door, threw the bag into the floorboard, and sank into the seat. The heater stung my already heated face.

"Well," I said. "Miss Weaver saw me and your test."

Daisy pressed her forehead against the steering wheel. "I'm sorry."

"It's fine. What else are friends for? If Momma asks, I'll say I bought it for Jenny."

I thought that may make Daisy laugh, but her head was still against the wheel, her shoulders jumping—and not from laughing. Damn, she was crying, and while I understood, I couldn't imagine what she was going through.

Staring through the fogged windshield, I rubbed her back. "It's okay," I said even though it wasn't.

It wasn't even close to okay, especially if that test came back positive, but sometimes when you know someone can't take much more, a little white lie doesn't hurt.

Daisy wiped her face and leaned back against the seat, arms straight and fingers clutching the steering wheel so hard her knuckles washed white. "Yeah. It'll be okay. I'll just like, move out or join a nunnery or just not tell them."

"You have to tell them."

"Nope. Sweatshirts hide all kinds of things." She jerked the gearshift into reverse, and we pulled out of the Piggly Wiggly parking lot, driving in silence until we reached the Circle K a few blocks over for her to take the test. Neither one of us wanted to try to explain a used pregnancy test in our trash.

We sat in the car with the headlights reflecting off the

white cinder block wall. Daisy fished the test out from the shopping bag.

"Want me to go with you?" I asked

"No."

The door shut, and I listened to the Christmas music playing on the radio while she disappeared into the bathroom to the side of the building.

"O Holy Night," "Frosty the Snowman," and "The Twelve Days of Christmas" had all played before Daisy emerged from the rundown restroom, eyes puffy and arms crossed over her chest.

She went straight to the pay phone on the corner. I watched in the rearview as she shook her head. I cringed when she banged her palm over the glass. I went to reach for the door handle, but then she slammed the phone back on the receiver, slipped out of the booth, and stormed back to the car.

"Asshole!" She pushed the heel of her hands against her eyes. "God. Ben's an asshole."

"What did he say?"

"Oh, he's really upset about football. You know." Her voice grew louder, bordering on hysterical. "How a baby will screw with his ability to play goddamn college football! Then he asked how I knew it was his!"

I sat frozen, unsure what to do. I feared calling Ben a dick may enrage her even more, but I sure wasn't going to suggest everything would be okay again. Because this was in no way okay. I couldn't help myself. I mumbled dickwad under my breath.

"Super." Daisy sucked in a breath. "Massive." And another. "Dickwad."

I leaned over the console and wrapped my arms around her, attempting to hold her while she sobbed. After about four seconds, she swatted me away, and there I sat, staring at the floorboard while "Grandma Got Ran Over by a Reindeer" hummed through her speakers, and a man dressed in a crummy Santa suit stumbled out of the gas station with a twelve pack of Milwaukee's Best. I turned off the radio, figuring festive, upbeat music wouldn't help anything at that moment.

Finally, I grabbed the tissues along with the Soft Batch, tearing both open and handing over a tissue followed by three cookies. "Here," I said.

Daisy glanced down at the items, frowning. "This blows." She took the cookies and left me with the tissues, and then we swapped places. I drove us back to my house where we pretended everything was the way it used to be when we were kids.

Before boys. Before sneaking around. When we all still had some hope.

30

ELIAS

Atlas made it halfway through the door before he dropped his end of the Christmas tree. "That shit is sharp!" He yanked a few green needles out of his shirt.

"Just pick the thing up, and stop being a sissy."

Scowling, he showed me his middle finger, and then grabbed hold of the tree again. By the time we had toted it to the corner of the room, we were covered in pine needles and sap.

"Why are we even putting up a stupid tree?" Atlas grumbled.

I went to my hands and knees, then laid on my stomach so I could tighten the knobs on the old, rusted tree stand. "Because it's Christmas."

He leaned around the branches, glaring at me. "We've never had a tree in our life!"

"Well, shit's changing."

"It's 'cause of Sunny." Judah sang from the hallway.

"Whatever." Atlas shook the tree to make sure it was

secure, and pine needles showered down on my shoulders just as the doorbell rang.

Judah grumbled, "Bahumbug" when he opened the door.

"I always pegged you for a Scrooge, Judah." I heard Sunny laugh.

"It smells like pine scented air freshener in here," he said. "Thanks to you."

"Everyone needs some holiday cheer."

Judah guffawed. "Holiday beer's more like it."

I crawled out from underneath the tree, brushing the needles off my shoulders. Sunny directed her attention to me and pointed at Judah. "How is he related to you?"

"It's questionable if he even is."

Shaking his head, Judah lumbered back down the hallway, and seconds later his door banged shut.

I took my keys from the counter and headed toward the door.

"How can he not like Christmas?" Sunny asked.

"Because we've never had one."

THE DRIVE to Daphne takes about forty minutes. It took fifty to get to the Walmart, away from the crowds of familiar faces. The air outside was crisp and cold. Our breath made tiny clouds against the dark sky as we fell into the fold of Christmas shoppers flooding the clusterfuck of a parking lot.

As we neared the entrance, the jingle of a bell rang out over the hustle and bustle surrounding us. Sunny dropped some change into the Salvation Army bucket, and the man in the ratty Santa beard gave a swift nod followed by, "*God Bless.*"

Sunny wrangled a buggy from the bay while I watched the wall of people gathered by the Rollback Bin arguing in the true spirit of Christmas.

We had been in the store a total of five minutes, and it was already proving to be too much. "Christmas shit's over there, isn't it?" I pointed over the bobbing heads toward the garden area.

An amused expression danced on her face. "It's not shit but yes."

Sunny kept muttering, "Excuse me. Excuse me" while we maneuvered our squeaky-wheeled shopping cart down the walkway, around screaming toddlers and overflowing buggies until she whirled down an aisle with ornaments and tinsel strewn across the floor.

"You wanna do the traditional thing or something fancy?" She picked up a discarded box of silver, glitter-covered ornaments. Some icicles. Some orbs.

I took the package from her, studying it even though I didn't care what we bought, just that it was what she wanted. Every single sweep she made of the decorations, her eyes always landed on the silver icicles and a tube of iridescent, white balls.

I tossed the icicle ones into the cart, then I grabbed two more boxes. "These and.." I snagged a few tubes of the white balls. "These." I tried not to smile when I saw her face light up.

"How did you know?" she asked.

"Just did." I kissed her forehead before picking out a strand of white lights—because you don't put colorful lights on a fancy tree—and we headed to the check out like a couple of adults.

WHEN WE GOT BACK to my house, Sunny put on Christmas music and tore into the boxes of ornaments like they were the best thing she'd ever been bought.

Elvis Presley's "Blue Christmas" played in the background as we decorated the pathetic, lopsided tree in my living room. I thought it was cute. Sunny sang along to the radio while making sure each ornament was in its rightful place.

I hooked an icicle onto one of the low-hanging branches, wondering if this was how Christmas felt to everyone else, full of hope and love and promise, or if that was just because of Sunny.

"We're gonna keep these forever, right?" she asked.

"Of course. I'm all about the sentimental crap."

She went back to singing.

I couldn't see her on the backside of the tree, but I took a handful of tinsel and threw it in her direction. A clump caught on the branches. She grabbed it and chucked it at me.

Before long, we were in a full-blown tinsel war. Metallic strands lay scattered across the carpet, the arm of the recliner, they hung from the fan blades. Sunny ended up pinned underneath me, out of breath and giggling with silver strands like moonbeams in her hair. I couldn't get enough of moments like this.

I was convinced what we had was something most people looked for their entire lives, few ever finding. Because the way I loved her was completely and utterly, a way that made me feel like I had a purpose. And to be anything in life, a person always need something other than themselves. Without words, men could not be poets, and without her, I could not be whole.

"Promise me," I said, laying my lips against hers. "We'll always be like this."

"I promise."

"You're my damn world, Sunny." I kissed her, hard then soft.

Her hand swept over my cheek. "Let's go to your room."

WE LEFT the tree half decorated and ended up naked in my bed, sweat-slicked and panting whispered I love yous while Christmas music played in the background.

And when it was over, we laid there, Sunny's cheek to my chest. "Can we play Have You Ever?"

"Of course." I shifted in the bed to get more comfortable. "Have you ever stuck your tongue to a flagpole?" I asked.

"That's a hard no. Are you running out of have you evers?"

"No. Your turn."

"Have you ever accidentally drank spoiled milk?"

My nose curled at that. "God yes. Pretty sure that's a passage in life. Have you ever seen a shooting star?"

"No," she said.

"That's sad."

She walked her fingers over my stomach, then drew in a deep breath. "Have you ever thought about if you would leave me if I got pregnant?"

The blood drained from my face down to my toes, my heart stalling as I lifted my head. All I could think about was how careful we'd been, about how much her father would hate me. "No. God no, I wouldn't leave you. Why would you think. . . Are you?" I gulped air.

"Oh. No, no."

My head fell back against the pillow, my skin tingling from an unwelcome dose of adrenaline buzzing through it.

"Daisy's pregnant," Sunny said.

The radio went to a commercial break, and we fell silent. I felt her swallow, and I stared at the ceiling, brushing my hand through her long hair while I contemplated what the hell would happen if that were us and not Daisy. We could be as careful as we wanted, but nothing in life was foolproof.

"Her dad's gonna lose it," I said finally.

"Yeah, and to top it off, Ben dumped her."

"What?" I got a sick kink in my stomach. "That's shitty. I thought he was better than that?" I pulled Sunny a little closer.

"Yeah. Well. Momma always preaches not to judge a book by its cover," she said, dragging a finger up the middle of my stomach. My skin broke out in goosebumps. "She's right. You shouldn't because some books with pretty words on the inside have terrible covers."

And wasn't that the truth?

31

SUNNY

NEW YEAR'S EVE 1999

Hailey Moore's kitchen was packed with students from Robertsdale, and a few randoms from Lockhart.

I plugged a finger in my ear and pressed my new cell phone to the other while Mother instructed me for the hundredth time not to leave Hailey's house. She went on and on about Y2K, and how, at midnight, we may experience a universal blackout because the computers would all crash. "Airplanes could fall from the sky..."

I rolled my eyes at that. You couldn't convince me that mankind could figure out open heart surgery and create the internet but that they hadn't planned for the calendars to tick over to 2000.

"I promise, Momma," I said. "I'm not leaving."

"And don't let Daisy leave either. Brandon. Ben. None of you leave!"

Laughing, I reassured her we were staying put, and then I slipped the bright orange Nokia into my purse while Hailey's dad made his way through the crowd, collecting keys.

When he passed by me, he stopped. "You aren't gonna tell your dad on me for letting you kids drink?"

"No, sir."

"Good." His eyes crinkled at the corners. "Rather you kids be here where at least I know you're not out driving around."

I dropped my keys into his waiting palm, then he moved onto the group of girls behind me.

"Two hours until triple zero, people!" Ben shouted from the dining room.

I clenched my jaw. I hated him for what he had done to Daisy—ditching her because he didn't understand what love meant.

Brandon leaned against the wall beside me. "Want me to punch him?"

"I wish."

"Maybe he'll come around?"

I watched Ben chug a beer and smile like his whole world was perfectly fine. And I guess, maybe it was. He didn't have morning sickness, he still had no responsibility. He had passed that all off on Daisy.

"Doubtful," I said, glancing back just in time to see Brandon's eyes lock on something across the room. I followed his stare which ended on Darren Hill the tall, blond laughing amongst a group of soccer players. Darren was Travis' new boyfriend. Aside from Brandon, Elias and I were the only people who knew about that.

"It's hard, huh?" I leaned against him.

"I think what makes it the hardest." A deep line sunk between Brandon's brows. "No one knows we were anything to each other. That kinda makes it feel like it never even happened."

I knew exactly what he meant. Most of the things we

tend to keep hidden are wrong or dirty, secrets we don't want anyone to know about. I'm convinced having to hide the dizzying bliss love creates takes a little something away from a person's soul, and who wants to feel like loving someone is shameful?

Daisy crossed the room, water bottle in hand. "I figured this will be the last outing I ever get," she said. "Soon I'll be grounded until my own kid's eighteen!"

It had almost been three weeks since Daisy took the test in the Circle K bathroom, and her parents were still none the wiser.

"You're gonna tell them?" I deadpanned her.

"I have to. I've got a doctor's appointment on the tenth, and they'll see the bill from insurance. Figured I'll tell them on the fifth."

"Why the fifth?"

"That's the day we go back to school." She took a sip of water. "I'll write a note on the dry erase board Mom puts to-do list on. Get milk, eggs, cheese. Daisy's knocked up." She almost smiled. "That should give them a few hours for it to sink in before I have to look them in the eyes." Resting her head on my shoulder, she exhaled. "I should've listened to you. I evidently have no idea how to do life."

I hooked my arm around her neck and swept my fingers through her hair. "Nah. I don't know how this whole life thing works out either, Daisy. But we'll figure it out."

Brandon moved to Daisy's other side and draped an arm around her.

And there we stood, three friends trudging into the New Year all with secrets that left us feeling a little broken inside for very different reasons.

At Thirty minutes to midnight, I was sprinting down Hailey's paved driveway.

The cold air stung my lungs, but I picked up my pace when the headlights of Elias' truck shined over the mailbox. I hopped in, scooting to the middle seat and pressing my lips to his before the door had even closed.

Elias finally broke the kiss and put the truck in drive, holding my hand and steering with the other as we drove off. I could never get close enough, and that was how I knew what we had was real. There were not enough days in a lifetime to grow tired of the way he felt like a sunrise and sunset all at the same time, warm and comforting. He was the promise of a new day and the possibilities of tomorrow.

We wove along the curved backroads that looped through the marshland, past the state park and down Rural Route 21 until the road teed off at the Parkway.

"Twenty minutes," Elias said when he pulled into the beach parking. He cut the engine, smiling like he knew some secret to the universe he'd yet to disclose to me. Then he grabbed his backpack from the floorboard, opened the door, and we took off, our shoes pounding over the cold, worn boardwalk as we raced toward the beach.

"When did you get so slow?" he called over his shoulder with a laugh when he hit the end of the walkway and nearly tripped. Sand sprayed up behind him as he hurried toward our spot by the water's edge.

By the time I caught up, I was out of breath, and he already had a quilt spread out.

"You know, you're like a foot taller than me, and"—I gasped for a breath—"you're stride's longer." Then I collapsed onto the soft blanket.

Elias pulled a small boombox out of his backpack followed by a bottle of Korbel and two plastic flutes. I felt my cheeks ache from a grin. While it was cheesy, it was sweet and romantic, and any girl would swoon over such a gesture.

"Aren't you fancy?"

"Only the best for my girl." He winked, then flipped the switch to the stereo. The speakers crackled, the CD whirred, and Elias hit the skip button several times before he was happy. The rumble of the waves nearly swallowed the easy-going strum of acoustic guitars. I adjusted the volume while Elias worked to strip the gold foil from the neck of the champagne.

"You do realize 'Crash' is super cliché?" I said.

"I do," he winked as he held the bottle away from us and pushed on the cork. It shot off with a loud *pop,* landing somewhere down the beach. "I don't know if you've notice, but I'm a helpless romantic."

"You mean hopeless romantic?"

"No. I mean helpless. Hopeless would suggest I'm in despair over loving you, all I am is powerless to it, Sunny Ray."

Leaning in, I smiled. "I feel like I have my very own Shakespeare." I kissed him while Dave Matthews sang to the rolling waves and the last cold air of the millennium whirled around us, until all I could taste was him, and it felt like we were breathing for each other. Until it felt like the world was spinning and spinning while we were sitting still, lips to lips. Heart to heart. Soul to soul.

We were Romeo and Juliet in Act II. Hopelessly—tragi-cally helpless—in love.

"I love you," I whispered against his parted lips.

He passed one of the glasses to me. "I love you, too."

I watched the tiny, effervescent strands dance along the

sides like pearls caught in a tumultuous sea, and when I went to take my first sip, Elias shook his head.

"We have to toast," he said.

"Right. How so very adult of us."

"To four more months," he said.

I cocked my ear, trying to figure out what his smirk was about. "What's in four months?"

"It's when you'll be old enough to marry me if you wanted." Elias held up his hand. A small diamond ring was gripped between his fingers. The moment was reminiscent of the day in my tree house when he promised he'd come back for me, except, this time he wasn't leaving, he was vowing to stay.

He slipped the ring on my finger. The stone was a speck of a diamond set on a silver band, and it was perfect because it was mine.

"You may be like the sun in a lot of ways," he said. "And I may be like the moon, because I'll fall for you, day after day. I'll chase you until the planets fade into an oblivion. But the thing is, the sun and the moon? They'll only ever spend a few minutes of their lifetime together. I don't want a few minutes. I want *every* minute." His lips pressed to mine in a featherlight touch. "You're my world, Sunny Ray 'cause the minute you're gone, some part of me stops existing."

Parting my lips, I clung to him and fell back—half on the blanket, half on the sand—and I brought him with me.

"Marry me?"

There was no hesitation, no wondering if we were possibly too young to understand what love was, because how could I be too young for something my heart was capable of? So I whispered *yes* over and over between kisses.

Fireworks crackled and fizzled far down the beach. The

muted echo of strangers singing "Happy New Year" rang out as we fought to gracelessly untangle ourselves from sweaters and boots and jeans. I let myself fall drunk on his promises and the way his fingers tangled in my hair, and even though it was freezing, the second his skin covered mine, the very moment he slid into me, I couldn't feel anything except the boy I would forever believe loved me in a way that was too good for me.

32

SUNNY

JANUARY 2000

I nstead of going back to school on January fifth, I ended up at Coconut Larry's with the rest of the early-bird crowd, waiting for Daisy to come out of the restroom. It was cold outside and about eighty degrees inside, which caused the windows to fog. I watched a drop of condensation trickle down the glass before I wrote Elias' name in a heart.

The table shook when Daisy slammed her palms over it and slid into the booth.

"Why do I have to pee all the time? The thing can't be any bigger than like a peanut or something."

The waitress sat a basket of steaming, grease-slicked hash brown tots on the table. Daisy took one look at them and gagged while shoving them as far away as she could.

"You love Larry's Breakfast Tots." I pointed at them.

"My mouth is full of I'm-going-to-toss-my-guts-spit right now."

I snatched the up basket and placed it in my lap, hoping if she didn't look at them she wouldn't vomit.

Daisy leaned back in the both, her face completely

drained. "Are your parents gonna kill you for skipping school?"

"My mom'll understand."

"Wait! You told her?" Daisy's brows shot up.

I crammed a greasy tot in my mouth and chewed it for a second, wondering how she could even rationalize that by now the phone lines weren't lit up with gossip about the pregnant preacher's kid. "No." I swallowed. "But I'm sure your mom has called my mom. *Someone's* mom has called her."

"People need to mind their own business." She sank down further in the booth. "I almost got out of there. The message was genius though, I started it with, *Guess what? I have my tongue pierced.* Then I added, *Also, I'm knocked up.* I figured it was best to come clean with all the things." She drummed her fingers on the table. "I was about to add *what a way to ring in the New Year* for a bit of comic relief, but that was when Mother came in from the garage. She evidently forgot her Weight Watcher's calculator and just had to come back for it. Foiled my entire plan."

"What did she do?"

"At first, she just stood there, looking at the board, then the marker in my hand. I kinda mumbled, *surprise*, and she started sobbing. Eventually, after a lot of screaming and crying, she prayed over me. Then she cried some more."

Cramming another tot in my mouth, I shook my head. "Does your dad know?"

"He was already at the church. Thank God. My guess is, I'll be in an all girl's boarding school by mid-week."

"You will not."

"Hopefully not. I figure I can argue that an all girl's school isn't going to un-impregnate me." Daisy's elbows hit the table with a thud before she buried her face in her hands. "What am I supposed to do, Sunny?"

The waitress stopped by to refill Daisy's Sprite, although it was nearly full. *Eavesdropper.* I waited until she moved on to the next patron before I answered Daisy. "What *can* you do?"

"Go back in time and never date that asshole?" She dragged her hands down her cheeks, pulling at her eyes until she looked like some mutant zombie with her lower eyelids stretched out and red. "It's not fair that Ben just gets to go on his merry way."

"When his parents find out, I'm sure they'll make him—"

"That's the thing, I don't want them to *make* him do anything. I was supposed to mean more to him than that. God, my life is over."

A teen pregnancy. Sure, I could see how it seemed like the end of the world, and in some ways, for Daisy, it would be. It would be the end of parties and most likely an ax in her plans to attend South Florida. It was a big kink in our plans to have kids when we were thirty so they could grow up together. It was losing the freedom to sleep in late and stay up until all hours of the night, and instead, going full-speed from adolescence into adulthood. But really, once the chaos of it ran its course, once the heartbreak and betrayal subsided, it wasn't the end of anyone's world. Just the beginning of a new one.

"It's not over, Daisy," I said. "It's just gonna be different."

She rubbed her lips together while bouncing her leg so hard her entire body shook. "Easy for you to say." Tears welled in her eyes. "The guy you're dating wants to marry you, and you aren't pregnant!"

"Look, Ben's a dick. You're knocked up, and sure, it's crap, but I'll still be here. Brandon will be here. Your parents will calm down and still be here. It's just not what you had planned, but really, I don't think anyone gets the life they planned."

TWO HOURS LATER, Daisy and I checked into school. Cramps were always an excuse the guy in the registrar's office never questioned.

And when I got home that evening and went to the fridge to grab a Coke, Momma was waiting at the table.

"Um." I offered a confused smile. "Hi?" I grabbed the soda and cracked it open before setting my backpack on the counter.

"Daisy's mother called me this morning," Momma said, her voice full of pity.

"Figured." I took a seat beside her at the table. Instead of looking at her, I focused on wiggling the can tab back and forth until it eventually broke off.

"How long have you known?"

I shrugged because that wasn't lying; it was a nonverbal, I'm not going to tell you.

"I know you aren't seeing anyone, but I also know that teenager's get urges, and I just want to make sure that—"

With a mouthful of soda, I shook my head and coughed. I did not want to go down this road with her. Again. "Mother, we had this talk after. . ." I swallowed Elias' name down. "Um, when I was fifteen. We don't need to have it again."

"Just. If the occasion ever arises." She tapped her hand on the placemat, and I caught a twinge of pink painted her cheeks at her choice of words. "I hope you'll use the proper precaution."

"Don't worry." I pushed up from the table, and just when I rounded the doorway, I heard Momma whisper, "She was such a good girl."

It seemed it didn't take much to strip the people I cared for of their "good enough" title.

33

ELIAS

FEBRUARY 2000

The temperature rarely dropped below forty degrees in Fort Morgan, so I was a little disoriented when I woke up an hour late with my bedroom freezing.

No lights. No power. Some transformer down the street had blown due to ice.

Ice, because it had dropped down to twenty-nine and rained.

I skirted through a stop sign, my back tires slipping on a patch of black ice. As luck would have it, I caught the flash of red and blue lights in my rearview.

Groaning, I pulled over on the corner of Seabreeze and Sawgrass, right in front of someone's manatee mailbox, then I sifted through the junk in my glove compartment looking for my registration.

The dreaded tap, tap, tap came on my window, and when I turned to grab the handle and manually roll it down, I froze. Mr. Lower had his head turned toward his shoulder, talking into the walkie-talkie clipped to his uniform. That was fucking great.

I wound the window down. "Hey, Mr. Lower."

"Elias?" He tipped the brim of his hat—out of habit I guess. "You had a taillight out, son."

"Shit. Didn't realize. Sorry, sir."

"Mmm." His chest inflated like one of those puffer fish, and the breath he finally blew out made a large, white cloud in the cold air. "License and registration."

"Yes, sir." I handed both items to him, watching his eyebrows pinch together as he studied them. "How's your aunt?"

"Good. Real good." Aunt Billie could have been dead adm I wouldn't have known. I clutched the steering wheel and nodded, then he passed the documents back, along with a ticket. *Asshole.* And I thanked him because what else was I going to do?

"I sure hope the things I've heard the guys at the station saying about you ain't true."

My heart stuttered. Enough that a slow sweat popped out on my forehead, pore by pore.

Surely to God, he didn't know about Sunny and me, not that it would have mattered in a few months anyway. As much as I respected him, as much as I refused to ever drive a wedge between his daughter and him—because I understood his concern, I did—what he thought about me wouldn't be able to keep Sunny away from me once he no longer had a legal hold on her.

"I'm not sure what you're talking about." I swallowed. "Sir."

His fingers drummed on the side of my truck. Another puff of fog. "All I'm gonna say is, don't follow in your daddy's footsteps, Elias. You're better than that." His lips flattened into a thin line, and he patted the roof of my truck before walking back to his cruiser.

Better than that. For some reason those three words ate at me, tugging and tearing like barbed wire.

Better than my paw.

Not anywhere close to good enough for his daughter. Even though I was determined to give her the world. Even though I would never, in a million years think of doing what Good Guy Ben had done to Daisy.

When I pulled off, I stuck my middle finger up. Even though he couldn't see it, it made me feel a little better.

WHEN I GOT home that afternoon, there was a message on the answering machine from Sunny. "I love you."

I sifted through the mail, smiling when I saw a letter from the University of Alabama. I slipped my finger underneath the seal, pulled the thick stock paper out and carefully unfolded it.

DEAR ELIAS,

Congratulations! You have an opportunity to become an educated man and play great football! University of Alabama degree is one of the most prestigious in America. As the head coach at the University of Alabama, I would like to formally extend a scholarship offer to you.

My team of coaches and I are committed to helping you develop your amazing athletic skills. My experience has allowed me to coach players from all levels from high school to college to the NFL. I am confident I can teach you the techniques necessary to take you to the next level in your football career.

Life-after-football opportunities await you at the University of Alabama. From law to business to education, the University of Alabama offers varying levels of degrees that I feel will lay the foundation for you both personally and professionally, paving the way to a successful life.

NCAA rules require that I disclose to you that this scholarship offer is contingent upon—

I DIDN'T NEED to read the rest. Those rules were the same no matter what college offered you a scholarship. I took the letter and tacked it to the side of the fridge, along with three others. And I wondered if Mr. Lower would consider an NFL player good enough because dammit, that was my goal.

Judah came into the kitchen and opened the fridge, grabbing a Coke. "Got another letter?"

"Yep."

He stared at the new addition to the fridge. "Ah, man. Alabama. Roll Tide Roll!"

"Did you sell the rest of that pot?"

"Yeah." He took a swig of soda. "Three hundred. Put it in the safe deposit."

I did a quick calculation in my head. "That's six thousand then. That'll cover us until August."

My emancipation approval came in the mail back in January, and I had already started on getting custody of my dingbat brothers.

"Just going to lay this out there, I would be more than okay moving to Tuscaloosa." Judah grinned. "The girls there are hot."

"You think girls everywhere are hot. You don't really have standards."

He snorted. "Whatever, man. So what's gonna happen with Sunny? She gonna go with us?"

Judah may not have been the brightest crayon in the

box, but surely, he had more sense than that. "What do you think, dipshit?"

"That you're pussy whipped."

I grabbed the paper towel roll from the counter and chucked it at him. "Hey. No more dealing either."

"All right, Captain Buzzkill. We'll be law-abiding citizens from here on out."

34

ELIAS

MARCH 2000

We'd spent nearly two hours at the mall in Daphne.

First, we looked for a pair of Doc Martins, and now, much to my dismay, we were looking at baby clothes for Daisy. Sunny held up a pink onesie with pale-yellow cat heads on the feet. "What do you think?"

I skimmed through the rack out of boredom. "I think it's baby clothes."

She rolled her eyes before grabbing another outfit, and I shoved my hands deep into my pockets, trying to ignore the women giving us nasty glares.

One woman whispered something to her gray-haired friend. They both looked right at me and shook their heads disapprovingly. I wanted to shout, "She's not pregnant. Her friend is." But I didn't.

We left the baby section, and Sunny dragged me straight over to the jewelry counter.

She traced her finger over the display case, finally jabbing at it. "Something like that?" she asked.

I circled my arms around her waist and looked over her

shoulder at the thick, silver wedding band beneath her finger. "Yep. That seems about right."

"That's just like the ring I saw at Macy's that was two hundred bucks, and lucky for us, I saved two hundred and fifty from Christmas."

Suddenly, it was more than real. "We're really gonna do it?" I asked.

"Yes." She twisted in my hold and pressed her lips to mine. "Two months?"

"Something like that."

It was exactly fifty-five days until her birthday, fifty-six until graduation, but who was counting?

Sometimes the thought of her running off on her parents made me feel guilty. Actually, ninety-nine percent of the time it made me feel shitty. And that's why I had planned to talk to Sunny's dad on her birthday.

My brothers and I had just started a lawn care business, and while it wasn't much, the fifty bucks we made from each yard added up. And it wasn't even close to illegal. I wanted to tell him I'd accepted a more than generous scholarship to Alabama where they had on-campus housing for married students.

I needed to make him understand I wasn't going to fuck this up. Then I'd ask him for Sunny's hand, whether we tied the knot in two months or two years didn't matter to me if he gave us his blessings.

If he didn't. . . I'd at least have a clear conscious.

Sunny went to kiss me but froze halfway to my lips. Her face crumpled, her cheeks went pink and then red, and I kept my eyes aimed right at her, terrified to turn around.

"Daddy!" Sunny grabbed my hand, and I spun around to meet Mr. Lower's weathered face full of silent fury.

His gaze drifted from her to me then back.

"Mr. Lower, sir—"

He held up his hand. That one motion must have possessed magical forces because it shoved the words right back down my throat.

"Sunny." He pulled his keys from his pocket and dangled them from his fingers. "The car's on level 2 of the deck. By the elevator."

"Daddy!" She clung to my arm, her nails digging into my skin.

"Young lady." One of his brows lifted. "Go to the car. Now."

I rubbed my hand over hers. "You better go," I whispered.

She kissed my cheek before snatching the keys and storming through the men's section, and I think that made Mr. Lower even more perturbed. She had listened to me and not him. I could see his heartbeat throbbing in his temples, and I could feel mine pulsing throughout my body.

"Elias, I asked you to—"

"I should probably tell you I'm sorry," I said, not wanting to listen to him tell me how I wasn't good enough. "But I love her. More than anything else in this world, so I'm really not sorry about anything but your inability to see that."

"I'm sure you love her." He dropped his chin on an inhale. "But love isn't what people get by on in this world."

Tension wound through me until every muscle felt tight, locked and loaded. "Bullshit!" I clenched my jaw. "It's the *only* thing people get by on."

I could have stood there and argued with Mr. Lower all day, but it would have only left me going in circles, so I turned my back to him and walked off.

Sometimes adults get so damn blinded by bills and work and whose house was bigger that it makes it impossible for them to see that nothing matters the way love does. Maybe I was only aware of that because I had grown up with clothes from the secondhand store; backpacks and bikes people had donated to us; an aunt who pretended to care just for a check. Every damn thing I had ever owned was charity, even my short time at the Lower's house came out of pity. But Sunny, her love had never been charity. It was real and pure, and it was the one thing in my life I could say was truly mine.

I could have all the money in the world, but if I didn't have her, my life would be meaningless. And I couldn't make him understand that.

Honestly, I didn't need to.

35

SUNNY

The drive home from Daphne was silent. Daddy turned the radio off, and he sat with one hand on the wheel and the other propped against the door to massage his temple. I thought, at that moment, that I hated him. And I felt guilty because daughters shouldn't hate their fathers, but fathers also should know when they're breaking their daughter's heart.

We pulled up beside the house, and I opened the door before the car had come to a complete stop.

"Sunny?" Daddy's door slammed shut, but I kept storming toward the porch, trying not to cry. "Sunny Ray!

I stopped on the step, fist clenched at my side and a tremor of anger rattling through me. "What!"

Daddy placed a foot on the stair, bending his leg at the knee and resting his hand on his thigh. "I know you don't understand, but one day you will."

I stared at him, fighting for a good breath. I was two months away from graduating. Two months away from being old enough to vote, and he was no closer to letting go of me than he was when I was fourteen.

"I won't, Daddy. I won't ever understand how you, of all people, could tell me that boy isn't good enough when he was good enough for you to almost adopt!"

"Sunny. . ."

"I love him." My voice echoed across the yard. "I love him, and he loves me, and I hate that you can't see that."

Daddy's shoulder fell hard. "I know you're upset."

"No. I'm upset when I make a *B* on a test. I was upset when my favorite book series ended. Right now, I'm shattered, but most of all, I'm disappointed in you." I went for the door, then ran up the stairs to my room, and locked myself inside.

I paced at the foot of my bed, glancing around at the pink walls. The tattered bear I once slept with on my dresser. Pictures of Daisy and me. Honor roll ribbons.

I was stuck somewhere between a kid and an adult. Almost eighteen. Almost out of high school. Almost in college. And almost married.

Almost still their baby. . .

I DIDN'T GO down for dinner that night. I didn't want to look at my father. I didn't want to be tempted to tell my mother she should be ashamed of herself for going against her life-long motto of not judging a book by its cover. Instead, I sat on my bed and thought.

I wondered if I had been wrong for going behind their backs to see Elias. I questioned if it made me a bad daughter or if it made them bad parents, or maybe if it just made us all bad. Most of all, as I crammed clothes into my backpack, I wondered if they would ever forgive me for what I was about to do.

I zipped my bag, grabbed my stuffed bear, and took one

last look around the room that had been mine for as long as I could remember. The door to my parent's room banged shut. I didn't have to press my ear to the wall to hear that discussion. It came through, loud and clear.

"David! Do you want to lose her?"

"No, Clara. Of course not."

"She turns eighteen in two months. She moves off to college in less than three months. She's not a baby anymore, and if she loves him—If she really loves him, we're going to lose her. So, you think about that long and hard."

I shouldered the bag, hopeful Daddy would have a change of heart.

"I see enough of his type come in and out of the station. It's a cycle, Clara! A cycle. And don't act like you didn't agree with me. You agreed months ago he would get her in trouble and—"

"Don't you think I remember that?" There was a pause, and I could imagine them standing at opposite ends of the room. "I've felt guilty over that for months because we don't know him."

"I know enough." But Daddy didn't know anything. He didn't know that boy would do anything to be my everything. He didn't know he had a scholarship or that he was the sole reason him and his brothers had even made it for the past three years. He knew only what he wanted to know, which was nothing.

"Do you?" Momma said, the volume of her voice teetering on yelling. "Because it seems to me, we're judging him because of his family, because of everything he had no control over. And how is that fair, David? How is it fair when he almost was our son?"

"Clara, I feel for the kid, I do, but he doesn't stand a chance at life."

"No. I guess he doesn't stand a chance when people like you refuse to give him one."

My eyes stung, my chest ached, and I reached for the door while Momma and Daddy continued yelling at one another.

My door swung open to Simon. He glanced at the strap of my backpack and frowned. "Who's Elias?"

"It's a long story, buddy."

He rubbed over his arm a few times. "Momma said if Daddy didn't give that Elias boy a chance, you'd leave. If I give him a chance, will you stay?"

My heart cracked, tiny fissures ripping in every direction.

Simon's little arms wrapped around my thighs, and he squeezed so tight it nearly broke me. "I'll miss you too much if you leave."

I bit at my lip, taking breath after breath so I wouldn't cry in front of my little brother.

"Hey." I placed the bear on the floor and knelt in front of him, swiping my hand through his sandy-blond hair. "I'll be back, okay? I would never leave you forever."

"Promise?"

Hugging him tightly, I buried my face in his hair. He smelled like soap, and that made the lump in my throat even larger. "I promise."

When I pulled away, I picked up the stuffed animal and pushed to my feet, then took his little hand in mine. "Let me tuck you in, okay?"

He nodded, and we walked the hall to the room that once belonged to Elias. After I turned on Simon's nightlight and folded back the sheets, he crawled into bed.

I covered him up before placing my bear on the pillow beside him. "Can you take good care of her for me?"

The beads in the bear's belly rattled when he grabbed it and squeezed it to his chest. "I'll take the best care of her. Even if she is pink."

"I love you, buddy." I kissed his forehead and whispered "sweet dreams" before I slipped into the hallway, then down the stairs, and through the front door.

36

ELIAS

C ountry roads are always dark. The kind of dark that makes you think someone should jump out at any second. But even in the cover of night, I could see Sunny's blond hair flying behind her as she made her way down the drive. I reached over to push open the door, and she climbed right in, dropping her backpack onto the floorboard. We stared at each other for a second, the glow from the dash the only thing creating light.

"Let's go," she said.

I gave one last glance toward the Lower's house, then put the car in drive.

Sunny turned up the radio and stared out the window. Neither of us knew what we were doing. We were just kids in love with each other, and sometimes, the thing that seemed to make the most sense ended up being the most senseless. We were running on emotions.

If I took her back to my house, what would that say to her parents? What would that do her, to us, to them? I made it to the public beach access, and instead of going straight, I pulled into the parking lot and cut the engine. The radio kept running, and I stared through the windshield at the dunes rising like ghosts in the distance.

"What are you doing?" she asked.

"I don't know."

Sunny looked at me, her lips slightly parted, her brows wrinkled. "Elias?"

"I don't blame him. I mean, I'm not the most upstanding citizen." I leaned back in the seat.

"Don't start that, Elias. Don't let him get in your head."

"Maybe all I've done by sneaking around with you is prove him right. If I help you run away, he's going to hate me even more."

"It doesn't matter what you do. He's stubborn."

Mr. Lower was stubborn. That was, at one point, why I liked him as a kid. He didn't take anything off anybody. But right then, that quality was a thorn in my side. But maybe, I was a thorn in his for reasons I couldn't understand. I looked at the way Sunny absently stared out at the beach, the way she was fidgeting in her seat. She didn't know what she was doing either, but I did not want to make things any worse between her father and her. That, I knew she would regret.

Clutching the wheel, I exhaled. "You need to go back."

"Why are you doing this?" she whispered.

I leaned over, and damn if the way her pouty lips trembled didn't stab me right in the chest. I took her chin in my hands and kissed her once. "Because I love you."

"Then take me home." She reached across and turned the ignition. The engine rumbled, the loose change in the ashtray rattling. "And by home, I mean with you."

I wanted to do the right thing, but the problem with that was I'd do anything that girl asked. Nodding, I put the truck in reverse and pulled out onto the highway, and I took her home. With me.

THE NEXT DAY, I woke to Judah calling from the living room, "Sheriff Lower's in our yard."

I shook Sunny. She rolled onto her side, halfway swatting a dismissive hand through the air.

"Sunny. Babe?" I tickled her neck. "Your dad's here."

Her eyes popped open, and she sat straight up. "Shit."

She grabbed her clothes from the floor and slipped them on before storming out of my room and down the hall. "Tell him to go away."

"I'm not telling the Sheriff to go away. He'll take me to jail," Judah said.

"He will not."

Groaning, I pulled on some jeans and made my way into the living room where Sunny and Judah stood arguing.

There was a loud knock followed by. "I need my daughter."

I pulled open the door to Mr. Lower, arms crossed and cheeks red. His gaze went straight over my shoulder, most likely landing on Sunny, and his eyes narrowed to slits. "All right. You had your fun. Now come on." He motioned her with his finger.

"I'm not leaving."

His jaw ticced. "You're only seventeen, Sunny, which means you're a minor. I didn't give consent for you to leave. If I wanted, I could take you in."

"But you can't arrest me." There was a pause where tension crackled through the air like a lightning storm. "If I come home, will you let me see him?"

"No." One, stern, powerful word.

"Then I'm staying."

Mr. Lower ran his tongue over his bottom lip, then his gaze shifted to me. "You think this is good for her?"

"She doesn't want to go home."

"And I don't want her here."

"You could just let her see me," I said.

"I'm not letting my daughter date a drug dealer."

"I'm not a dealer." My blood pressure elevated like a slow rising tide.

"Sunny." He frowned. "Let's go."

From the corner of my eye, I caught her walking toward my room. The door slammed, and Judah mumbled "damn."

I tapped my hand on the doorframe a few times.

Mr. Lowers expression went from hard to soft. "What have you done to my little girl?"

"Loved her. That's all."

Shaking his head, he let out a disbelieving laugh.

I stared at him, wondering why he disliked me so much, questioning how he couldn't see that he was the one causing harm to Sunny—not me. Had he just given me a chance, there would have been no sneaking around, no reason to make her feel the need to run away.

"Mr. Lower, with all due respect, sir, have you thought about what *you're* doing to her? Trying to make her chose between the two of us? 'Cause that's not really fair to her."

Mr. Lower looked dumbfounded and as bad as I felt for him, I didn't want to deal with this mess any longer. "Mr. Lower, since you don't have a warrant, I'm closing the door. Sir." And I did, latching the top lock before I turned around.

37

SUNNY

It had been two days since I'd left my parent's house. Two days of Mother calling me and me assuring her I was fine. As upset as I was with Daddy, I wasn't upset with her. I knew Daddy was at work, which was the only reason I went by to grab a few more clothes and talk to Momma.

Elias parked his truck in the drive beside my Honda. I'd left the car on purpose. I didn't buy it. My name wasn't on the title. It was theirs for all intents and purposes.

"Want me to come in with you?" he asked.

"No. I won't be long."

It was a weird sensation to knock on that door instead of just walking in, but I felt it was the right thing to do, or maybe I did it to make a point. The wooden door opened and before I could step inside, Momma threw her arms around me.

"Oh honey," she whispered beside my ear.

I rested my head on her shoulder, fighting the emotions moving through me like a riptide. "I'm sorry if I hurt you."

She squeezed me harder before she took a step back.

Deep bags sat below her eyes. She looked tired, and I felt guilty. It was my fault, and it was Daddy's fault that she had been put through the ringer.

"I don't want you to do this. . ." She paused, and I prepared myself for an argument. "I wasn't ready to let you go yet, Sunny. I was supposed to have a few more months of being your momma."

There went that tug in my chest that had become all too familiar. "You'll always be my momma."

"It isn't the same once you leave." She cupped my cheek, and I leaned into her touch, remembering how she used to comfort me when I came in crying from a skinned knee. I felt she was trying her hardest to mend the heart my father had broken.

Momma sat on the bottom step of the foyer, then patted the place beside her. Over the years, we'd sat in this exact spot a total of eight times—every time we'd seen a foster child off. It was the place where we tried to figure out how to fill the hole, the place we decided, after Drew, that we wouldn't take in any more foster children.

I guessed that was exactly what we were doing that day, too. Filling holes that could never really be filled.

"Believe it or not," she said. "I do remember being your age, and it's not easy. But then again, no stage of life is easy."

I stared at the picture by the door, the family portrait from when I was four. I breathed in the familiar aroma of freshly baked bread and wood polish that had seeped into the floorboards over the years, and it hurt. Because regardless of whether Daddy had approved of Elias from the start, this chapter of my life—the one where I lived with my parents—was over. And when I really thought about that, it hurt more than I expected.

"Do you think Daddy will ever give him a chance?"

"When he calms down. He's hurt Sunny. To him, you've chosen Elias over us."

"It's not that. It's just. . ." I tried to find the words while Momma brushed my hair away from my face.

"At some point, you grow up," she said. "It's not choosing. It's simply living your own life. That's all. Parents raise their children, knowing they'll one day let them go, but this wasn't how we had it pictured." She pressed a kiss to my forehead. "I promise, as hard as this is on you. It's just as hard on him."

"I don't want him to hate Elias." I chewed at my lip, imagining what the rest of our lives would be like with that stress. "Because he's not going anywhere."

"I believe that."

We sat on the step for a long time in silence. I was thinking about Daddy, and I was sure Momma was thinking about me.

Finally, I pushed to my feet and started up the stairs to my room.

"You know you can come home?" Her voice sounded strained, and I stopped on the first landing. "I won't stop you from seeing him, Sunny."

There was a small part of me that wanted to come back. I loved my parents. I loved Simon, but I was deeply, irresistibly, absolutely *in love* with Elias. I was desperate for every second with him. "I. . ."

"Sunny? How do you know you love him?"

There were so many ways I could answer that, but no combination of explanations could define what I felt. I could say that from the way my chest ached when I wasn't with him, every love story seemed dull and petty. Or I could try something cliché like he was the last thing on my mind when I fell asleep and the first thing I thought of when I woke. But those arguments seemed cheap and powerless. So instead I said:

"I know I love him because there are no words I could use to possibly describe it."

38

SUNNY

APRIL 2000

I picked up a weekend job waiting tables at Coconut Larry's to help with bills. As easy as it looked to serve people food, it wasn't. People, I quickly learned, were rude. A four-hour shift ended up feeling like twelve, and I left smelling like a tater tot. But, I wouldn't dare complain because I was making my own money.

When I pulled into the drive, two cop cars were parked by the house. Judah, Atlas, and Elias stood in the side yard, faces red and hands in their pockets.

I knew whatever this was, my father was most likely behind it, and it sent hot fury through my veins. I slammed the door to the truck. "What's going on?" I asked Elias.

"They evidently have a warrant to search the house for drugs."

"Daddy did this, didn't he?" I marched right up the stairs and into the living room.

The cops had torn the cushions off the couch, ripped up the air vents. Emptied the kitchen cabinets.

I spotted Joe, one of Daddy's friends who had been on

the force since I was little, and I strode up to him. "Who issued the warrant?"

Joe closed one of the cabinets. "Your father."

My heart hammered and hammered until I felt short of breath and found myself clasping at my chest. Meanwhile, Joe and the other officers continued their raid.

"You're not gonna find anything here," I said.

"Sorry, Sunny." Joe gave a curt nod, then walked down the hall to Judah's room.

I wanted to scream, so I did just that. I grabbed the remote from the coffee table and slung it against the wall, shouting over and over that I hated my father. Instead of making things better, he only made them worse, and it pained me. It was almost as though he didn't care that he hurt me, and that was a new, unwanted sensation.

My father had always tried to protect me, but now I felt he was trying to destroy me. Bit by bit. I didn't want him to hate me; I just wanted him to see what I saw in Elias. Someone who loved me unconditionally. Someone who made me happy. All Daddy saw was a delinquent, and Elias was so far from that it was ridiculous.

Eventually, I went outside and sat on the steps. Elias strolled toward me, cigarette in hand. "It's all right," he said, a stream of smoke slipping through his lips. Despite his house being ransacked on pure principle that my father disliked him, Elias laughed.

"How you aren't livid is beyond me."

"I like to find beauty in all things."

"And what beauty is there in this?" I asked.

He took another slow drag, the smoke swirling around his face when he let the breath go. "Your dad's gonna feel like an asshole when they go back to him with nothing."

"You give him more credit than you should." I took the

cigarette from his hand, and he gave me a crazy look before stealing it back.

"You're kidding, right?"

"No. It's bad for you."

"You're supposedly bad for me, too." I snatched it away again, this time placing it to my lips. One puff had me doubled over and coughing. I tossed the thing to the dry grass and stomped it out.

"Told you," Elias said with a smirk.

THE POLICE CAME out with nothing but a six pack of Miller Lite. Joe tipped his hat, and I glared at him, even though he was simply following orders. "Be sure to tell my dad that was my beer you just confiscated!"

Joe frowned before climbing into his patrol car.

"Lies. Lies. Lies." Elias tsked. "You don't even like beer."

I stomped up the rickety steps and into the pillaged living room, cursing and swearing under my breath as I picked up the couch cushions and shoved them back in place. Elias and his brothers came in behind me, and without a word, began putting the dishes away in the cupboards.

"So mad," I mumbled as I folded a blanket over my arm.

"Hey." Elias rubbed his hand over the small of my back and placed a tender kiss to my neck. "It's okay."

My entire body was tight, swirling with anger and sadness, misunderstanding and disappointment. Daddy was furious, and every move he made caused an unrivaled hatred to bubble inside me. I didn't understand how, if he loved me, he could try to hurt the thing that meant the most. And what would he have done if the cops had stumbled across something? Would he have arrested Elias? Sent him to jail? Surely, he wouldn't expect forgiveness from me if it had come to that? But the thing that caused me the most grief was the thought that, maybe, he didn't expect my forgiveness at all.

LATER THAT NIGHT, I laid in bed, the almost cool air of the AC blowing across my face as I stared at the ceiling.

Elias shifted next to me, draping his arm over my waist. "It's bothering you?"

I nodded. I felt like I was drowning, and every time I swam close to the surface, something grabbed hold of my ankle and tugged me farther down. I was lost in a whirlpool of what I should do and what I wouldn't do; pride and grief. Elias and my father.

Elias inhaled a deep breath, his fingertips dancing over my ribs. "I don't want you to regret this."

"Regret what?"

"Me."

My body bristled. "I would never regret you. Why would you say that?"

"I don't know what it's like to have a family, but. . ." He shook his head. "I don't know. I just hate to see you upset like this, knowing I can't do a damn thing to fix it."

The air conditioner kicked off, and the hum of the cicadas filtered through the window. I thought about the things Daddy had said regarding Elias. About how he seemed hell-bent on tearing us apart. My father was the world positioned between the sun and the moon, determined to never let the two collide.

"I don't know that I'll ever forgive him," I said.

"You need to talk to him, Sunny. Life's too short for bullshit."

My face heated, and I sat up, looking at Elias from behind tears. *Tears?* I wasn't even sure why I was near crying, but I was. "It's not bullshit, Elias."

He pushed onto his elbows, moving in toward me until we were nose to nose. "In the grand scheme of life, this is bullshit. No matter what happens, I'll still be right here, and he'll still be your father."

"How are you not mad at him, Elias? How?"

"Because just like me, he's only doing what he thinks is best for you. And love, well, it makes you crazy sometimes."

I just needed time.

There were some days you knew would stick out in your mind forever, like the day I met Sunny or the day I found out my maw's body had been found up in the Talladega Forest. The first day of spring that year would turn out to be no different. Forever lodged in my brain like a bullet.

On my way to cut Magpie's yard, I passed by Krispy Kreme, and just like every morning, Mr. Lower's cruiser sat at the far side of the building. That man was predictable if nothing else.

I tapped the brakes, debating whether I should stop or not. Right when it was almost too late, I jerked the wheel to the right and flung my truck into the lot, parking beside his car. I sat there gripping the steering wheel until my knuckles washed white, and then finally, I slung my door open, pocketed my keys, and headed to the glass entrance.

The bell dinged, and the warm, inviting aroma of sweet pastry and glaze slapped me in the face. Mr. Lower sat at a booth in the back, alone. A cup of coffee, a notepad, and his Bible on the table. His eyes were closed, and I was pretty sure by the way his hands were clasped on top of that tattered book, he was praying.

I maneuvered past a mom with two crying toddlers in tow and past several empty tables before I stopped at the end of his.

My insides shook, my stomach tying knot after knot. I didn't want to make things worse, and I wasn't sure that I could do anything but just that. But I loved Sunny, and deep down at the heart of everything, I loved Mr. Lower, too, simply because for those two years I stayed with them, he was the closest thing I came to having a real father.

"Mr. Lower?"

His eyes opened, bloodshot and tired. Without a word, he tore a page from the notebook and folded it once before slipping it between the pages of the Bible. His hand tapped on the tabletop, then he inhaled.

I couldn't take the silence anymore.

"I just want you to know, I was never trying to take Sunny away from you."

"I know, Elias."

I swallowed. "And I may not be the kinda guy you had envisioned for her. I'd promise you that I'd turn into that kinda guy, but I can't. If life has taught me one thing, it's that not much is certain." I paused, trying to gather my thoughts into something more coherent than babble. "The world kinda likes to work against people sometimes, so I can't say that I'll ever be what you consider good enough. I don't really know what good enough is to you, but I love her, so I'm sure gonna try. And that's all I can do, promise that I'll try."

His chin dipped, and he nodded a little before thumbing through the pages of the Good Book. He pulled out a faded polaroid which he handed me. "Give that to her for me, would you?"

It was a picture of Mr. Lower and a tiny Sunny in front of the water, the sun setting behind them. "Her momma and I tried three years for a baby before we had her." He cupped his hands around his empty coffee mug and stared down into it. "I know she hates her name, but we named her Sunny because she was the center of our universe. And now I guess she's the center of yours. That's how life works. The sun never sets where it rises. . ."

I grappled for words, for anything to say, but I fell short because he was already pushing out of the booth and hitching up the waist of his uniform. "I just hope she can forgive me."

"She'll be off work at five," I called when he neared the exit.

He nodded, then the bell over the door dinged. He walked to his cruiser, leaving me with the photograph that had *Sunny 1986* scribbled on the bottom.

Sometimes, just sometimes, things work themselves out.

THE TRAFFIC on the Parkway was at a crawl. Horns blared. People leaned out of their open windows and craned their necks to see what the holdup was. I had just picked up Judah from cutting Miss Weaver's lawn, and we didn't have anywhere else to be, so had it not been for the AC in my truck being on the fritz, I wouldn't have particularly cared that we were stuck on the two-lane highway.

"What the hell?" Judah grumbled, snatching his ball cap from his head and using it to fan himself. "You'd think it was the fourth of July with this crap."

Red and blue lights went flashing by on the shoulder. Soon after, an ambulance sped past, sirens wailing.

By the time we reached the T, my shirt was soaked with sweat, and Judah had already tossed his to the floorboard.

"Oh shit!" Judah hung himself out of the window.

Two cars had collided head-on in the middle of the highway. As we inched along, I noticed a third crashed against a telephone pole, nothing but a smoking heap of metal.

"That person's gotta be dead," Judah said.

Firefighters stood in a huddle on the shoulder, extinguishers at their side. Policemen were scattered across the median in an attempt to direct traffic.

It wasn't until I flipped my signal to turn on the county road that I noticed *Sheriff* in tan letters across the side of the crumpled car. My heart thumped at the back of my throat.

I wanted to say that there was hope, but really, all that existed within the site of Mr. Lower's demolished cruiser was hopelessness and proof that life refuses to become bearable for anyone for very long.

It's a cruel, bitter bitch.

SUNNY

The doctors said thanks to a massive heart attack, my daddy was gone before his car slammed into a telephone pole at sixty miles an hour. The thought that he didn't suffer was meant to bring us comfort, but all it did was bring me to my knees. I would forever believe that I had literally broken my father's heart.

I would never have his forgiveness, and he would never have mine. I'm not sure which was worse, believing I had an invisible hand in his death or believing he died thinking I hated him.

I slept with Momma and Simon for the first three days after he passed, realizing what emptiness truly felt like for the first time in my life. Understanding just how unfair things could be.

We didn't choose to be born. We didn't choose to die. Yet, here we were. Expected to trudge through the hardships, expected to smile at the happiness, even though it can all be ripped away in an instance.

THE DIGNITY FUNERAL HOME stood across from the public beach, a one-level brick building with navy shutters. I'd driven past that building countless times and never noticed it, but I was sure it would never go unnoticed again.

Elias leaned against his truck in his gray dress shirt and black tie, smoking a cigarette.

That time, when I pinched it from his grasp, he didn't stop me, and I didn't cough, but I did cry.

His arms wrapped around me right along with the smell of leather and spice, and I broke even more. I shattered into a million, jagged pieces of pain and regret because I knew he would hold me together as best he could.

"Hey," he breathed against my ear. "I love you."

I fisted his shirt while my legs threatened to give way. At seventeen, I hadn't appreciated how quickly my world could be sucked into a black hole. Up until then, not being able to kiss the boy I loved seemed like the end of the world. Oh, how foolish that seemed now. As long as there was still the hope of maybe one day, the story wasn't finished. And with my daddy, I now only had "remember the day".

In life, there were no rewrites, no edits. Only painful rereads.

I buried my face in Elias' shoulder, my chest burning and heaving until I couldn't catch my breath until I wanted to scream.

"Sunny," Elias whispered, the scent of cigarette swirling around me. "We've gotta go inside."

"I don't want to."

"I know."

I clung to him for a few more seconds before finally pulling away and turning around. He drew me into his side to steady me, and we walked toward the entrance packed with people whose names I didn't know.

I glanced down as not to meet the pity on everyone's face. I didn't want to talk to them. I didn't want to listen to them tell me how sorry they were. After my father was buried, they would all go home to watch their television shows, laughing before they retired to bed.

And what would I do?

I would go home, and the guilt would take a little bit more from me. I would go home and see the absolute heartbreak on my mother's face. And I would tuck Simon into bed, listening to him pray that God would tell Daddy we loved him.

So, I told myself it was okay to be a little bitter, and I looked at the ground as Elias opened the door and ushered me into the lobby. It was nearly silent apart from the instrumental music playing over the speakers and hushed conversation.

Elias squeezed me a little tighter. "You still with me?"

I gave a half nod, and he led me through the people, not letting a single person stop him like he understood if I heard someone mumbled the words, *it'll be okay*, one more time I would completely break down.

When we stepped into the chapel, the earthy scent of flowers surrounded me, and the conversation disappeared, leaving only the soft melody of "Amazing Grace."

"I'm right here, okay?" he said.

Another half-hearted nod.

Someone brushed my arm, and I glanced up at one of the teachers from Robertsdale. Her mouth began moving and her eyes watering, but I didn't hear a word she said.

Elias thanked her for the condolences, then led me to the front of the tiny chapel. He moved his hands to my shoulders and leaned down until his forehead touched mine, his watercolor eyes peering into mine. "I'm not gonna lie to you; this is gonna be one of the hardest things you ever do in your life." He wet his lip with his tongue, dropping his chin while shaking his head. "You won't ever get over this, but you'll learn to live with it, okay? And don't you dare try to be fucking strong. You crumble if you need. I'll be right here."

I stared at the maroon skirt surrounding the table first, then the steel-gray coffin, the arrangement of white roses, my daddy's hands—the hands that had held me as a baby, that had held onto the handles of my bicycle; the hands that had wiped away tears.

And then my gaze slowly moved to his face.

That was the hardest part, looking at his waxy skin powdered with makeup to hide the raw appearance of death and saying, *that doesn't look like him.*

Blinking away tears, I looked at the ceiling. I traced my fingertip along the cool edge of the casket, trying to comprehend a life without my father. But some things you just can't fathom. Death, I was convinced, was something I'd never understand. It was cruel and senseless, and the absolute worst, non-physical pain I'd ever experienced. The person lying in that casket was nothing but a shell, and maybe that was why it was so difficult to bring myself to touch him.

My hand trembled, my throat threatened to close, but I needed my goodbye. "I'm sorry, Daddy," I whispered on a choked breath, squeezing his cold hand. "I love you." My jaw ached from how hard I clenched my teeth. "I love you." I repeated those words until they were nothing but sobs. But no matter how many times I said them, I'd never hear him answer me.

FOR THE REST of the funeral, I sat between Momma and

Elias. When Pastor Fulmer went to the podium, Simon refused to move away from the casket so the funeral home director could close the lid. Elias was the one to finally pull him away, promising the box was a rocket ship that would take Daddy to God. Then Pastor Fulmer spoke about the Godly man my father was, but I didn't hear much of anything. Words hold no meaning in regards to love or death.

THAT NIGHT, Daisy's mom and a few ladies from church sat at the kitchen table with Momma, talking about all the great things my father had done in his life. I couldn't bear it, although it seemed to bring my mother comfort. The ladies eventually left, one by one, and Mother went to bed while Elias and I watched *Power Rangers* with Simon.

My little brother fell asleep in my lap, clinging to the stuffed bear I'd given him, and eventually Elias carried him to his room.

I didn't like being alone. After tucking Simon in, Elias stopped at the bottom of the stairwell, rubbing at the back of his neck. "You wanna come outside for a minute?"

I turned the TV off, and in a fog, I followed him onto the front porch.

The humid blanket of southern heat swathed around me, and the cicadas hummed their song while the fireflies flashed out in the field. Elias leaned against the wooden railing, and I sat on the swing, emptiness sitting down right beside me. That house felt different, the porch. The world felt emptier, and to me, it was. I lost myself in thoughts and regrets, numb tears seeping from my eyes.

"I love you," Elias said as he pulled a cigarette from his pocket and placed it to his lips. The flint to the lighter caught, and I watched the flames dance over his face as he lit the smoke.

As wrong as it felt to think about in light of the tragedy we were all drowning in, I couldn't help but think how much I loved him. "I love you, too."

His eyes narrowed when he blew the smoke out. "I might as well. . ." he mumbled before dragging himself off the porch and to his truck. The interior light turned on, and Elias leaned across to open the glovebox. I tried to focus on him when he shut the door and started up the path, because focusing on him didn't hurt. He threw his cigarette out on his way back up the steps. The swing bounced under his weight when he sat next to me.

"I've struggled with this," he said, "because I don't want to put any more on you."

My heart seized, my already confused mind spiraling into the darkest of places.

Elias bit at his lip, then exhaled. "But at this point, I don't know if it'll do you good or send you over the edge. The day your dad. . ." he swallowed those awful words, then handed me a Polaroid, backside up. "I went to talk to him, and he asked me to give you this."

I felt my brows pinch together when I flipped the picture over, and any bit of strength I had clung to fled from my body in a bitter sob.

The picture was off-center and faded, but it was perfect. The soft pinks and deep reds of the sunset behind the near silhouette of my father holding me in front of the expansive ocean—it was a snapshot of life when I still innocently believed my father was invincible and when I was still his baby girl.

A heart is hard to capture, but that polaroid did just that.

Elias pressed his forehead to mine. "He knew you loved him, Sunny. Please stop worrying about that. He knew."

I choked on my next breath, placing my hand over my struggling heart. I don't remember what the last words I said to my father where, but I remember that I thought I hated him the last time I saw him, and that's something I don't know that I'll ever get over.

Love hard. Forgive fast. That's what my father's death taught me.

41

SUNNY

AUGUST 2000

Our last day in Fort Morgan was the first day it hadn't rained in over a month.

That had to be an omen.

Elias, Daisy, and I sat shoulder to shoulder at the tideline. Elias on one side, Daisy on the other while Brandon stood in front of us, staring out at the ocean. The four of us had survived whatever adolescence was. All the heartbreak and drama, the lies and the hate, and the chaos of trying to find our way—all the unimportant things in life that, at one point, seemed so incredibly important.

And I had survived my father's death, only because I had no choice.

That summer, I decided death wasn't half as cruel to the people it took as it was to those left behind to find their way through the heartache.

"I can't believe you're leaving me here to rot," Daisy said, taking a broken piece of shell and tossing it into the rolling waves.

I nudged her. "I'm not leaving you here to rot. We'll come back."

"You better come back for the baby shower. I had high hopes you'd be in charge of the music selection. Mother's gonna to try to play gospel music. I just know it."

"That's gotta be sacrilegious or something, playing gospel at the baby shower of an unwed preacher's kid," Elias laughed, and Daisy shot him a menacing glare.

"True." Brandon threw over his shoulder.

Daisy huffed. "If she plays gospel music, I swear, I won't be in your wedding."

"That's a lie."

"She's got a few years to come around, Sunny. Don't let her guilt you into being a DJ," Elias said.

We'd decided to wait until after college to get married because we knew that's what my father would have wanted.

Brandon turned away from the water and took a seat on the sand beside us. "Was it just me or did graduation seem anticlimactic?"

"Yeah," we agreed in unison.

I had always expected graduation to be some pinnacle that launched me into adulthood. But it was nothing like that. It was boring and hot, and when the ceremony was over, only half of the graduating class of three hundred tossed their caps. It wasn't at all like I'd seen in the movies, but then again, most things in life had proved not to follow the expectations Hollywood set forth.

"It was stupid," Daisy said. "But that after party. . ." She fist pumped.

Elias gave her a dumbfounded look. "You didn't go to the party."

"Oh, right. Because I'm the size of a bluebell cow, and it looks bad for the pregnant girl to be at a kegger." Daisy rolled her eyes, and I patted her back.

"I can only hope your kid has half your sarcasm."

The sun began its slow descent behind the water, and Elias pushed to his feet, wading knee deep. "You know, this is the last time we'll all be here for a while, I feel like we should all scream 'Goonies never die' or some shit."

Brandon snickered, and Daisy cocked a brow while pointing at Elias. "He may be hot and swoony and like love you a lot, but he's a grade *A* dork. Don't let those tats fool you." She cupped a hand around her mouth and whispered, "They definitely aren't from prison."

I stood, and Daisy held out her arms, wiggling her fingers for me to help her up. And then, the four of us stood there, letting the warm Gulf waters rush over our feet as we watched the sun set on a chapter of our lives, thankful that there was always so much more than the page we were on.

42

SUNNY

MAY 2015

T he day Elias and I packed up to move to Tuscaloosa, Momma handed me a letter she found stuck between the pages of my daddy's Bible.

To say it had crushed me in the most beautiful way would be an understatement.

I carried that letter with me everywhere. To college, I tucked it underneath my garter on mine and Elias' wedding day, and I finally framed it and set it on my nightstand, so it was the last thing I saw when I fell asleep and the first thing I saw when I woke.

It never gets any easier to read, though.

April 18, 2000

Sunny Ray,

I'm not a man of many words, but I've had to take a good, hard look at life lately.

As your father, it's been my job to provide for you, protect you, and that's something hard to let go of. Sometimes I think I'm turning into a stubborn old fool, but know, I'm a stubborn old fool who loves you. And I know you love me.

There's an old saying from a story, "The sun loved the moon so much that he died every night to let her breathe," and I think maybe I need to heed to the metaphor in that message. If I love you, I need to let you breathe. So breathe, my dear Sunny Ray, and know I love you enough.

I'll always love you enough, and I think that boy will, too.

I'm proud of you. Both of you.

Love,

Daddy

I PLACED the frame back on the table just as Stella came barreling into our room, her blond pigtails flying behind her before she grabbed that very picture frame and hopped onto the bed, snuggling between Elias and me.

"Tell me the story grandpa was talking about, Mommy."

Pressing a kiss to her chubby cheek, I brushed a strand of hair behind her ear.

"I was a girl who fell in love with a boy who fell in love with me, and the most beautiful thing of all in life is that there is always a part waiting to be written."

The End

If you enjoyed this book you may also enjoy Whiskey Lullaby or A Love so Tragic FREE on KU.

ALSO ON KINDLE UNLIMITED

Whiskey Lullaby

A Love so Tragic

Falling in Between

QUOTE THAT INSPIRED THE SUN

The quote that inspired this entire book:

"Tell me the story of how the sun loved the moon so much she died every night just so he could breathe." - Anonymous

ACKNOWLEDGMENTS

First, I must thank Jen Lum for reading the 17,000 different endings and always acting as my sounding board. I love you! You are one of the most amazing people I know.

Thank you, Kerry for being squirrel-tastic as always.

Thank you, Emily for all your hard work to make sure The Sun got out to people and keeping me on track. You've been there for the long haul!

Autumn, thank you for all of your help and organization and for not wanting to strangle me. I'm lucky to have you.

Jesus in heaven to GFY Edits. Bless your soul and thank you for all the magic glitter you sprinkled in here. You are amazing and ALL THE THINGS! You can send me the therapy bill now...

Lauren. You are my ninja squirrel cat forever. And totally Daisy...

To all the bloggers who took the time to read The Sun, thank you so much. I appreciate you more than you can know.

To all my readers, thank you so much for giving this

book a chance. I hope you loved the book as much as I loved writing it. I never want to let you guys down.

And lastly, to my husband who has picked up all the slack while I finished this book. Who listened to me plot out plot after plot. Caleb, I love you more than anything. The minute your gone, my world stops existing.